ZOMBIE FEINT

A Samuel the Vampire Novel

ZOMBIE FEINT

—ᴍ—

A Samuel the Vampire Novel

By

James T. Carpenter

This is a work of fiction. All the characters, events, and organizations in this book are fictional, and any resemblance to real people, events, or organizations are purely coincidental.

Cover art by Bethany Fast

ISBN 13: 978-1075808616

Interior design by booknook.biz

To my sister
Who won't read this book
Because she won't read any book or watch any movie or
television show
With vampires, werewolves, or zombies.

I

A Zombie a Day

Samuel

The creature ambled along. Its skin was pale, almost the white of newly fallen snow. Its eyes were glazed over with a film, were almost as white as the creature's pale skin, and were colorless—lacking the blue, green, or brown that made one human's eyes recognizable from another's. The creature stood at six-one with long arms and legs. Its head was mostly bald. If it had been alive, I would have guessed it was in its mid-forties. It wore a button-down shirt that wasn't tucked in, a pair of slacks, and a pair of tattered athletic shoes. Its arms hung limply at its sides. It smelled of decaying flesh. By all appearances, this creature appeared to be harmless.

It strolled along a sidewalk on a residential street in West Des Moines, Iowa. Since the time was nearly 2 a.m., these streets were deserted, the houses all darkened, the birds silent. Nearby streetlights illuminated the creature as it walked slowly along.

I followed on foot not too far behind, but far enough that this creature, or more accurately zombie, didn't notice me.

My name is Samuel Johnson and I'm a vampire. Following zombies isn't my usual job. In fact, dealing with zombies in any capacity isn't my job. Well, unless I'm assigned to such a task.

I'm an agent for Vampire Against the Evil or VATE as we like to call it. The evil we fight are Evil Ones, vampires who hunt, kill, and drink the blood of humans directly from their bodies. We also fight aliens, who, disguised as humans, infiltrate human organizations and businesses intent on destroying them. In more recent years, aliens also have hatched other plots in order to kill vampires like me. We consider ourselves Protectors since we protect humans against the evil of both vampire and alien kind.

Because I was a VATE agent and on duty, I had a sword as well as a pistol at my side. Not that I believed I would use either, at least not until I heard I should from my boss.

I pulled my cell phone from its place on my belt, and dialed my boss's cell. His phone rang once, and he picked up on the second ring.

"This is Samuel."

"This is Beryl."

"I'm following the zombie."

"Anything unusual happening?"

I found that to be an odd question. I happen to be a vampire following a zombie. Not exactly what you would expect on a residential street at 2 a.m. My guess was Beryl was referring to the zombie doing anything unusual besides the fact of its existence.

"No, it's simply walking along."

"If you see any sign of dangerous activity, kill it."

"You mean destroy it?" I asked. After all, by their nature, zombies are dead.

Beryl sighed. "Yes, whatever." And hung up.

I guess that meant I might have to use my sword. According to lore, one way to kill zombies is by slicing off their heads.

My boss and his superiors insisted I write narratives about the more unusual cases I worked for VATE and felt that I should write my accounts as if I was writing for an audience of humans. Those of you who have never read any of my works may believe that since I'm a vampire, therefore I'm dead. Wrong. In reality, we vampires are mutations of the human race. A stray gene here or there and we could be human. The most important part of this digression is to say that, similar to humans, we are born, grow old, and die. Of course, when we die, we melt into ash. A much cleaner solution than that of humans who become corpses and can be brought back to life—similar to this zombie I was following.

As for how I look, I'm six feet tall with black hair in a buzz cut, have a thin nose, small ears, and dark green eyes. My hands and fingers are long and bony. My skin is pale and incapable of becoming tan. That's one reason we vampires like to hang out at night. We don't particularly like daylight, but, if the truth be told, the sun's light doesn't kill us, despite the claims of popular literature.

My following of the zombie may seem strange. I, too, thought this activity was a bit odd at the time. But that wasn't where the weirdness ended. Two other VATE agents were following two other zombies within six blocks of where I was. Since Beryl hadn't told me about these other agents' progress or lack thereof, I had to assume they were calmly following their undead subjects in a similar fashion to me. Our worry at VATE was that the zombies might try to go into nearby homes and kill humans. That hadn't happened so far, or at least I hadn't heard about it.

Not too far away, a door opened and closed. I glanced around the area at the large two-story homes with two-car garages that lined either side of this street. Some houses were all brick; some had siding painted in any number of colors: dark blue, white, tan, and one even a neon yellow. In most of the homes, all the windows were darkened. In a few, a light was on in one of the second story windows. In a house to my right, a window on the first floor was lit.

The zombie in front of me halted. I stopped walking so I could keep the same distance between us. In the lawn to our right, a German shepherd roamed. It sniffed the ground as it walked in circles, finally stopping at a spot where it relieved itself. After doing so, it scratched the ground with its two rear paws. Then it sniffed at the ground again. It looked around, back at the house from where it had come, and toward the street where the zombie and I stood silently.

I don't know whether the zombie was paying attention to the dog or not, but it finally resumed its amble toward some unknown destination. Since the zombie was moving again, I began walking as well.

The German shepherd loped toward its home, then stopped, and again sniffed at the ground. It raised its head and looked in our direction. It barked twice.

From the nearby house, a door opened and a voice shouted, "Bonnie, don't bark!"

The dog looked from the house to us.

With the door still open, the owner shouted, "Bonnie, come home!"

The door closed.

Gazing from us to the house and back at us again, the German shepherd stood still. Then it dashed toward the zombie.

I can't say that I'm a big animal lover. Some vampires are. I've known some who have tried to have pets, a few with success, others with none. Quite a while ago, I knew a female vampire who tried to have pets—dogs, at that—and young boys at the same time. That hadn't worked out because the boys had kept drinking all the blood from the dogs. Not a good pet situation. I've never tried having a pet. Still, I think the pet would be safe with me because I'm not a fan of animal blood.

In any case, I let my hand drop to my sword hilt. I was afraid that the zombie/dog encounter wouldn't be good.

The German shepherd ran up and stopped in front of the zombie. Its brown eyes stared up at the glazed eyes of the creature. The dog panted from its run. It hopped up so its front legs were on the chest of the zombie. The zombie stopped walking and looked down at the dog that was seeking attention.

For those of you with a queasy stomach or who happen to be dog lovers, I'd suggest you skip this next paragraph.

Because the zombie grabbed the dog's head, twisted it, broke the dog's neck, then yanked the head from the dead dog's body. The rest of the body fell to the ground with blood seeping from the neck. The zombie cracked the dog's skull, lifted the broken skull to its mouth and sucked out the brain.

That activity counts as dangerous. I pulled my sword from its scabbard, walked up behind the zombie, and beheaded it.

II

Wild Ones

Joe

Life. It's lived in each moment. Seize the day. Seize the moment. Make the most you can out of every second of life. That's what we werewolves believe. Other paranormal creatures think every moment should be scripted, as if in a play or a television show or a movie. They're so wrong. I won't mention names. Yeah, I will. Vampires.

I'm a werewolf. That's cool, isn't it? My legal name is Joseph Butler. I prefer to be called Joe. Joey is okay, too, but I only let people who knew me as a cub call me that. Once I worked with a vampire who wrote all about our adventure. I didn't think that was fair. I told my pack leader, Grant. He didn't care. He said, "Leave the writing to those over-thinkers." We call vampires that lots of times. We call them many other names that are even more insulting. Anyway, this vampire wrote about us and always called me "Joseph" and said I always called him "Samuel." I didn't. I called him "Sam" or "Sammy," or "Yo, you," but he was the writer, so what can I say? I'm Joe. That's who I am. If I'd written that tale...

Cub, kid. For us werewolves, it's all the same. In our wolf form, we're cubs. In our human form, we're kids. Oh, but I have a story to tell. Better get to it.

One night I was on assignment. I work for the Werewolf Organization Of Fighters or WOOF. I think that's a great name. When we're wolfed-out, we woof, so it's great that we have an organization that's got the same name as the sound we make. WOOF is vitally important for werewolf kind. See, there are good werewolves and bad werewolves. And, my gosh, I've written all kinds of stuff and not gotten to the whole reason I'm writing. I'll get back to this stuff later. That's all it is. Stuff. When it's relevant, I'll add it.

It was a dark and cool night. A cold, stiff wind blew through the city. I walked along in human form. That's what we seem to be most of the time. We look like humans. We act like humans. Fiction writers say we're created by the bite of a werewolf. That's wrong because we're born this way. We also grow old and die this way. Only, when we die, a white fur covers our bodies.

Almost a block ahead of me was another werewolf. I hoped he wouldn't turn around or sniff the air too much. *He might detect my presence.*

Even as humans we have a heightened sense of smell. We also have better eyesight and hearing than the standard human, if we choose to use them. That's what makes what I do dangerous. But I'm a member of WOOF, and we're used to danger. That's one of the characteristics WOOF looks for. Spontaneity is another. We're werewolves, and that ability to improvise comes with being one of our species.

I was following a Wild One. They're werewolves who like to wolf-out, hunt, and kill humans. A long time ago, we all lived like that until the human race took offense and began hunting us. To avoid extinction, we figured out other ways to survive—mostly by eating livestock. When we go to the grocery store, we load up on meat and not much else. Grocery stores have made our lives much easier. Except if you're a Wild One and still want to hunt humans.

I'm five-eight with a stocky build, shoulder-length brown hair, a bushy beard and mustache, and huge eyebrows. I've got broad hands with short, stubby fingers. They work for me. They transform into paws faster than if I had long narrow hands and fingers.

The Wild One in front of me was very hairy, too. The hairy part came from his being a werewolf. He had long, shoulder-length black hair tied in a ponytail behind his head and a very bushy beard. He didn't have a mustache, so he must shave twice a day. We werewolves are hairy, and controlling it takes a lot of effort. Sometimes I wish we were a bit more like vampires who tend to have too little hair rather than too much.

The Wild One was on his way to a meeting and walking along a street in downtown Des Moines. Up until about ten years ago, they didn't have much residential housing in downtown. Then the city decided that young professionals might like to live downtown close to where they worked. So apartment buildings, many with other commercial establishments on the first floor, sprang up all over downtown.

This Wild One, named Henry Borman, had parked his car a few blocks away, and I'd done the same. I'd been following him for most of the day. My pack leader, Grant, had intel that Borman was meeting in town with a newly formed group of Wild Ones. Many streets in downtown Des Moines had traffic almost all night long. Others didn't. We were on one of the "others."

I stopped. About a block ahead of me, a female came from a north-south street that intersected with this east-west street and joined Borman. The female had long hair that fell down her back. She was quite muscular, too. Had to be a werewolf.

As the two met, they stopped for a few moments, probably to greet each other and find out how each of them had been doing. We werewolves are like that. We genuinely care for one another and other sentient beings. Some humans do that. Others don't. We understand the first group but not the second. Finding out how someone else was doing was always a good thing.

I let my powerful werewolf hearing come into play.

Borman said, "...why we have to be all cloak and dagger about this."

The woman responded. "We've got something going we've never done before. I don't know the ultimate plan. Maybe to get rid of WOOF."

Both laughed at that.

Hey, I took offense. It's a good name.

I ducked into the shadows of a nearby building. Both of the Wild Ones looked around suspiciously. One might have smelled me or seen me or they might simply have figured out they shouldn't be discussing such stuff out in the open.

They both broke into a run, dashed to the next corner, and turned right.

I waited a few second, then sprinted to the corner where they'd turned. Looking right, I saw nothing.

Oh, shit. Grant's gonna be mad.

III

A Meeting with Beryl

Samuel

Before I relate the following meeting with Beryl, as is customary with my writing, I wish to address my various audiences. Prior to that, I want to apologize to all who are reading this work because, by now, they realize that I'm not the sole narrator. Joseph, my companion from a prior adventure, is telling his side of the tale while I relate mine. My readers will surely see who is the better storyteller.

Regardless. First, I welcome vampires. I'm sure you know and love my prior narratives. This one will be no exception. Well, except for the fact that Joseph is giving his version of events.

Werewolves. I fear you will favor Joseph's narration above mine due to the sheer fact that he is one of you. However, if you read our opposing tales well, you will certainly determine that mine is written more elegantly and thoughtfully than that of my fellow narrator.

Finally, humans. For you I explain aspects of vampire life that my kind already understand and werewolves have at least heard of. To my other two audiences, if at times my writing seems far too explanatory, this is the reason why. Beryl and his bosses want me to write in such a way that even the stupidest humans will understand.

A side note: The observant reader has noticed that each chapter is labeled according to who is writing. Although our styles differ, I advised our doing this for the less intelligent readers who might have been confused without such a labeling mechanism. Joseph, of course, agreed.

But I must continue the narrative.

I sat on the couch in Beryl's living room with two other special VATE agents. Sitting on his couch and meeting with two other VATE agents wasn't the way I usually began a mission. Traditionally, both Beryl and I sat in his recliners and drank mugs of blood warmed to just the right temperature. So I wasn't happy. I wasn't happy at all. To add to the insult, I was drinking a small glass of cold blood.

The other two VATE agents were Ernie Aims and Mindy Rogers. Ernie was a tall—six-six, muscular—African American. He was on loan to us from Cincinnati, Ohio. Mindy Rogers was a petite woman of five-six with bright red hair, on loan to us from Minneapolis, Minnesota. I envied both of them. I'd never been on loan to any other city. I guess Des Moines has had enough problems with Evil Ones and aliens, so that I couldn't be sent to another city to help with its issues.

Beryl sat in his recliner. My boss is taller than I am, with bright red hair, green eyes, and large ears. I'm in my fifties but appear to be in my thirties. Beryl appears to be in his fifties, but his age is rumored to be almost one hundred and fifty. My boss is smart and tough. He's able to fight three Evil Ones simultaneously and kill them all. If I were in a similar battle, I'd want to take the Evil Ones on one at a time.

I looked at the other recliner enviously.

"I think we need to review what happened last night," Beryl said to start the relevant conversation. We'd already gone through introductions. Prior to today, I'd known other special VATE agents were in town, but I hadn't met them.

My boss looked over at the three of us. "Please explain to us what happened with each of your respective zombies. Samuel, you go first."

I detailed how I'd been following the zombie, how it had eaten the dog's brain, and how I'd destroyed it after this atrocious act. Ernie went next. He'd followed his zombie until it turned up a driveway and walked toward a residence. Ernie had properly disposed of it. Mindy told how she'd been following her zombie and followed it and followed it. Until it had collapsed and decayed.

Beryl shook his head. "This is the fourth night we've had zombie sightings. WOVACOM noticed the first three nights when only one appeared each night."

WOVACOM is an organization called Watchers of Vampires and Cleansers of Messes. They watch agents belonging to such organizations as VATE to make sure we don't do anything that might reveal our vampire existence to humankind. WOVACOM agents tended to be in law enforcement or the media, in both cases to cover up when VATE assignments go awry. After I'd made a mess of an assignment, WOVACOM sent me to the Aspen Retreat Center in Colorado where I'd learned to be a special agent. By the way, not all Protectors return from Colorado.

"Five corpses had been in funeral homes, waiting for the embalming process," Beryl continued. "They came from three different funeral homes. We don't know where the sixth corpse originated."

Mindy sighed heavily. "I think you aren't taking this plot seriously enough. We have some undead walking around. We've sighted six. Each night the number keeps growing. Ernie and I can help, but we three aren't nearly enough for the threat we face."

Ernie gave her a sideways glance. "I disagree. This all seems like a waste of time to me."

My boss laughed softly. "I realize what's going on, Mindy. But we've never seen the undead before. We know humans view us as such, but we all know we're alive and well—"

"Or we're ash," I said. I wanted to add something to this conversation.

"That still doesn't justify either Mindy or me being here," Ernie put in defiantly.

Beryl stared at the two visiting agents. "I understand. Some higher-ups in VATE think the sixth corpse could have been one of the aliens' pseudo-humans."

In the first case I'd been on when I was a special agent, we'd discovered that aliens can clone people and clone the same person multiple times. With each cloning, that person becomes less of a human, only a pale image of the original. Of course, if what Beryl said was true, he probably also meant to imply that aliens were behind this zombie threat.

Mindy nodded in agreement. Ernie snorted in disgust.

The latter was one of my favorite responses. I was glad I wasn't the only vampire who did it.

"We think aliens may be behind these zombies," Beryl said sternly. "Besides, you two came here to help with our Blood International problem. You proved flexible and useful. That's why I asked for you again when WOVACOM started sighting zombies."

The "Blood International problem" had been one of my bigger cases to date. I was the lead agent, but I'd received lots of assistance. I never got to know most of the out-of-town agents who'd helped, though, partly because they didn't want to get to know me. Being one of the only special agents in Iowa can be a lonely job.

"On that case, we had specific duties," Ernie said. "Following zombies that aren't causing any harm seems to be a task hardly worth doing."

I knew better than to say something like that. Beryl was similar to bosses in other professions. Sometimes your boss will tell you to do something you think is nonsensical. You do it anyway. Once I had a case where I had to work with a werewolf.

Yes, a werewolf. If Beryl hadn't forced me to do it, I wouldn't have done it.

Beryl gave Ernie a stern look. "You two will remain here and at my command until I decide otherwise. I'm contacting your chapter leader, Ernie, to let him know that you've been insubordinate. I doubt he would put up with the comments I heard today." He shook his head as he gazed at Mindy. "I think you're taking this seriously enough, Mindy, perhaps too seriously. I feel we have plenty of agents for the time being."

Ernie didn't speak. Mindy shrugged.

"That's more like it," my boss said. "You two may leave. I have a bit of business I'd like to discuss alone with Samuel."

The two other special agents grumbled, then said their good-byes as quickly and efficiently as possible. Beryl didn't see them to the door. I could tell he was angry. He'd sometimes been angry at me, and often I'd suffered for it.

"I don't know if having those two on loan is a good idea or not," Beryl said.

"Will I have a chance of being loaned out someday, too?" I asked.

"Yes, maybe." Beryl downed the rest of his blood. "I don't get Ernie. Doesn't he see that these zombies may be part of some much larger plot? I understand that three zombies in one night might not seem much of a threat, especially three zombies that don't threaten any humans. The aliens may only be playing with us here, or perhaps testing their zombies."

"And Mindy thinks we need more agents," I added.

"That doesn't help either," my boss said in annoyance.

I drank a little bit more of my blood. It had begun as cool and now had gotten almost cold.

"If zombies appear again tonight, you'll be on duty again," he said.

"That's what I thought." And I didn't say any more.

IV

A Meeting with Grant

Joe

Time to give a shout-out to my many audiences:

Werewolves of the world! Hey, this story will be great. Well, I'm writing it so it will be. Yeah, I realize you probably already know a lot of what I have to tell about us human-lovin' beasts. That's cool. But I can tell you a whole bunch of other stuff that you'll find entertaining.

Humans! You'll enjoy this, too, because you'll learn that not all werewolves are evil and want to eat you for lunch. I'm going to provide lots of detail about werewolf life, so you'll find this an educational experience.

Oh, yeah, and you vampires. I know you think all of my kind (and humans, too) are stupid. Sammy's writing a portion of this and, since he's a vampire, you'll probably prefer it. Try to be tolerant. Like your human cousins, you may learn something.

By the way, despite what Sammy says, I think our styles are different enough that anybody can tell who's writing what. But agreeing with him that we should label the sections was easier arguing about such a trivial point. You know, those stubborn vampires.

Back to the show!

A meeting with Grant. Good times. He'd been an older member of our pack since when I was a cub. He treated me as if I were his own. My parents had suffered a quick death at the hands of Wild Ones, so the pack had adopted me—Grant first and foremost among them. When he became pack leader, we both wolfed-out, howled happily, and had a good romp around a state park.

Meetings with Grant are great. We get together. He always has some raw meat waiting for me. Often, it's ground beef. Sometimes, he combines ground beef, pork, and veal. A scrumptious feast! Other times he has raw slabs of steak. Or pork chops. And other times raw chicken. The type of meat varies. The degree of rawness never. If you haven't guessed, we werewolves don't like our meat cooked.

This particular afternoon I met with Grant to talk about my non-encounter with the Wild Ones. He'd put together ground turkey, cubes of steak, and raw chicken legs. Yum, yum, yum. After we'd exchanged greetings and pleasantries, we sat down at his kitchen table to get to business.

Grant popped a beef cube, chewed it, and said, "Too bad you lost them last night."

For you interested readers, Grant is taller than I am with shoulder-length black hair, and a beard and a mustache similar to those of any self-respecting werewolf. He has brown eyes, a hawk nose, small ears hidden by his hair, and short arms and legs with stubby fingers and toes.

I took a spoonful of ground turkey, chewed it up, and said, "Good selection today."

"I thought you'd like it. A sampling of meats is always best."

"Any meat is best." We werewolves aren't too picky about our meat. At least the werewolves I know.

Grant smiled. "All well and good. We have the matter of the Wild Ones to consider."

"Sorry I lost them."

"Not your fault. They took off at a run and were out of sight before you could do a thing about it."

We werewolves are a very forgiving lot. Some events aren't within our control. We do the best we can, given the conditions we have to work with.

After eating a cube of beef, I asked, "What's so special about these Wild Ones?"

I belong to WOOF. WOOF's most important job is dealing with Wild Ones. We also kill packs of ferals—werewolves who have lost all sense of humanity. They're like animals. When a pack of ferals comes to town, humans die. Lots of humans. WOOF agents kill them off as fast as possible.

As for Wild Ones, they're always coming up with some plan against us Friends of Humanity or FHs as we like to call ourselves. Humans really are great. I go to a bar once or twice a week to commune with humans, in all senses of the word. Women are hot for wild and impulsive werewolves like me.

Being a WOOF agent, I've dealt a lot with Wild Ones and their nefarious plots. I personally stopped a farm designed for hunting humans, a human breeding program, and efforts to take over all the hog and chicken farms in the state. Also, once I helped a vampire vanquish a vampwolf. I think he and I would have gotten along if the vampire had only had a sense of humor. That was Sammy, the vampire I mentioned earlier. He lacked a sense of fun. An open perspective. Any one of these characteristics would make vampires a better species. Sammy is a good guy anyway. I can't hold a grudge.

Sorry for that digression. This narrative is my first. If I do a good job, Grant will let me write up more of my cases—those three I mentioned previously and so many more. They were all fun. And dangerous. The danger in them was what made them fun.

Back to my conversation with Grant.

"We had other WOOF agents following other Wild Ones," he said.

That statement didn't really answer my question as to what was special about these Wild Ones. I said as much to my pack leader.

"I know," Grant answered.

Vampires may say they don't lie. They're wrong. They do. We werewolves don't lie. Sometimes we may withhold a bit of information, but we don't lie outright.

Grant took another bite of ground turkey. After he swallowed, he said, "We have two worries. One is that some of the Wild Ones have come from out of town."

After I finished a beef cube, I replied, "We've dealt with out-of-towners before. Most cases I've worked have had werewolves from out of town."

'Yeah, I know," Grant admitted. "But that's not the really bad news."

"Was it about last night's meeting?" I asked. "I didn't like that I lost them. I should have been closer to them. When I saw Borman meet that woman, I was worried my cover might be blown. I could have taken them. But you wanted us to avoid any fights this early on."

"That's okay," my pack leader said. "The Wild Ones from out of town aren't our concern. Our problem is the other people who attended the meeting."

"Other people?"

I found that strange. Wild Ones and FHs usually gather as a pack. Packs for both of us are our main social units. We become a pack either through common interests or blood relations, if not both. If we gather beyond a pack, we usually get together with other werewolves such as at parties. We FHs have parties as well, but without the human hunts. If a new pack comes to our territory, within a generation at least one new member is breeding with someone from a local pack. That's a positive because we face the danger of inbreeding. Occasionally, a pack goes under because it doesn't breed enough with other packs.

"Yes, other *people*. People who aren't werewolves."

This time I didn't eat anything. Grant wasn't eating either. I waited. I fidgeted in my chair. I never can stand suspense. I want an answer, and I want it now. Grant knows better than to lead me on.

"And?" I said.

"Other WOOF agents saw vampires going to the meeting. We don't believe they're the Protectors like the ones we worked with on the vampwolf case. We think they're what the Protectors call Evil Ones."

Werewolves and vampires meeting? That doesn't make any sense at all! I said as much to Grant.

"Exactly," he said. "We're in contact with the Protectors. They are busy with another matter. They want us to handle this problem ourselves. We'll pull them in if this conspiracy gets too out of control."

And what could be more important than evil werewolves and vampires meeting?

I was going to be very surprised when I found out.

V

Where Do Zombies Come From?

Samuel

Another night. More zombies. Ernie, Mindy, and I were on zombie patrol the night after our meeting with Beryl. Ernie wasn't happy to be on this duty, but he might not have been happy on any sort of duty in Des Moines. Mindy seemed content but a bit wary, probably because she thought more of us should be working on this case. In my mind, this zombie case still hadn't proven to be large enough to need many agents. Granted, the case was strange since, according to Beryl, no other VATE agent had ever dealt with zombies, but strange did not a great case make.

I drove my Ford Focus through residential West Des Moines. That was where the zombies had been seen the last few nights. Now that WOVACOM knew VATE was watching for zombies, WOVACOM agents were handling their regular cases: VATE agents going astray, the petty crime humans commit against each other and the like. I had a pistol in a holster under one arm, a sword in a scabbard lying on the passenger side's front seat.

Of course, we vampires don't have to rely only on the weapons we carry. We have our own set of amazing powers. Personally, I have the strength of three men, the speed of a cheetah, the vision of an eagle, and the hearing of a coyote—all abilities if I choose to use them. I also have the capability to change into a cloud of mist or a bat—granted, not a very big bat and I couldn't remain in either of these forms too long.

I also have special mind powers to either detect sentient life close by or a full-blown mind attack on one or more minds. I have the ability to appear to be dead and not be. Similar to my mind powers, I can also attack electronic devices.

The previously mentioned are very useful abilities that require me to drink plenty of blood before performing. If I remain my human self and only use my basic human abilities, I can survive on two pints of blood a day, one in the morning and one in the evening. However, if I use any of my special vampire abilities, I need to drink more blood because each ability drains my energy that much more.

So far with this zombie case, I hadn't needed to use any special abilities. I hoped tonight would be the same.

Of course, to use our special powers, we needed blood. Since we're Protectors seeking to protect humans from evil, we obviously don't get our blood by drinking it directly from human bodies. Instead, we have the Vampire Blood Supply or VBS, a blood bank run by vampires for vampires. VBS holds daily and weekly blood drives to collect human blood, then stores it, and delivers it to important figures in the vampire community, who distribute it to the rest of us. Beryl is my contact. Recently, I had a case concerning VBS where I learned far more than I wanted to about that organization. For instance, its conducting blood drives at companies to obtain blood in which one of their employees walked through the establishment using mind attacks to get more volunteers. A horrible task if you ask me. Although I can perform mind attacks on humans, I prefer to avoid contact with humans in any capacity.

As I drove, I saw a human walking along slowly. My headlights revealed its skin was pale, even paler than my own, and its walk was almost a shuffle. Parking my car, I grabbed my sword, exited the vehicle, and strapped the scabbard to my waist. Before advancing further, I sent texts to Ernie and Mindy. Beryl wanted us to contact each other when we saw zombies. I hadn't heard from either of my fellow agents, so I assumed I was the first to see one of these strange undead tonight.

I walked up behind it. The creature continued its ambling walk, not making any noises. In so many zombie movies, zombies are always moaning or groaning when they walk. This creature did neither. I thought that might make it all the more dangerous.

On this night, Beryl didn't simply want us to follow the creatures. He wanted us to dispose of them as fast as possible. He thought if we disposed of them quickly whoever was bringing these zombies would be forced to put more out on the street. Ernie and Mindy were indifferent to this scheme. I thought this was one of Beryl's better strategies.

I strode swiftly behind the zombie and walked on the grass to its right. I continued my pace until I was about ten feet in front of it, then turned and faced this undead creature. As before, the zombie's clothes hung loosely on its body and its arms hung limply at its side. Its eyes were glazed over as if it couldn't see a thing.

Before doing anything else, I took out my cell phone and photographed the creature. Beryl wanted us to photograph each zombie, so others could track where each individual came from.

I drew my sword. The creature moaned, raised its arms, and advanced toward me. I swung my sword. The zombie parried my sword with its right arm. My sword cut into the arm, and white pus oozed out.

Although I held my ground, the zombie continued to advance. This time I attacked, not with the intention of destroying the creature, but with the idea of wounding it. I swung my sword and sliced off the right arm at the elbow. The zombie stopped, stared at its wounded arm, from which white pus dripped, then advanced again. Next, I sliced off the left arm at the elbow. And took a few steps back. This time as the creature advanced, I jumped forward, swung my sword and sliced off its head. The zombie tumbled to the ground. Each of its parts melted away into a decayed mess of white pus.

Putting my sword back in its scabbard, I carefully wiped off the white liquid. Then I texted my fellow VATE agents and Beryl, telling them what I'd done.

In the next half-hour, I received texts from Ernie and Mindy describing how they'd killed zombies in the same way I had. We weren't letting these creatures get too far this night. In the next hour, Ernie and Mindy each sent me a text saying that each had destroyed another zombie.

So went our second night of zombie hunting.

The next afternoon we three had follow-up meeting with Beryl in which Ernie didn't complain—my boss had been in contact with his boss and that had made Ernie give us grudging support. Mindy again said this operation was larger than we imagined and we needed more agents. Beryl ignored that comment again and said our plans remained the same. Of course, that night we were on zombie patrol once more.

I drove my Ford Focus on the route my boss had designated. I'd slept in this day because our meeting with Beryl was in the afternoon and I knew I'd probably have another zombie patrol at night. Not that I had a problem working at night. I actually preferred it. We vampires might not die in direct sunlight, but we could be very unhappy in it. So night duty was fine with me. Ernie and Mindy seemed to be good with it, too, although at our meeting with Beryl earlier in the day both had been their typical selves: Ernie saying this case was nonsense, Mindy insisting on the need for more agents.

We didn't begin our patrols until about 11 p.m. Darkness had fallen many hours prior, and most people had gone to bed so that only night shift workers or those who stayed out late at bars would be on the streets. Other cities might have a bustling nightlife, but in residential West Des Moines we had practically none.

I covered a certain area of town; Ernie and Mindy covered other specific areas. If any of us felt our situation was getting out of control, we were to contact the others to pull in reinforcements. Our encounters with only one or two zombies so far hadn't been anything worth worrying about. Mindy had had a few problems with her first zombie the night before, but she was a special VATE agent and handled it appropriately.

Again, my headlights revealed the shambling outline of a zombie. Again, I parked my car not far behind it. *Here we go again.* Yet once more, I strapped my scabbard to my belt.

Tonight, I had a silencer on my pistol in case I chose to use it rather than the sword. Ernie had used a pistol with a silencer on his zombie the night before and hadn't been too impressed with its effectiveness. He'd used a whole clip to down one zombie. In a cost-benefit analysis, Beryl said that probably wasn't the best weapon to use. Unfortunately, Ernie lacked a significant talent with a sword.

I walked up behind the zombie. This time as I approached, it turned toward me. It moaned as if in pain. Or so I guessed. These zombies were decaying too fast for any vampire scientists to examine them, and that wasn't on the agenda yet because Beryl hadn't told us to try to capture one.

I drew my sword and advanced around the tall, slow-moving zombie. This creature stood six-five with huge broad shoulders, a bald head, and those same glazed-over zombie eyes. It lunged at me. I jumped out of the way.

Maybe the pistol should be my weapon of choice.

The creature wasn't letting me come close enough to use my sword without putting myself in danger. I backed away from it, keeping my sword between the zombie and me. The zombie was between me and my vehicle.

Shouldn't be a problem.

Then I heard a moaning far behind me. I glanced over my shoulder to see a black van at the corner. Between the van and me, but closer to the van than me, another zombie ambled along.

I backed away from the huge zombie closer to me and yanked out my cell phone. I had it auto-dial Beryl. His phone rang once, twice, and he picked up on the third ring.

"This is Beryl."

"This is Samuel. A black van just dropped off another zombie while I was still dealing with one I'd spotted a few minutes earlier."

"Get its license number?"

"No. I was lucky to see the van." Then I gave him my location.

"I'll alert Ernie and Mindy. Take care of your zombies then start searching for the van." And Beryl hung up.

I knew the importance of the van. That's why I'd called it in. Yes, I wanted to discover more about it, but I had two zombies to deal with.

I took a photo of the one closest to me, turned, took a photo of the second zombie, then slapped my phone into place on my belt. *Time to divide and conquer.* The second zombie approaching was shorter and thinner than the one I was currently facing. The second zombie would probably be easier to defeat, but right now it was also farther away. Regardless of which one I attacked, I had to destroy one or the other so I wouldn't be forced to fight both at once.

I lunged toward the zombie closest to me and swung my sword. The zombie grabbed my sword in its huge hands. I tried to yank it out, but the creature's grip was as strong as a vise. *Swell. Now we have zombies who like to fight back.* My next course of action was obvious. I pulled out my pistol—luckily, I'm ambidextrous, as many of us vampires are—and shot at the hands that decayed away as one bullet after another pummeled them. I tugged my sword from the mess that had been the creature's hands and sliced off one arm.

The zombie moaned loudly and took a step back. I quickly sliced off the second arm. *At least these creatures still are in the process of decay.* The undead took another step back. *Am I hurting it?* Now wasn't the time for analysis. Not far behind me, I heard the moans of the second zombie. I lunged forward and sliced off the huge zombie's head. Head and body tumbled to the ground and dissolved into white pus.

I turned toward the second zombie approaching me. As I heard my phone buzz—probably with a text from Beryl or one of the other two agents—I charged this zombie. Its hands swatted at me. I sliced at the hands with my sword. The creature leaped forward and grabbed my sword arm with both of its hands. It moaned loudly. I tried to free my arm, but the zombie's hands had a tight grip on me. I kicked the creature in its abdomen. That failed to affect it. I sighed heavily, drew my pistol and shot off one hand, then the second. *Decay can be a wonderful thing.*

With gun still in hand, I shot the creature between the eyes. A whitish puss oozed out of the wound. The creature took a few steps back. I advanced and sliced off its head. Similarly to its comrade, it dissolved into white pus. If I'd been human, I might have been grossed out by this development, but we vampires have strong stomachs.

These zombies seem to be smarter than those we encountered before. I checked my phone and read a text message from Ernie. He'd found another zombie and gave his location. I re-loaded my pistol, put it back in its holster and my sword in its scabbard, then dashed to my car. I drove toward Ernie's location. If what had happened to me was a sign of what was to come, another zombie would soon be dropped off close to Ernie.

My phone buzzed once, then again. Checking it, I saw that another zombie had been deposited close to Ernie, but Mindy had spotted the van. She'd included the license number in the text.

We'll get them now.

As I drove in the direction of where Mindy was pursuing the van, I hoped Ernie was doing well with the zombies. One zombie was easy. I wasn't sure what I'd do if I had to fight two at the same time. *Ernie better be using the same strategy of fighting and killing one, then the other.*

My phone buzzed again. Mindy reported a zombie had been let out by the van and she asked whether she should pursue the van or take care of the zombie. Seconds later, Beryl returned with a text to follow the van. As I sped through West Des Moines—WOVACOM was keeping the police from arresting us if we speeded—Ernie reported he'd taken care of his two zombies and was going after the one Mindy had reported.

Turning a corner, I saw Mindy's red Ford Fusion following a black van about a block ahead of her. I texted all that I was close behind Mindy.

In front of us, the van stopped and another zombie was pushed out its side door. The door slammed shut, then the van sped off, leaving little room for doubt that it had finished delivering zombies for the night and was returning home.

Both Mindy and I texted this development. Ernie texted us that he would take care of the zombie, and once we knew where the van had stopped for the night he'd meet us there. Beryl texted a note of confidence and thanks to Mindy and Ernie.

I didn't care that he didn't thank me because, if all went well, we could close up this zombie case.

Our cars sped into the darkness.

VI

A Wild Party

Joe

Wild Ones. What can I say about them? So much and so little. They aren't ferals, who've lost all sense of humanity. We werewolves don't like when that happens. If that happens to any FHs, we kill them immediately. Better a quick death than a life beyond reason. However, reason isn't everything to us. We like having our rational faculties, but we live in irrationality with our emotions, fears, loves, and lusts.

Putting reason and rationality in perspective, we FHs still believe in living life large. Wild Ones believe in living life beyond *large*, beyond *huge*, beyond *everything*. We call them Wild Ones for a reason.

Wild Ones are even better than we FHs at attracting humans, at least certain types of humans—the humans who like to live life on the edge. Who skydive. Who travel to exotic places. Who love to drink, to use drugs, to have sex, and all with wild abandon. We FHs attract a calmer crowd. Still, a regular human who thinks too much will have little in common with any werewolf.

Wild Ones have parties. Packs of Wild Ones from all over Iowa gather once every few months. We werewolves are social creatures. We enjoy being with our packs, and we enjoy being with other packs. If any question ever arises as to who's in control, we fight it out for dominance. A fight can break out anywhere and at any time. Hey, that's who we are.

Henry Borman, his female companion, and all the werewolves, who attended the meeting we knew took place but didn't know where, were bound to attend any party held by the Wild Ones.

Grant said I was to attend the party on the second night after our meeting. The party was to be held on a hobby farm southwest of Des Moines. Hobby farms were run by city folk who own the farms but don't expect them to be their primary sources of income. Some maintain their farms for recreational purposes, many to keep horses or other fun livestock. They operate more like country homes than solely as money-making enterprises. And entertaining was what this particular farm was for. The owners kept it, so every few months they could throw their wild parties far from city lights and city controls.

This farm consisted of a house, a barn, and a few other outbuildings, one for horses, another for hogs. The couple, who owned the farm, worked in both insurance and banking.

I was glad I worked for WOOF because many werewolves had to work among humans all the time within their institutions. Of course, I did, too, in a way because WOOF tracks down evil werewolves who seek to do humanity harm. At this party, I was to take as many photos of Wild Ones as possible. During our current operation we might not want to take them out. Once this case was finished, though, we'd operate by different rules.

But about the farm. A field in front of the house was used for parking. The party itself was being held in the barn, converted to a huge reception hall and rented out by its owners for weddings, funerals, and the occasional high school dance. The Wild Ones needed to receive some income, after all. For those events, they resisted their urge to hunt and kill people. Money sometimes speaks louder than the stomach. For a werewolf, that's saying a lot. Our stomachs mean a great deal to us.

I parked my car in the field at around 11 p.m. About fifty vehicles were already parked in the lot, showing this party was going to be a crazy, raucous affair. *My favorite.* Wild Ones were always easier to manipulate at a party, where their wildness was an asset to me. I left my car and tromped through the tall grass toward the house.

For these parties, the house was always lit up. Lights glowed from every window even if the windows belonged to bedrooms and bathrooms. Parties like these let us be us. Werewolves be werewolves. And that meant being wolves as well. We were far beyond the city, so wolfing-out was not only an option but encouraged. The house was lit up because Shirley and Dick, the hosts, wanted their home to be appealing. Besides, inside the house was where they kept the reserves of food and booze. Ground pork and beef. Hanger steak and red wine. Whiskey with any raw meat. Usually as part of the night's entertainment, Dick threw in a human hunt, an activity we FHs abhorred. *Sick Wild Ones. Sick, sick, sick.*

As I walked by the house, I heard howls from inside. One of the lights switched out. Yeah, Shirley and Dick let partygoers have sex in their house as long as the participants remained in human form. If the participants wanted to rut as wolves, the outdoors provided plenty of space. I'm not sure which is my favorite form in which to rut. I've done it both ways. With humans, of course, I have to be human. For tonight, I didn't care.

Walking around the house and toward the barn, I noticed to my right a circle of partygoers had surrounded two wolves fighting. The wolves were the size of St. Bernard dogs. A few of us transform into wolves even larger than that. I'm not one of them. I wondered what the two were fighting about. Or the fight could be a member of one pack trying to be respected by another pack. Fighting was the only way to gain approval. So I knew tonight I'd have to fight.

Tables with spreads of all kinds of raw meat presented in a variety of ways stood around the barn. Ground meat. Slabs of meat. Meat on the bone. Whole carcasses of animals. Anything a werewolf could desire. A little way inside the barn were tables with bottles of hard liquor and wine, and coolers filled with beer. We werewolves can hold our liquor. Mostly, because we really enjoy our liquor.

"Hey, Joey!" a partygoer shouted at me.

"Hey, Vince!" I yelled in response.

Vince Brown was my best contact among the Wild Ones. He knew I was an FH. Vince didn't care because my pack, FH though it was, left him alone. We also left Dick and Shirley alone, although at times we'd wiped out almost all of their partygoers. Vince was about five-five, had a very stocky build with broad shoulders, large arms and legs, large hands and feet, shoulder-length red hair, and, as with most males, a beard and mustache. Vince was tough as a human, and tougher as a wolf. When I visited these parties, he knew I was always on a case. Because that's the only time I attended them.

Vince came up to me. We shook hands, then gave each other bear hugs.

"Good to see you, man," Vince said.

"Likewise, brother."

"Bet you came here for a reason besides having a good time."

I gave him a wolfish smile. "Got that right."

As we talked, we approached the barn. We stopped at one of the food tables and each grabbed a few cubes of beef. After we ate them hungrily, we stepped a few feet away from the crowds gathered in the barn.

Farther away, the fight continued. Even from this distance, I could see the black wolf with white around its face was pummeling the brown wolf. The groups around the fight were obviously two different packs. This fight must be for honor.

"Those two packs are always going at it," Vince said. "One's from eastern Iowa, the other from western."

I rolled my eyes. *Vince, I know that. They fight at every party.* They were also far enough from Des Moines that we FHs usually left them alone. Besides, they ate a fair amount of purchased meat and kept their hunting of humans to a minimum. As long as they did that, we could tolerate their existence. *But don't push it. You two both are on Grant's radar.*

Other packs had come from out of state. Rarely did we get any who had traveled from another country. We were in Iowa and werewolves in many countries didn't even know Iowa existed.

"Yeah, fighting like they do every party," I said. "I'm interested in any packs new in town, say within the last month or so."

We stopped at a table with coolers of beer. Each of us reached into the cooler, grabbed a bottle, popped off the cap, and downed the beer. Each of us smacked his lips contentedly and dropped his bottle into a recycle bin. We werewolves may be wild, but we're ecologically sound.

"I've heard of a pack with a Henry Borman," I continued. "I really want to meet them."

"Oh, that pack," Vince said hesitantly. "For being new in town, they're quite social."

"That should make my job easier," I said.

If a pack was isolating itself at a party, getting to know its members would be more difficult. Packs came to parties to deal with other packs, whether in a friendly or hostile fashion. The fighting wolves and their packs were examples of the latter. A party wouldn't be a party for them unless one of their members fought a member from that other pack. For a pack to come to this party and not at least talk with another pack was strange. Luckily, the Koman pack wasn't that way.

Vince shrugged. "I'd think so. The Koman pack wear yellow and brown outfits. A few others are, but you should be able to distinguish your targets."

Especially Henry Borman.

In the middle of the barn was a dance floor where men and women alike were dancing to recent hits. Off to one side a group was sitting on steel folding chairs, sipping wine, and playing with their cell phones. I didn't get that either. Come to a party then spend the whole time on your cell phone. What's the point?

Glad the Koman pack is behaving more sociable than those werewolves.

Vince motioned at the various groups between the barn and the house. "Koman pack is spread out in this area."

Indeed, they were. People in brown and yellow outfits dotted the mass of werewolves. Some women wore yellow blouses and brown skirts. Others wore brown and yellow dresses. The men wore either brown shirts and yellow pants or yellow shirts and brown pants. All seemed to be in intense conversations with members of other packs.

I recognized Borman immediately. His being one of the few werewolves without a mustache gave him away. He stood next to the female with long brown hair. The two of them were in a deep discussion with four females and three males.

About ten feet away from Borman's group, a six-foot tall woman in a yellow blouse and a brown skirt was conversing with an even larger group of more mature looking individuals.

When some packs attended parties such as this one, they dressed in similar colors so other packs could easily identify them. Other packs wore whatever outfits each individual felt comfortable in. I preferred the latter over the former because I consider myself a free spirit.

Okay, if Grant attended a party with my pack and told us we all had to dress the same, we would because he may be our friend but he's also our pack leader.

"You wanta make contact?" Vince asked.

"'Course, that's why I came."

"Want me to introduce you?"

I gave Vince a quizzical look. "You already know them?"

My Wild One contact gave me a grin. "I know everybody here. That's why Dick and Shirley put up with me."

Vince can be obnoxious. He likes to bait others into a fighting. That's how I got to know him so well. One time he baited me into a fight, and I beat the meat out of him. We've had a cordial relationship ever since. But Vince lies a lot, too. I didn't believe he really knew everybody here.

"So?" Vince asked.

"Nope. If I want to get their respect, I have to approach them alone."

"Hey, it's your life."

Indeed, it was. And being a member of WOOF, I often had to put my life at risk. That was one of the fun things I got to do. I get a thrill out of it. Especially if I know a fight as a wolf is coming. Wolfing-out is the best part of being a werewolf.

I went to a beverage table, grabbed another beer, popped off the cap, downed the beer, and dropped it into the recycling bin. The bin was getting rather full. Our hosts were letting down on the job.

Having received some liquid courage, I took a deep breath and advanced toward Borman, his female colleague, and the group they were with. Vince followed a few feet behind me.

"That's why we think it's important you join our cause," Henry was saying.

Two of the other males scrunched up their faces. One female laughed nervously.

I bumped into Henry and stepped into the group.

"But is your cause worth fighting about?" I asked.

Borman turned. "Who the hell are you?"

I smiled. "Well, hello to you, too." Being kind to hostile werewolves always makes them angrier.

Borman stared at me. His female companion and the rest in the group turned and stared at me as well.

"Is it?" I persisted.

"Yeah, we think that's a good question," one of the males agreed.

"Henry," his female companion stammered.

"My name is Joe Butler," I said and extended my hand in greeting.

"I don't give a shit who you are!" snapped Henry.

I'd already implicitly challenged him to a fight. His slighting me by not offering his name or shaking my hand now necessitated that he fight me.

Two nearby werewolves backed up in shock. Three smiled maliciously. A few snickered.

My reply was obvious for any werewolf reading this tale.

"I challenge you to a fight," I said.

A hush fell over the surrounding werewolves.

VII

The Surprise in the Van

Samuel

The van sped through the residential streets with Mindy's red Ford Fusion almost right behind it and my Ford Focus about a block behind them.

Mindy texted me that she could handle the situation.

I texted back that the van probably contained aliens and these aliens were probably more than capable of killing one vampire.

Mindy texted back she could easily handle two aliens.

Beryl, who'd been receiving all of our texts, sent one saying the two of us should tackle the occupants of the van.

The van sped onto a main street, driving through red lights and stop signs. Mindy's car sped through the same lights and signs, and as I gained on the two vehicles to the point I was almost tailgating Mindy, I followed suit. The van drove east onto I-235, the interstate that went through Des Moines and its suburbs, with Mindy and me almost on its tail.

For the last five minutes we'd driven silently. I assumed Beryl had contacted WOVACOM, so we wouldn't get police cars in pursuit. We didn't need that, and that was one of WOVACOM's many duties. When VATE agents were breaking the law to solve a special case, WOVACOM agents made sure that law enforcement didn't notice.

I will spare you the details about our chase because, unless you live in Iowa or even Des Moines, you probably don't care about which streets we took following the van, what red lights we ran, or which stop signs we failed to obey. In an action movie, all of those activities might add some excitement to take up a little screen time—even if this action didn't move along the plot significantly. That was Hollywood for you. In any case, the van led us on a chase through town and was unable to lose either of us.

The van pulled into a dead-end alley. Mindy's Ford Fusion pulled in a few moments later, and my Ford Focus a few seconds after that. As I climbed from my car, I put my scabbard at my side, checked my pistol to be sure it was loaded, and made certain I had extra cartridges in my pockets. Mindy appeared to be doing the same as she exited her vehicle. We'd both left our headlights on, so they illuminated the black van in front of us.

A tall, thin, pale man emerged from the driver's side of the van. He was six-seven, thinner than I am, with a bald head, little beady green eyes, and small lips. At his side was a sword. On his back was a shotgun. A shorter, thick-set man emerged from the passenger side. He was about five-six, stockier than any of the other three of us, with shoulder-length brown hair, a fluffy beard and mustache, and large hands with chubby fingers. At his side was a sword. On his back was a shotgun.

As the tall man yanked the shotgun from behind his back, the shorter man leaped forward. His hands expanded into paws, his fingernails becoming long claws. Brown fur erupted all over his body; his face stretched forward, his nose and mouth extending into a long muzzle with sharp teeth; his arms and legs stretched into narrow legs with paws at the end.

I recognized this transformation. When I'd teamed up with a werewolf previously, turning into a wolf was his first response to everything. I don't think I ever got used to that reaction. Now I liked it even less since Mindy and I had to face this werewolf and, I guessed, a vampire using a shotgun.

"I'll take the wolf," I volunteered.

"Shotgun guy is mine," Mindy said.

As the shotgun barked pellets toward us, we both dissolved into mist. I floated a few feet away from both of our vehicles. Even as a cloud of mist, I could tell the wolf had stopped its charge and was sniffing the air for each of us. The vampire had ceased shooting because, as any vampire knows, ammunition shouldn't be wasted when your opponent is in mist form. I re-materialized as a bat. The world around me appeared to be huge and strange since I felt movement and objects through my radar and sense of smell instead of sight. I detected that Mindy had re-materialized as a human.

Ignoring whatever Mindy's plan was, I flew toward the wolf, which charged toward me, snapping its massive jaws at the small bat that I was. Diving under the wolf's belly, I re-humanized, yanked out my pistol and shot twice into its stomach. Unfortunately, I didn't have silver bullets. If I'd had silver bullets, I could have inflicted some real harm. Lead bullets aren't bad. They simply aren't as effective against werewolves as I'd like.

The wolf jumped ahead of me, screaming in pain. I stood to face him. To my left I heard another shotgun blast. *Now a shotgun could inflict some real harm on this beast.* Of course, the only available shotgun was in the hands of the vampire attacking Mindy.

The wolf growled at me. I shot it in the face. Three times. The wolf began to pounce on me. I dissolved into mist. As I floated as a cloud of mist, I was aware I couldn't keep up these transformations for too much longer. I'd drunk more blood than usual for an evening meal, but even three pints of blood was going to be exhausted if I kept up these changes.

The wolf prowled around the cloud of mist that was me. I felt another shotgun blast. *If Mindy would take care of the vampire, I could take care of this wolf.* Or maybe that was the wrong way of thinking. I floated away from the wolf, which continued to pace, growl, and paw at the ground. As mist, I could detect movement.

Unfortunately, as a cloud of mist, I moved slowly, though I moved fast enough to find the vampire hiding behind the van and occasionally stepping out to shoot at Mindy. I guessed Mindy was doing the same behind one of our vehicles.

I re-humanized behind the van and behind the vampire.

"Hello," I said loudly.

He turned.

I slapped the shotgun out of his hands.

"Beckman!" shouted the vampire.

As the vampire drew his sword, I dissolved into mist again. Even as mist, I could feel shots fired behind the vampire. I re-humanized on the ground next to the shotgun. I grabbed it. The vampire put one of his feet on my arm.

"You won't get away that easily." He looked down at me with his sword drawn.

I dissolved into a cloud of mist. I'd swear the vampire cursed. The wolf bounded up behind the vampire who turned toward it and said some very angry words. I didn't understand any of them, however, since after all, I wasn't human. I floated behind both of them and re-humanized.

"Surprise," I said quietly.

I shot the vampire in the back and the wolf in the head. The vampire collapsed to the ground. The wolf transformed back into its human self. Mindy charged forward and sliced off the head of the vampire who melted into ash. The werewolf glanced from Mindy to me. Blood ran from his head. He leaped forward, transformed into a wolf, and dashed out of the alley and into the night.

"Well, I took care of my vampire," Mindy said.

I wanted to say that I didn't have the proper weapons for dealing with a werewolf, but Mindy would ridicule me over that. Because, as VATE agents, we know we have to use the resources available.

"I find it strange that a vampire and a werewolf were releasing the zombies," I said to change the subject.

"Why?" asked Mindy. "We've never seen zombies before. I think this is another sign we need more agents on this case."

Ignoring her "more agents" comment, I said sarcastically, "As if vampires and werewolves would cooperate."

"These two obviously did."

"If they'd coordinated their attack better, we might not have triumphed."

Before Mindy could say anything, Ernie drove up in his large pickup and pulled to a stop near our two cars. Climbing from his vehicle, he looked over the scene.

"At least you have the van," Ernie said. "Maybe somebody can pull some information from that."

Swell. These two make working with a werewolf look good. I never thought I'd think such a thing.

VIII

A Fight for Honor

Joe

Borman stared at me in anger. I looked at him nonchalantly. *Trying to figure out what I want. Well, duh, I want to fight.*

Other werewolves, including the blonde female, from nearby groups gathered around us

Behind me, Vince chanted, "Fight, fight, fight, fight..."

Borman's female colleague patted him on the shoulder. "You know what you have to do."

"Or are you afraid to fight me?" I asked.

We werewolves don't like being called cowards. We may be foolhardy, but we aren't cowards. Well, some of us may be. Agents of WOOF aren't.

"Fight, fight, fight, fight..." Vince continued chanting behind us.

A large crowd, including many wearing yellow and brown, gathered around us. Fights at parties always drew crowds. I think some of the Wild Ones come to parties simply to see the fights that break out.

"I'll fight and kill you," Borman said icily.

"We'll see," I told him.

And we transformed into wolves.

Black and white world. Smells of humans. The dampness of the ground. The grass against my paws.

All around humans chanting. Chanting words I can't understand.

The smell of another wolf. Smell of mold, antiseptic soap, and musty linen sheets.

Look forward. See Borman as a wolf.

Borman growls. [Fight!]

I growl back. [Yes, fight!] No fear. Fear not for one like me.

Borman paws the ground. [Ready, ready.]

I paw ground in reply. [Yes, ready.]

I snarl. Growl. [You will die! Fight!]

Borman howls. [For glory!]

Humans chanting. Chanting. Chanting.

Borman pounces.

Jump to one side. Then pounce. Borman turns to meet me.

Claws. Teeth.

Slash with claws. Bite with teeth. Our front paws meet each other as we rise on our back feet.

Snap at each other.

Fall away from each other. Jump on Borman. Bite his back.

Pushed over. Roll over. Borman's teeth snap at me. Miss.

Back up. Smell Borman's blood. Smell my blood.

If human, I would laugh. More wounds on him than on me.

Bark quickly in triumph.

Borman jumps at me.

Jump sideways. Borman skids in grass.

Pounce on Borman's back. Bite his fur. Bit his flesh. Slash his back.

Whimpers from Borman. [I'm hurt! Hurt!]

Borman can't escape my grasp.

Move to the side. Still on top. Shove Borman over.

Borman rolls over on back.

Still on top. Borman's claws flail. Teeth snap. Don't bite.

Have the advantage. Slash with claws. Bite with teeth. Move up to bite his jugular.

Ready for death blow.
Chanting all around.
Borman whimpers. (Stop! Stop! I surrender!]

And I transformed back into human. Borman did as well. And he still whimpered.

"Death blow! Death blow!" the crowd around us chanted.

The chants died as the participants saw that we'd both transformed back into humans.

"I simply want your respect," I said magnanimously.

"You should have killed me," Borman whispered. "At least I'd have my honor."

"Then you owe me," I said very quietly.

We both stood.

Vince stepped through the crowd. "A well-fought match. And honor is done when a life is spared. We all know the winner. And what is the prize?'

I smiled. "I want to join their pack. I want to hear more about this idea."

Borman shook his head. "What the winner wants, the winner gets." Then he smirked. "But you may not like it."

Since we'd stopped fighting, the crowd dispersed. They didn't care about any deals we reached. They'd come to see bloodshed. Both of us were still wounded, with blood staining our clothes.

My opponent gave me his hand. "Henry Borman."

"Joe Butler."

The brown-haired woman who'd met Borman on the street introduced herself as Victoria and the tall blonde woman as Theresa, their pack leader.

I was in the pack that met with vampires.

IX

Zombies, Zombies Everywhere

Samuel

When we'd reported our finding a vampire and werewolf in the van delivering the zombies—and another zombie that hadn't been released, Beryl determined that this zombie plot was more than a random experiment. He called in more special agents from nearby states. His—and my—theory was still that aliens were behind it. Neither Wild Ones nor Evil Ones used surrogates to cause us trouble. Okay, Evil Ones often had detailed, complicated plans that we had to thwart and in these plans deceit and cunning were used. So far, though, we'd never seen them use other beings—such as zombies—to achieve their ends.

Two more agents arrived the day after Mindy's and my vampire/werewolf encounter. They were William, a thin, short man from Kansas City with large hands and bright red hair, and Hannah from St. Louis, a petite, young woman with shoulder-length black hair and blue eyes. Both of them were intrigued by the zombie element.

We sat around in Beryl's living room in the early evening before venturing forth on zombie patrol. Ernie, Mindy, and I told of our adventures of the previous night. My boss explained how the van had been examined and only had the fingerprints of the vampire and werewolf and the zombies they'd released.

Unfortunately, nothing could be established about the identity of our escaped werewolf.

The vampire and werewolf had been in the front seats, and, at each stop, had opened one of the side doors to release the undead to the world. Unfortunately, the zombie had decayed to a pool of white pus, and following the examination of the van, a green slime had dissolved the van into a pile of rust.

Beryl looked around at all of us. "Any speculation as to what the end game with these zombies is?"

"From what's been discussed," William said. "I'm not so sure the zombies are the ones who have the end game."

After drinking some blood, Hannah added, "I think William is right. The Evil Ones/Wild Ones are ones with the plan."

Ernie groaned. "Vampires and werewolves don't work together. We hate each other and nothing more needs to be said."

Mindy shook her head in annoyance, "I disagree. I think the seeing vampires and werewolves working together is further evidence—"

"We need more agents," Ernie and I said simultaneously.

I continued, "The two who fought us didn't even have a coordinated attack. I think that shows they're somewhat disorganized." I didn't want to lend any credence to Mindy's exasperating request for more agents.

For readers of my previous works, you know my opinion of werewolves and having vampires work with them. I worked with a werewolf on a very short-term mission and concluded that both my time and his had been wasted, although we had vanquished the monster we'd been sent to kill. (All right, the tale is more complicated than what I just said, though the scope of this narrative doesn't allow space for me to tell anymore.) To conclude, werewolves are wild, impulsive beasts who think little, if at all—at least in any rational fashion.

Beryl laughed softly. "I don't care if vampires and werewolves working together doesn't seem logical. That fact is they did. And they were releasing the zombies. And another two might do so tonight since you...” He paused and looked at Mindy and me. “...let the werewolf escape.” Then he stared at Mindy again. “And as you can see, I have more agents.”

Mindy began to protest, but my boss raised his hand.

He continued, “Now isn’t the time for pointing blame. Even if you’d killed the werewolf, we’d be exactly where we are now. All of you are on zombie patrol again tonight. We’ve got WOVACOM agents watching all funeral homes and city morgues. Last night’s zombies came from both places. So far WOVACOM was only watching these places at night, but beginning today, they’ll be watching all morgues and funeral homes 24/7. Whatever is turning these corpses into zombies, the process doesn’t seem to be too lengthy.”

“I think we have a bigger issue,” I said. I wanted to make my views known in this discussion. “Granted, the vampire/werewolf team delivering the zombies shouldn’t be underrated, but I think the bigger predicament is that the zombies were fighting back last night. That’s okay with one, but with two or more, that could become a major problem.”

Beryl laughed softly. “As per Mindy, I did bring in more agents.”

That must be his solution to the issue I posed. I wasn’t sure that two more agents would make that much difference, especially considering what I’d had to say.

I went on, “And I find that the drivers of the vans dropping zombies off on the routes we take is strange.”

The others, including my boss, simply looked at me.

“Well, it is.” I gazed at Beryl. “You design these routes and only give them to us the night we’re going out. Granted, the drivers might randomly be able to drop off a few zombies on our routes, but the last two nights they have dependably put them specifically on our routes. I think that’s hardly coincidental.”

“Duly noted,” my boss said.

Then I didn't have a chance to make another comment. Beryl broke up the meeting and told us which areas of town each of us would patrol later that night.

Zombie patrol. Each of us driving around in his or her vehicle looking for zombies. Each of us quite confident that we would see one or more black vans delivering these undead to the local neighborhoods.

Our real objective of the night wasn't to find zombies, although if we found any we were to destroy them as fast as possible. Our real goal of the night was to find the van or vans releasing the undead, follow the vans back to their source, and destroy that location. If we destroyed the source, we would stop having zombie patrol every night. Beryl had explained this target to us. I stayed after everyone else had left, and both my boss and I agreed that reaching that result might be much harder than the other special agents wanted to admit.

As I drove through my designated streets in a computer-generated pattern, I saw my first zombies at about 11:15. Instead of the lone zombies of previous nights, I spotted two ambling along the sidewalk. Neither undead seemed to notice the other, but each kept an approximately equal distance from its fellow. Both moaned as they walked. One appeared to be a young man in his twenties; the other was an older woman, possibly in her seventies.

His skin, although paler than mine, was smooth and clear. Her skin, equally pale, was wrinkled and splotched. Not that I cared much about what these undead looked like. I did care that I was driving up behind instead of in front of them because, in all likelihood, I could approach and kill them from behind without having to fight either of them.

What we want when we meet zombies.

I was disturbed that two zombies were together. Whoever was behind these undead kept increasing the number they released each time. So far, we hadn't heard of the zombies attacking humans; however, I thought it was only a matter of time. After all, the first night I'd seen one of the undead kill a dog. Obviously, killing was in their fluids—I didn't use the term "blood" because, if the zombies had any blood, the blood wasn't what poured from their wounds.

I parked my car, exited it, put on my scabbard with its sword, and walked behind the two undead. I pulled out my pistol with its silencer and fired a bullet into the back of the head of each zombie, then did it again. Of course, each bullet hit where I intended because I'm a vampire and our sense of aim is perfect—or close enough.

The zombies stopped walking forward as white pus gushed out of the back of their heads. They each slowly turned. Before they could complete their movements, I charged forward, swung my sword, and beheaded them, one after the other. Their heads and bodies collapsed to the ground where both melted away, letting off the smell of a huge landfill.

That was easy. Although, as I'd said, disturbing. *If they're dropping off two zombies at a time now, will they continue to increase the number of undead they're releasing?* After this thought, I cursed because I'd forgotten to take photos of either of my zombies. *Beryl will be mad.* Because identifying who the zombies had been prior to death seemed to be important.

Back to my car. Called my boss and explained the situation. As expected, he wasn't pleased. He couldn't do anything about it, but he still was unhappy.

Again on zombie patrol. I sent a text to all other agents explaining what I'd seen. A few minutes later, William reported destroying two zombies. Fifteen minutes later, Mindy reported the same. Twenty minutes later, Hannah reported in. She'd destroyed her zombies, but was wounded and heading back to Beryl's. Bad news. Our first casualty of the night. A few minutes later, William reported he'd destroyed one zombie. Not too long after, Ernie reported in and said he'd fought three. All three were destroyed. Ernie had a few wounds but believed he could finish out the night.

Beryl sent out a text that told all of us to park our cars and rest for a few minutes.

About fifteen minutes later, my phone rang.

"This is Samuel."

"This is Beryl."

"Rest time over?"

My boss chuckled. "Definitely. We've got a new development."

"Besides having three zombies at once."

"Yes. We've got a new location."

Although I wanted to make a smartass remark, I refrained.

Beryl continued, "Seven zombies are strolling around that sculpture park in western downtown."

Des Moines has a sculpture park in the western part of downtown. Certain wealthy people like to support the arts and promote downtown Des Moines. This sculpture park fulfilled both objectives. In an area about two blocks long and one block wide, this park—displaying statues or huge works of art and areas of grass and sidewalk—ran through the western part of the downtown. On one side was a series of restaurants with unusual, yet not too pricey, food. On the other were large office buildings of companies with a huge presence in Des Moines.

Among the statues in the park were a donkey dressed and sitting thinking on a rock; two large snowman-like statues, one black, one white, with a smaller sphere placed upon a larger sphere; bizarre shaped rocks with faces on them; and a circle about fifteen feet in diameter of glass plates about the size of doors. I'd only seen this park from a vehicle but I'd always been meaning to examine the sculptures in more detail. If the park hadn't been overrun with zombies, this night might have been the perfect time.

"I'm on my way," I said.

"I've also contacted Ernie and Mindy. You three make a good team, so I thought all three of you should check it out."

I withheld a groan. "I'll get there as soon as I can."

"I sent texts to the other two while I was talking to you."

"I feel so special." I hoped my words weren't too sarcastic.

I didn't discover Beryl's opinion of such because he'd hung up.

I started my car and raced through town.

As I approached and parked by the sculpture park, I saw a fair number of vehicles driving on both east-west streets north and south of the park. A few vehicles were parked there, and groups of teenagers were loitering on the sidewalks. One group of about ten teenagers stood around, drinking beer, chatting with each other, and texting or surfing the internet on their cell phones. A good way not to socialize in a social situation. I approved. One or two in this group must have seen the zombies ambling around the park.

Swell. This is exactly what we don't want. At all the prior zombie drop-offs, no people had been present. Beryl was correct that this was a new twist on the zombie game.

Having parked, I called Beryl and told him we needed WOVACOM here as soon as possible. Vehicles kept passing by the park and I saw at least two groups of teenagers. My boss replied that Mindy had already called in, requesting the same. He said WOVACOM was a good ten minutes out.

That's the luck of working with other agents. Sometimes they steal your news.

I exited my car, strapped on my sword, and walked into the park. Then I gazed around and tried to see either Ernie or Mindy. Across the park, I saw three creatures ambling along. *Obviously zombies.* Unfortunately, I also saw two teenagers, holding beers by the look of it, point at the creatures, and shout at them. When the zombies failed to respond, the two teenagers strolled in the direction of the undead creatures. I strode toward this unlucky meeting as fast as I could. Since both security cameras and humans were around, I knew I had to use as few of my vampire abilities as possible.

I still didn't see either Ernie or Mindy.

The two teenagers dashed into the park toward the zombies. The humans stopped, shouted again at the creatures, then tossed their slightly full beer cans at the undead. Moans echoed through the park.

Damn! They made the creatures angry. If these had been the undead of a few nights before, I wouldn't have worried, but the creatures of the prior night had shown the ability to react and fight back. Besides, I still remembered my first night on zombie patrol where the undead had eaten the dog's brains.

Before the teenagers could move, the three zombies were upon them. Let me say a very grotesque scene proceeded. The remains of the teenagers were not a pleasant sight.

The other teenagers from their group saw this scene, screamed, hopped in their cars, and sped off. I caught almost all the license plate numbers and texted these numbers and a description of the scene to Beryl. He texted back that WOVACOM had gotten held up, but they would handle this crisis in addition to the previous requests.

In the meantime, four other zombies met the three who'd just eaten the brains of the two raucous teenagers.

I sighed. I still hadn't seen Ernie or Mindy. *Doesn't matter. I have to stop the undead.* I drew my sword and charged forward.

Behind me, I heard shouts. I skidded to a stop and saw three people emerging from a black van.

Where are my other special agents?

X

Prior to an Important Meeting

Joe

Success. The feeling of winning a fight is always glorious, the feeling of winning a fight and making progress on an elusive case even more so. After a wolf-out and a fight, I'm always supercharged. I want to race around in circles, drink a few beers, howl at the moon, hug my friends, and roll around in the grass. When I beat Borman, I restrained myself from doing any of the previously mentioned activities. (But I really, really, really wanted to.) Other people at the party wouldn't have blamed me. Once, after a fight, I saw the victor remain in wolf form, dash around the party, and howl at the night sky for almost an hour. That was a little much.

Theresa told me the time and place of their next meeting. She was so disgusted Borman had lost the fight that she gathered her pack and they left the party immediately. As they left, Theresa and Victoria kept staring back at me angrily and muttering under their breaths.

Vince sidled up to me. "That guy was a wimp."

I shook my head. "Got that right. He hardly put up any fight."

I had a few cuts and bruises. Borman had been bleeding profusely under his shirt. Humiliating.

"I've done my damage," I said.

"Hey, come again," Vince said.

I smiled. "I've gotta get a few selfies with the packs here, then I'll vamoose."

"Always on the job."

"It's what I do."

Theresa's pack met two nights later. This time I knew the location. This time I was invited. This time I was given instructions to walk around downtown for a while to be certain to lose anybody tailing me. *The way I had followed Borman a few nights before.* This time WOOF didn't have any agents following any Wild Ones. Since I was attending, why waste another agent's time? We werewolves aren't into redundancy. If one agent is enough, why waste the time of others. I think vampires use lots of redundancies because they fear failure too much. Big risks, big gains.

Victoria met me at the door to the apartment and invited me in.

"Welcome, victor of fights," she greeted.

"Thank you," I said politely. "I'm one of you now."

As I walked in, I discovered this apartment was hardly set up for a domestic lifestyle. The main room was filled with rows of chairs facing a podium. A whiteboard that looked as though it could be used for PowerPoint shows as well as for brainstorming ideas stood behind the podium. Six laptops sat on a small table close to the kitchen, currently being used by two males and four females. Three other males talked together in a corner.

Victoria smiled at my discomfort. "Did you think we'd use one of our actual homes?"

I gave her a malicious smile. "Not if you have a clever operation in the works."

Well, what did you expect me to say? "Oh, yes, I hoped you were a pack who loved to have orgies." Orgies do take place. Some parties of Wild Ones exist only for that purpose. I'd been to two and learned nothing about the pack I was pursuing. Well,

I did learn something at those parties. But modesty prevents my writing about it.

Borman emerged from the kitchen, chewing on a raw drumstick and carrying a beer. He strode up to us. "Vic," he said to my hostess.

"Henry, don't be so rude to Joe," Victoria said. "He beat you in a fair fight."

My former opponent ripped off the remaining meat from the drumstick, chewed it up, and tossed the bones in a nearby trash can. "He beat me. Doesn't mean I have to like him."

"Same to you," I snapped back.

Henry growled.

I growled in response. I bit back any crueler response as Theresa walked across the room. Turning away from Borman, I delivered a mock bow to the female leader.

She gave me a mischievous smile. "Joe, or do you prefer Joey?"

"Joe is fine."

She patted me on the shoulder. "You have superior fighting skills. Henry boasts a lot, but that's about it. You showed us how a true master works."

Henry growled again.

Theresa shook her head. "Henry, he beat you in a fair fight. I'd thought you'd drunk a bit too much at the party. Perhaps that's why you fought so poorly."

"I was perfectly sober," Borman snarled.

"So Joe's fighting skill appears even greater."

Victoria grabbed Borman's elbow. "Henry," she stammered.

He looked from her to me to Theresa, pulled away from Victoria, and walked away quickly.

"You're a new pack in Des Moines," I said.

Both females gazed at me. Theresa said, "Duh."

"Some packs come here for parties like those at Dick and Shirley's," I said. "I check out the parties to find new blood. Mixing with new blood is always fun."

Werewolves know exactly what I'm saying. Humans, you're smart, so you should be able to figure it out, too, especially after my comments about the orgies. If any vampires are reading this, I don't give a shit whether you know or not.

Both women snickered at my comment. Victoria took my hands and squeezed. Theresa gave me a wink. Rutting comes from winning fights, too.

Across the room, Borman snarled. Victoria went and took his hand, then led him toward the kitchen.

"You'll have to watch him," Theresa warned. "He doesn't like you."

"The feeling is mutual."

The leader left me to go examine a laptop that sat on the podium in front of the rows of chairs. I glanced from the rows of chairs to the kitchen and to the table where the werewolves were working on their laptops. Two of the females caught my eye. One whispered to the other. Both giggled. One was about my height with long black hair, dark blue eyes, and a small face. The other was a little shorter than me with shoulder-length blonde hair, green eyes, a thin nose, and large lips. Both wore blouses and jeans. Then the brunette typed a bit on her laptop, closed it, stood, and walked toward me.

"I'm Ellen," said the brunette. She motioned at the blonde, who waved at me. "That's Leslie."

"Joe," I responded.

"We know," Ellen said. "You beat up Henry like he was a pup."

I shrugged. "All in a night's work."

Ellen stepped closer to me and said very quietly, "He's Theresa's pup. He'll do whatever menial chores she gives him. That's why he's tolerated despite being a pissant poor fighter."

"Yeah, his fighting skills suck," I admitted.

"But you fight like a true wolf."

"Do you?"

She smiled. "Do you need to ask?" She glanced at Leslie, who looked up from her laptop and grinned. "I do other things like a true wolf, too."

Her coming on to me may seem strange to some of you, but not you werewolves. We're a lusty race. Often when I infiltrated Wild Ones' packs, I had some sexual dalliances with the enemy. No harm, no foul. All is fair in love and war.

"I'm a loner in this area," I explained regarding her unasked question. "I was ostracized from my last pack." I paused. "Long story."

This was my standard line in getting in good with Wild Ones' packs. Ellen nodded, as if understanding. The "long story" always causes them to let me change the subject.

"This pack is new to the area. Why did you come?"

"Ah, an interested party," Ellen said. "Our story, not so long. Before Theresa became our pack leader, we were in the Chicago area. Lots of packs there. Large ones. Vicious ones. Our last pack leader was Benjamin. Tougher than most of us, but not smart strategically nor tactically. We fought lots of fights, but the victors always gave us mercy at the last moment."

"Humiliating?"

"That's not the half of it. About a month ago, Theresa showed up in Chicago. One time we were at a party. Theresa saw Benjamin, challenged him to a fight, and beat him even more soundly than you defeated Borman. That's how she became our pack leader."

"A female pack leader is rare," I commented. That's not as true now as it was for centuries. As human females have made inroads to success, so have werewolf females. Still, we're chauvinistic race.

"But she's good. She led us to victories in Chicago, then we came here."

"And why did you come here in particular?" I asked.

"Theresa has a plan to kill off all the pets. Wimpy werewolves," Ellen muttered.

"Yeah, I hate those pets."

If my readers haven't guessed, "pets" is the derogatory word Wild Ones use to describe us Friends of Humanity.

"And that's what this meeting is about?"

Ellen gave me a malicious smile. "Oh, and so much more."

Theresa barked three times as she stood behind the podium. Using wolf aspects of our language when in human form sometimes is more efficient than using human equivalents. We all know what each bark or growl or snarl or howl means even if we're not wolfed-out. In this case, our leader's barks meant the meeting was about to begin.

The werewolves left whatever they were doing and sat in the chairs. Henry and Victoria sat next to each other. Ellen and I sat in one row behind those two. Leslie joined us.

Theresa barked once. All conversations of those in the chairs ceased.

"Welcome to tonight's meeting," the pack leader said to us. "We welcome Joe to our fold." She paused. "I'd like to introduce our other members, Joe." She glanced at Victoria and Henry. "I realize you know a few of our members, but I'll introduce you to all to be sure." As she said each name, she indicated the individual in question. "Victoria, Henry, Ellen, Melody, Leslie, Irina, Roy, Bill, Chuck, Jake, and Nick."

Roy, Bill, Jake, and Nick howled. Irina, Melody, Leslie, and Ellen barked a few times. Henry growled. Victoria patted his shoulder and whispered soothingly into his right ear. Chuck growled, too, but nobody was around to soothe his anger.

Then something pounded loudly at the door to the apartment.

XI

Zombies and Hit Squads

Samuel

I glanced from the three people advancing from the van to the seven zombies. The seven undead milled around, moaning and groaning as was the wont of their non-living lifestyle. One picked up a loose leg left by one of the unfortunate teens and chewed at the blue jeans covering the flesh.

Where are Mindy and Ernie?

Of the three people hurrying toward me, one had drawn a sword, the other a shotgun, and the third a pistol. Two were male, tall—each over six feet—thin, lanky types, who could very well be vampires. The female was only about five-eight with long flowing black hair. Possibly a werewolf. That is, if the categories of our adversaries tonight were the same as the prior night. This time I was ready. My sword was made of silver and the bullets for my pistol were silver as well. *Not going to catch me unprepared again.*

Both zombies and those emerging from the van ignored me. I thought the mix of two vampires working with one werewolf was strange. I figured we vampires would get the better deal than our less intelligent cousins and force the ratio of those coming into danger to have the werewolves outnumbering the vampires. *Not in this case.*

Ernie and Mindy emerged from behind one of the hills spread throughout the park. Both had pistols drawn and both were firing as they rounded the hill, shooting bullets into each of the zombie's heads. Silencers on their pistols quieted the shots, but, using my vampire hearing, I could hear each shot, and, using my vampire sight, I saw each bullet plunge into each zombie's head. One through the forehead. Another in the side of the head behind an ear. Another in the back of the head. And so on. *Ernie and Mindy might complain a lot, but I can't criticize their work.*

White pus oozed from these wounds. The zombies turned toward their attackers, moaning even more loudly. The undead that had been chewing on a leg tossed the limb at its attackers, who jumped out of the way as they raced confidently toward the creatures—none of whom had fallen. On the prior night, a bullet to the head had caused a zombie to fall. Not tonight.

In the meantime, the three from the van advanced closer to the zombie horde. I stopped and looked from the zombies to Ernie and Mindy, then to the three living people from the van.

As Ernie and Mindy approached the zombies, they continued firing their pistols. The bullets splatted into the undeads' heads. Even from this distance, I could hear Ernie cursing. Mindy was too focused on the job at hand to curse. The zombies seemed impervious to my colleagues' assaults.

Both Ernie and Mindy holstered their pistols and drew their swords.

That won't be a fair fight, especially if the vampire/werewolf team arrives.

Despite my dislike for each of these special agents, I knew what I had to do. If the three of us disposed of the zombies before dealing with the van occupants, we could then take on the vampire/werewolf team. Slipping my sword into its scabbard, I dashed across the grass adorning the sculpture park.

A shout echoed behind me. Then guns fired. Both a pistol and a shotgun.

Damn, the squad's not going to let me do what I want. Or if they were, they weren't going to let me dispose of zombies without making it more difficult for me.

As I reached the zombies, one or two turned, but not the ones closest to me. I drew my sword and beheaded two of them. Two others surrounded Mindy. Three closed in around Ernie.

A loud howl echoed not too far away from me. A black-furred wolf the size of a St. Bernard charged toward me. Neither vampire was in sight. Still holding my sword, I yanked out my pistol with the other hand and fired at the wolf dashing toward me. *Silver bullets do your stuff.* Aiming for the wolf's head, I fired. Three times. And hit the wolf between the eyes each time. *We vampires are good.*

The wolf collapsed on the ground, transformed back into a human covered with a layer of white fur.

One down.

I turned to see Mindy slice off the head of one of her zombies. And to see Ernie drop his sword and a zombie rip off one of his arms. I have to give Ernie some credit. He refrained from screaming. I'm not sure I could have done the same. Blood gushed from his wound as the zombie holding Ernie from behind bit into his neck. The zombie with Ernie's arm chewed away at it. The third zombie grabbed both side of Ernie's head and squeezed.

Behind me, more gunshots rang out. I dove to the ground to see two tall, thin assailants emerging from behind a small hill. I let my sword drop, grabbed my pistol with both hands, and took aim.

The vampires must have heard me because they dissolved into clouds of mist. *Damn.*

Holstering my pistol and grabbing my sword, I turned to see a pile of ash between three of the zombies. Mindy beheaded the last undead attacking her. The three free zombies immediately turned toward her. I quickly jumped behind one and beheaded it. Head and body fell to the ground to decay away.

I dove to the ground again as gunshots echoed behind me. The shotgun blast hit the back of a zombie. The pistol bullet hit Mindy in the arm. I wondered if that bullet had been aimed for my torso but had missed. I fired twice at the head of the vampire carrying the shotgun—after all, the shotgun could do further harm, so I wanted to eliminate its user first. The vampire with the shotgun tumbled to the grass. And I dissolved into a cloud of mist as the other vampire shot repeatedly where I had been lying.

As a cloud of mist, I floated across the ground. Behind me I could feel the movement of air while Mindy fought the last two zombies. I felt other bullets fly through the air. A few might have hit zombies. *Most might be hitting Mindy.*

I re-materialized into bat form. Using my bat radar, I detected the last attacking vampire who stood still and was re-loading his pistol. *Now's the time.* I flew low to the ground until I was behind this vampire. I re-humanized with my sword drawn. Swish. Off came the head of this vampire. As head and body fell to the ground, both melted into ash.

I turned to see Mindy collapsing. Blood spurted from her chest and her head. The bullets from this vampire had done their work. Although the zombies were wounded with white pus oozing from their wounds, neither had fallen. Each one dropped to its knees to continue its attack on Mindy. I quickly sprinted to the vampire injured by the shotgun blast and beheaded him.

Dashing across the open lawn, I decapitated first one zombie then the second. Both bodies fell to the ground and melted away to white pus.

I knelt next to Mindy.

She gave me a wan smile. "To think Ernie thought this was a stupid case," she said weakly.

All around us police sirens rang out. Finally, WOVACOM had appeared on the scene. I looked around the sculpture park, at the businesses and restaurants near it and at the streets all about that were becoming steadily more deserted as the WOVACOM police officers cleared the scene.

"You put up a good fight," I told Mindy.

"We should have had more of us here." Mindy wheezed. "Beryl doesn't have near enough agents. Somebody higher up should be put in charge. Something awful is happening."

I shrugged. "Be quiet. I'll call Beryl and ask for assistance. We'll get you fixed up."

Mindy smiled.

Two police officers approached. "Are you Samuel?" asked one.

"Yes, and this is Mindy. She needs medical attention."

"We've already contacted Vampire Medics."

"Will you take care of all the camera feeds in this area? Two carloads of teenagers also saw some of this action."

One police officer shook his head. "You VATE agents certainly made a mess of this. We're on it, but we have to keep this struggle secret. Encounters such as this one could reveal vampires to the world."

"And the zombies and assailants we dealt with could also put humanity in general in danger," I said.

"That's your job, not ours," the second police officer said.

I refrained from replying. If zombies kept appearing in downtown, we'd not only need more VATE agents, but we'd need more WOVACOM agents to keep these future battles secret.

Maybe Mindy was right all along.

XII

A Meeting with Evil Ones

Joe

"Roy, answer the door," ordered Theresa.

Roy stood and walked to the door. He opened it and backed into the room. His eyes widened. He stepped away from the door to let our visitors enter.

"The rest of the attendees of the meeting," he said meekly.

As ten pale vampires entered the room, Roy sat down, and the rest of us moved to one side of the set of chairs. Each row had ten chairs with an aisle between leading to the podium behind which stood Theresa. All of us werewolves moved to the right side facing the podium. The vampires occupied the left side.

The vampire who came in first was six-nine, thin, black skinned with black hair in a buzz cut and menacing brown eyes. He was followed by nine other vampires. Six, both male and female, were the classic tall and lanky build, typical of bloodsuckers. The other three weren't so much the typical types. One female was short and chubby, the second, petite both in height and breadth. The atypical male was short, stocky, but with lots of muscles. Whether the typical body build or not, none of the males sported mustaches or beards and all had short hair, three a buzz cut. The females had long, but thin hair, not the luxurious hair that we werewolves enjoy.

The tall black vampire advanced to the front while his companions surveyed the crowd, and we stared at them.

"I don't like this," Ellen whispered.

"Leeches don't make good friends," I whispered back.

"'Cause they're hairless bloodsuckers."

We both giggled.

Borman and Victoria growled at both of us. The vampires looked our way and frowned. I didn't care. The remark was funny.

"Welcome to our partners," Theresa said.

Henry and Victoria gave plastic smiles to the vampires across the aisle. A few other werewolves followed their example while a couple simply scanned the floor. *It's best if I show I like this arrangement.* I waved at them. Ellen winked at me and waved as well. Chuck gazed with hatred at our hairless partners. The vampires on the other side of the aisle gave us nasty glares.

"Cecil, it's good to see you," the werewolf leader greeted her counterpart. They shook hands as Cecil took his place beside her.

"Theresa, we are pleased to be here."

Most of his followers passively surveyed the leaders. Others cracked their knuckles and grumbled to themselves. Sammy, my old vampire colleague, had been a happier companion than any of these angry leeches.

Cecil nodded for Theresa to continue.

"Now that we're all here we can discuss our plans." Theresa scanned the small group. "For you vampires, we have a new recruit, Joe Butler." She motioned at me. Nobody, not even any of the other werewolves, gave me a look. Ellen nudged me with her elbow. "You still have your same crew," Theresa added.

"Quite so," Cecil said. "For your newcomer, let me introduce my 'companions.'" As he gave each name, he pointed at the individual. "Helen. Tricia. Dexter. Lucille. Morgan. Kelsey. Troy, Matilda. Irma." None of the vampires even glanced at us werewolves, let alone acknowledged our existence. Troy and Dexter snickered during the introduction only to have Cecil look at them and clear his throat.

Following these introductions, the vampire leader continued. "We have gathered more of our kind—"

"But they keep dying on us," interrupted Troy.

Tricia, Kelsey, and Morgan giggled. Seeing vampires acting as if something was funny was strange. They're generally a serious lot. Because they think any being who isn't a vampire is stupid. I learned that after my assignment with Sammy.

Cecil gave Troy a nasty look.

"Regardless, you've lost some vampires recently," said Theresa.

"A werewolf died last night, too," Cecil countered.

"That's why we need new recruits. We werewolves have various get-togethers—"

"Parties," Ellen whispered.

"Good times," I whispered back.

Henry, Roy, Bill, and Leslie, werewolves all, gave similar comments almost as quietly.

"—where in one fight we can gain one or more," Theresa continued. "Right now, both groups of us need plenty of reserves."

"It's damn dangerous duty," Chuck cut in. "We should be able to deliver the cargo and be done."

"Vampires aren't afraid of risky jobs," Troy said across the aisle.

Chuck, Ellen, and Bill growled.

Dexter and Morgan smiled, pointed their index fingers at us, and used the finger to motion for us to come and get them.

"That's why they die so easily on assignment," Bill shot back.

"We die because we fight with honor," Troy retorted, standing.

"You die since you're lousy fighters," said Bill as he stood.

"Take that back!" shouted Troy.

"Make me!" Bill yelled in return.

Troy's eyes reddened, his incisors grew, and his fingernails turned into claws. Then he jumped toward the aisle. For you werewolves who don't know, that's a bloodsucker "vamping out."

Across the aisle, Bill leaped into the air and transformed into a wolf.

Cecil dashed across the room, grabbing Troy as Theresa tackled Bill.

"Troy, calm down!" Cecil ordered.

Theresa whispered soothing words into wolf Bill's ears. Our wolf comrade let his body transform back into his human self.

Not too far away, Troy ceased to be vamped-out.

Having calmed down their respective followers, the two leaders strode back to the front of the room. Bill sat at the far right end of one row, Troy at the far left end of another row.

"We are not here to fight over which race is the better or more honorable," Cecil said sternly.

"We're working together," Theresa said harshly. "Our fights should be focused on killing pets and human-lovers, not each other."

"Because that is our true aim," the vampire leader added. "All of our lives will be much easier once we eliminate the human-lovers and pets in this area. Neither group suspects a group of vampires and werewolves cooperating in their destruction. We have plans to first kill the most powerful of our enemies, then we will clean up the rest."

"Danger is danger," Chuck cut in again. "We deliver the cargo. We shouldn't have to fight if the cargo isn't doing its job. If I hadn't fled when I did, I wouldn't be here tonight."

"I agree," spoke up Matilda. "Last night nobody survived. And why do we send more vampires than werewolves?" She studied us werewolves. "The Hairy Ones deserve to die as much as we do."

"We need to continue doing these runs at night," Cecil said. "That is our agreement with the third party of this operation. As long as we get the cargo where it needs to go each night, the third party promises it will do its part to destroy the human-lovers and pets."

Now this discussion is interesting. I wonder what all of this has to do with our destroying all FHs and Protectors. Sammy was, and probably still is, a Protector. I hoped I wouldn't be sent on such an assignment because I wouldn't want to be on opposite sides with Sammy.

"Only the experienced will be set on these assignments. I have requested from the third party to keep you safe, and they have agreed," Cecil explained.

"I've complained too," Theresa added.

But who is this third party? I figured that could answer many questions. None of the other audience asked questions. To fit in, I kept quiet, too.

"As we said," Theresa continued, "Recruitment is our primary aim. We werewolves will be going to a party similar to the one where we recruited Joe. This time we will attend with the idea of increasing our number exponentially." She paused and stared at Cecil. "Do you have a similar plan?"

"Partying is not something vampires do." The vampire leader snorted. "However, our organization is nationwide. If needed, as is the case in this circumstance, we can gather followers from other parts of the country to join us in our quest to destroy the human-lovers. More have been arriving every day." He stopped and looked at Theresa and all of us werewolves. "The less they have to work with your kind, the more likely they are to come to this area. They agree that, if enough of us are here, we can rid this region of those human-lovers."

Theresa told us. "The third party wants our continued involvement in the deliveries, so we may be stuck working together."

"Not if more than one vehicle is involved."

Our leader smiled. "Yeah, and I think from here on out that'll be the case."

Both the vampires in the audience and we werewolves muttered our approval of this development. I wanted to ask about the vehicles and the cargo. I didn't. I like to look for opportunities. In this case, there was none, at least to discover that information.

"With our losses as well as for our upcoming attack, we have to gather as many of each our races as possible," Cecil said. "The third party has decided that they will not use us as cannon fodder when making deliveries."

"That's true," Theresa agreed. "We have a good estimate of the pet fighters in this region, but we also have a mole in their organization to ensure we will kill plenty of their agent types during the attack."

"We also have a good estimate of the human-lovers in the area. However, as more strong human-lovers come to this area concerning the cargo issue, we will be able to kill the most powerful before we clean up the more insignificant ones," Cecil said. "We also have a mole who is encouraging more agents to come here."

Our leader sighed heavily.

Their leader snorted in disgust. He pulled out his cell phone. "I've made out a list of who needs to work when in the next few nights."

Theresa shook her head. "All right, send it to me. In the end, I'm sure the third party help will prove to be invaluable."

"The cargo is performing its job better, so may eventually aid our cause," Cecil said. "When the third party helps us, it will be in a good way for us as well as them."

Both werewolves and vampires grumbled assent.

What the hell is the cargo? Obviously, everyone but me knows.

"We will kill all the pets and human-lovers!" Theresa exclaimed.

We werewolves howled happily. The vampires applauded.

Werewolves and vampires might not like each other and not want to cooperate with each other. But if we find something we can agree upon, we'll work in tandem for the accomplishment of this goal. *That's what I'm afraid of.*

XIII

A Need for Corpses

Samuel

We met with Beryl yet again. This meeting wasn't a happy affair. Not that any meeting with Beryl can be called a happy affair. Before, during, and after my assignments, my boss rarely makes meeting with him a fun event because most of the time, he's evaluating my performance and telling me what I should have done, what I could have done, or what I could have requested that would have made my last case more acceptable. I think Beryl's problem is that he's not out in the field enough, and he's become an armchair agent. Not that I'm ever going to tell him that.

The five of us met with him in his living room. William, Hannah, Ronald, Ingrid, and I sat either on the couch or in one of his recliners—William received that honor. Beryl sat in his own usual recliner. We were all drinking cold blood. *Ah, for the good old days of having a small enough assignment that I could talk with my boss alone.* This mission definitely wasn't shaping up that way.

Ernie was dead. Our first major casualty. Mindy was severely wounded. According to Beryl, she should recover fine, but her healing would take a few days since the zombies had nearly killed her the night before. Although Hannah had been injured as well, she'd recovered enough to attend this meeting.

Ronald and Ingrid were new. We seemed to be getting a number of stereotypical vampires to help us on this case. In fact, Ronald was a thin, lanky vampire with a bald head and he reminded me some of Bald Guy who had once been a member of my chapter. Unlike Bald Guy, though, Ronald had a sense of humor. He was from Omaha, Nebraska. Ingrid—also tall, thin, with blonde hair—was from Madison, Wisconsin. She lacked a sense of humor. Well, you can't always get what you want.

"Give me a rundown of what happened last night," my boss told us. "Samuel, please go first."

I explained how we'd encountered the zombies in the suburbs and how zombies had been spotted in the sculpture park and the ensuing battle. William told about his individual fight with his group of undead. Hannah told how she'd been injured but still had done away with her zombies. We were all in agreement that these zombies were becoming progressively tougher to destroy.

Ronald and Ingrid paid careful attention, and each occasionally posed a question or two. Beryl listened almost in silence, absorbing every detail and asking a random question, sometimes questions that seemed hardly relevant until one of the three of us had adequately explained the answer.

"All of this is very troublesome," Beryl concluded.

He's right about that.

"The zombies are becoming a bigger force," my boss continued. "And we tried to have our people examine the van, but it melted into a pile of rust before they even arrived."

Sometimes he thinks out loud. I find it an obnoxious habit. Each of us should be able to think to him- or herself and reach logical conclusions, and I find it exasperating when someone, especially someone I believe to be an intelligent vampire, needs to talk it out. However, the information about the van was new and distressing.

"Those vampire/werewolf teams are strange as well," Ronald said.

I wished either Mindy or Ernie were here. I was the only one among the five special agents present who'd actually fought against these teams. Even being more adequately prepared the prior night, I still hadn't been able to save Ernie.

"I don't quite understand their existence," I said. "The zombies have to be an alien creation. Why would they be recruiting vampires and werewolves to deliver their creatures?"

"Why are vampires and werewolves even working together?" Ingrid asked.

At this point, I could have told the story of my working with a werewolf to vanquish a vampwolf in a shopping mall. However, I preferred to think about that case as little as possible regardless of its possible connections to this one.

Beryl must have thought along the same lines because he said, "I would like to say that the growing strength and number of the zombies and the vampire/werewolf teams were our only worries, but, unfortunately, we have a new issue that, we believe, is connected to our overall case."

We sat and gazed silently at Beryl.

Beryl continued, "As you know, WOVACOM agents are watching all morgues and funeral homes in the areas. They've been doing it the last two nights."

That's supposed to be a good thing. If the aliens couldn't acquire corpses, then we wouldn't have zombies. Problem solved. Extra WOVACOM agents had probably been called into town for this duty, and these new agents were probably as little thrilled by this assignment as Ernie had been. *But if Ernie had been properly worried about our case, he might not be dead. And Mindy said we needed more agents, and she seems to have been right. If she doesn't recover from her injuries, she'll never know that Beryl finally took her suggestion seriously.*

My boss looked at me. "Listening, Samuel?"

"Of course," I replied.

"Good. Because yesterday we had a very strange scene. In the middle of the day, a shooter appeared in a department store and shot seven people. As expected, WOVACOM and the police quickly surrounded this store in the mall and found the shooter, but they were unable to capture or kill him. What was even stranger was that all the corpses were swooped up by medical personnel in black uniforms and put in black vans." Beryl stopped to let us absorb this information.

"So?" asked Ronald. "That should be a police matter."

"The corpses weren't taken by coroners. Witnesses say the medics—or what they supposed were medics—were average-built men and women. Nothing special except they weren't real emergency personnel," my boss explained.

"Were these vans similar to those dropping off zombies?" I inquired. *This must have some connection to the zombies, or Beryl wouldn't bring up this issue.*

My boss smiled at me. "Exactly. We think our culprits may need other sources of corpses. VATE contacted me and said similar incidents have occurred in nearby cities such as Cedar Rapids, Omaha, Minneapolis, and Kansas City. None of the shooters has been caught or killed. None of the corpses of the victims has been found."

"And you expect they'll be showing up as some of our zombies soon," Hannah said, completing his thought.

Beryl laughed softly. "I'm afraid so."

"There must be some reason why these culprits...," I refrained from saying "aliens" since we hadn't proved whether aliens were behind this plot or not, "...want more zombies."

"Maybe they want to kill off the vampire population," my boss said, a bit sarcastically.

"You might need to call in more agents," Ronald advised.

"You're not the first to suggest that," Beryl conceded.

Of course, we could ask the local werewolves. But that's a stupid idea.

Beryl's phone rang. He stood up, walked away from the group, and answered it.

"These zombie appearances aren't logical," said Ingrid. "If whoever is behind this plot wanted to kill us, I'd think they'd find where we're meeting and set loose their zombies on us. That would have a better chance of killing all of us than doing these random drops."

"If these zombies keep getting stronger, they won't need to be helped by the vampire/werewolf squads," William countered. "Both Hannah and I had difficult times subduing our zombies—"

"And zombies alone killed Ernie," Hannah said, cutting in.

Our time for random comments was up. Beryl returned to our group.

"There's been another shooting. I want all of you on the scene. Some of you help the police and WOVACOM with the shooter while the rest of you get rides with these fake medics or replace the medics to find where these black vans are taking their corpses."

XIV

Another Meeting with Grant

Joe

Fun times again! Update meeting. One of my favorite times in mid-case. A time of give and take. An exchange of views. Recommendations. Brainstorming. And all that good food, too! Fun, fun, fun.

Good thoughts like these spun through my mind as I sat at Grant's kitchen table adorned with a plate of beef cubes and another of raw chicken legs. Good ol' Grant. Always with the food to whet our appetites in our discussion of my current case.

I was glad to be able to report because that werewolf/vampire meeting had been disturbing. Disturbing like eating rotten meat. And not keeping it down. That kind of disturbing.

We talked about the Wild Ones' party, my fight with Borman, and the Wild Ones/Evil Ones' meeting. We spent the most time on this last item. Grant found the discussion as unsettling as I did. If werewolves working with vampires wasn't bad enough, the delivery of the strange cargo, a mole in our organization, and the plans to kill off us Friends of Humanity brought chills up both our spines.

"This group was really excited about killing off FHs and the friendly vampires," I said as I finished. "We gotta contact VATE. The vampires gotta know. Sammy needs to know."

Grant chomped on a beef cube. "I don't want to contact them prematurely. Your friend's boss doesn't have any sense of humor."

"This isn't about anything funny. Their lives may be at risk," I countered.

"True, but the last time you worked with Sammy, his boss was a pain to work with." My boss snickered, knowing how much the vampire hated that name. "We need something more concrete before making contact."

"But the Evil Ones are planning to kill the most powerful Protectors. That's gotta include the VATE agents. Sammy's one powerful dude."

Grant shook his head. "Okay, that's true, but as far as you know they don't have all their forces collected yet."

I ate another beef cube. "But they have a mole in the good vampires' organization."

"You also said they have a mole in ours."

I rolled my eyes. "Yeah, I know."

My boss chewed thoughtfully on a chicken leg. "Do you have any idea who it might be?" he asked.

"Everybody in our pack is reliable," I replied. "I can't imagine anyone betraying us to Wild Ones."

"I've contacted other WOOF packs nearby to bring their agents here."

"That's good because Theresa is planning on getting as many Wild Ones as possible to attack us. We'll need lots and lots of agents to fight back."

"We'll definitely surprise them," Grant said knowingly.

Grant's smart that way. Sometimes it's like he and I are thinking almost the same thoughts. That's why he's such a great boss.

"Their talk about the cargo and third party bothers me too, but they didn't give any details on either."

"I got that from your description," Grant acknowledged. "Interesting that both the Wild Ones and Evil Ones said delivery duty was dangerous."

"And they had to fight," I added. "One werewolf even got injured."

"And they didn't say what they were fighting?" asked Grant.

"Nope. But it had something to do with the cargo and the third party. Supposedly, the third party will help them kill us FHs and the human-friendly vampires."

"You gotta learn more about this third party."

I shrugged. "Yeah, I know, but after the meeting Borman told me the next few deliveries already have volunteers."

"So they volunteer for this duty?"

I grabbed a chicken leg and took a bite. "That's what Borman says, but I don't trust him. He doesn't like me and could've been lying. Besides, the others didn't like the deliveries at all."

"Any idea who the third party might be?" asked Grant.

"Nope, I've got nothin'," I responded. "But I don't like it. Both Theresa and Cecil seemed to be good about whoever they are, but all the rest less so."

"Maybe the two leaders have a special relationship with the third party or somebody in it," Grant suggested.

"Yeah, maybe." I didn't think that was true. Both leaders hadn't liked the idea that the deliveries were dangerous. *Although nobody said* why *they were risky.*

"But the plan for right now is recruitment by both the werewolves and the vampires."

"That's what they said. They're looking for a big fight from both us and the Protectors."

"That's right, that's what they call themselves," my boss conceded.

"But you're calling in more WOOF agents?"

"Definitely. I contacted some in our region even before last night's meeting. Something big is going down, and we'll need more than our small central Iowa pack to stop it."

I chewed on a chicken leg.

"I'm arranging for a party to coordinate our efforts once all of the out-of-towners arrive."

"Good plan."

"It's best to know our friends for an upcoming fight."

"And even better to know our enemies," I added. "By the way, the evil pack is going to a party in the next few nights to recruit."

"You'll be there."

"Of course."

Grant gave me my instructions. My job was to keep my deep cover going with the Koman Pack. Like it or not. Usually, Grant and I are akin to two wolves howling at the moon together. Our howls in unison. Our goal the same. That wasn't true today. My gut was telling me we were missing something. Something very, very important.

But I didn't tell Grant. So I pulled the rest of the meat off the chicken leg and chomped away at it.

XV

Vampires and an Active Shooter

Samuel

A second lone gunman shooting up people in as many days in Des Moines, Iowa—that was ominous. Luckily, WOVACOM was keeping yesterday's and today's incidents out of the news. I wasn't sure how WOVACOM succeeded in this venture, but as long as they did, we wouldn't have national media swarming through the city.

I pulled my car into a parking lot across the street from the restaurant where the shooting was occurring. Even if I'd wanted to use the restaurant's lot, I couldn't have, because police vehicles filled all the spots other than where customers were parked. The lights flashed on the police vehicles, and the police officers stood or crouched behind their patrol cars with weapons drawn. A plainclothes detective held a megaphone, probably attempting negotiations with the assailant. *Hopefully, most of the police are from WOVACOM. If so, we VATE agents aren't the only vampires on the scene.*

Exiting my vehicle, I strapped on my sword. I had my holster with a pistol already at my side. Although I carried cartridges with silver bullets, my gun was currently filled with standard lead shot. This time I wasn't alone in getting out of my vehicle. Ingrid and Ronald had come with me.

Our drive to the crime scene hadn't been pleasant. Beryl had told us to team up in our cars since so many police vehicles were already at the location. I'd hoped to go with William or Hannah because both had fought zombies on the previous night and I wanted to compare notes in terms of the best way of neutralizing these undead. Instead, I had the two newbies—newbies at least in the fight against zombies—in my Ford Focus.

I'd thought Ronald wouldn't be too bad to deal with, and he wasn't. At the meeting, he'd offered a few insightful comments. Ingrid had struck me more like Ernie and Mindy at earlier meetings. All the way to the crime scene, like Mindy, she'd complained that not enough agents were on this case, and, like Ernie, that Beryl's plan was stupid. In addition, she said that this shooter affair was WOVACOM business, and that I was a horrible driver. I kept my cool through all of these comments because Beryl would make life miserable for me if I criticized visiting special VATE agents. Luckily, Ronald cracked some jokes to alleviate my misery.

Regardless, the three of us exited my vehicle, each armed with a pistol and a sword. We converged with William and Hannah.

The five of us crossed the street, cordoned off by police at both nearby intersections. They let us through because each group had one officer who was in WOVACOM. We approached the plainclothes detective. From inside the restaurant, we heard more shots.

The plainclothes detective was about five-nine, short brown hair, brown eyes, and the appearance of someone determined but not knowing exactly what to do. He looked us over.

"You're from VATE?"

"Yes," I answered. It was my duty was to be in charge since I was the local in our group.

"You know the situation," the detective stated.

"Only in general terms."

The detective explained what was going on in detail that Beryl hadn't received from his call. During a typical lunch rush, more so than usual at this Italian restaurant, at about 12:30, the shooter arrived, took a table, ordered a red wine, and a pasta dish. When the red wine and pasta dish failed to arrive within ten minutes, the shooter had stood and begun firing. A few people snuck out the back, called the police, and fled. The kitchen and restaurant staff had also fled. The customers in the dining room area of the restaurant were being held hostage or had already died. The police had arrived within fifteen minutes. We'd arrived ten minutes later.

"I think we can talk the shooter down," the detective told us.

"We're also worried another party may come to snatch the corpses," I said.

Luckily, the detective was a vampire and knew about the previous day's incident. "That's why we called you in. From the description the witnesses gave, this shooter is the same as yesterday's."

"Then you probably won't be able to talk him down."

"Beryl thinks the shooter is an alien," William commented.

"That explains how the shooter escaped yesterday," the detective said. "Okay, one or more of you can enter through the back. We've got snipers set up there, but I'm worried about the people in the black van, too. Yesterday they took out our officers guarding the entrances."

"We'll see what we can do about them," I volunteered. "However, our more important objective is to discover where the vans are taking the corpses."

"Just get this shooter to stop the killing," the detective said, disregarding the latter part of my statement.

Leaving the detective behind, the five of us crept in back of the police cars and other vehicles in the parking lot. Glancing at the restaurant, I saw that all the front windows were intact, so the police and the shooter hadn't engaged each other in combat. Beryl had given us a description of the previous fight, which had followed along the same lines. The shooter hadn't wanted to deal with the police; the shooter had wanted merely—if such a word was appropriate given the circumstances—to kill many people.

We circled around the building to the alley behind where deliveries were made and the staff had parked their cars. No deliveries were currently being made, and the staff's cars had left quite some time ago. On a rooftop about a block away, we saw the sniper, who waved at us.

This shooter must be an alien. And the people in the black van may be as well. We could be dealing with at least two aliens and possibly three or four. The shooter had to be a warrior type. I'd encountered these sorts of aliens on more than one occasion, which hadn't always ended well, because, unlike your typical aliens—who were excellent fighters even if that wasn't their "alien" occupation—alien warriors were tougher, faster, and smarter than your usual alien and were specifically trained for fighting.

The five of us decided that Hannah and I would go inside to take down the (probably) alien shooter and the other three would wait either inside the door or in hidden spots in the alley to watch for the black van we knew would soon break upon the scene.

As we opened the door and snuck into the back storage room, Hannah whispered to me, "Now this is more what I expected. A fight with an alien."

"They must want to handle this part of the operation themselves," I whispered back.

The storage room was filled with shelves covered with large cans of tomato sauce, tomato paste, and chopped tomatoes; huge bags of onions; smaller bags of garlic and mushrooms; drying herbs; bags of a variety of pastas: penne, linguine, spaghetti, and others; cheddar, mozzarella, and pepper jack cheese; and unlabeled boxes and cans that held ingredients we could only guess about. In the corner were mops, brooms, and a vacuum cleaner.

Entering the kitchen, we saw the staff had ceased in mid-preparation of many dishes as evidenced by vats filled with water and pasta partially cooked; large pans with partially browned veal and chicken breasts; pots filled with marinara and Alfredo sauces; bottles of opened wine sitting next to cold burners; lettuce and spinach lying on the counters close to large cutting knives; lemons next to zesters; herbs partially cut; and a pile of cut mushrooms. All probably needed for a large lunch crowd.

Neither Hannah nor I commented on this assortment of food. Both of us had drunk a pint or more of blood before leaving Beryl's because we knew this upcoming fight could be tough.

We stopped at the kitchen doors to the dining room and listened.

From outside the restaurant, we heard the detective on his megaphone. "...give up. Come out with your hands up and your weapon left inside. We can still reach some sort of understanding."

Whispers echoed through the dining room. Followed by two shots. A few gasps.

Okay, our shooter has killed two others. Might make the job easier. The shooter's goal was to kill humans to make corpses for zombies. No amount of negotiating could change that objective.

Within the dining room, we heard a few humans still breathing. *They aren't all dead yet. Considering the fact the alien wants to kill them all, for stupid humans, they're probably acting as smart as they can.*

I looked at Hannah. She nodded.

Each of us dissolved into mist. We hadn't told each other that would be our plan, but from what we'd heard in the dining room and not knowing the geography of the kitchen doors to the dining room, we each knew that if we pushed open the doors and charged in the alien might very well shoot both of us in the head, thus ending our mission rather ignominiously.

When transforming into mist, one moment your mind is within your body, specifically your head, the next it's filling all your body, that is, your cloud of mist. I slid under the door and into the dining room. Even as mist, I could tell that the kitchen floor had been linoleum while the dining room floor was carpeted. I floated among the tables, noticing two corpses close to the kitchen door.

Easier for the van people to pick up.

I kept floating until I found a booth. Keeping track of other movements in the air, I calculated that the alien—if the shooter was indeed that—was in the middle of the room and at least five or six humans were dead, another ten or so still alive. *Perhaps not for long.*

Re-humanizing, I found myself behind a half-wall with a table and chairs on the other side. Not too far away someone was talking in a language I failed to understand. As I looked over the top of the wall, the shooter had his back to me and was talking on his cell phone. His language was garbled and strange. In a case not long before, I'd met another alien who'd talked on a cell phone. That time such talking had helped me out. This time I wasn't so sure.

Where is Hannah?

I didn't have to wait long. As I glanced over the table again, Hannah appeared behind the shooter. She grabbed his head with both hands. Only to be smashed in the face with the butt of the rifle. She stumbled back.

The shooter dropped his phone, turned, and fired at my fellow vampire. The bullet hit her in the chest. Not the best place to hit a vampire since it wouldn't be a fatal blow. I yanked out my pistol, still with its silencer, and shot at the shooter. And hit him in the leg. The shooter gazed around the room. Hannah was out of sight and probably lay on the floor. I quickly ducked behind my table, then dissolved into a cloud of mist again. Bullets sailed over the spot three times where I'd been humanized as I floated to another place in the dining room. Many people shouted and charged the shooter.

Idiotic humans. Trying to be brave to save a vampire who should have known better. Well, Hannah should have.

I re-materialized behind another booth that had a partial wall. Many gunshots rang out and screams echoed belonging to the humans who'd so courageously charged the shooter, believing that was the right thing to do. It wasn't. I glanced over the wall. The shooter had raked down five humans who'd attacked after Hannah's unsuccessful attempt. The shooter might have failed to kill his attackers with his shots, but he was able to cripple them or wound them enough that they would bleed out eventually.

Hannah was still hidden from sight. After the five attackers had fallen—*so that leaves five humans still alive?*—the shooter walked around their bodies and stopped somewhere in the wide area that he'd used as a base for his attacks. He raised his rifle and aimed it at something—Hannah?—on the floor.

I yanked out my pistol and took aim as well.

When the shooter fired toward the floor, I shot at him. His shot successfully hit something—and the few remaining humans gasped at the sight—Hannah must have melted into ash—at the same time my bullet hit him between the eyes.

Even a shot like that can kill aliens. The shooter looked up as green ooze slid out of his forehead. He muttered something in a strange language and collapsed to the floor.

I stood, walked through the dining room, and gazed around. Various human corpses either sat limply in chairs or booths or lay on the floor. Close to where the alien lay were eleven humans, all males—probably trying to act like heroes for their families or girlfriends—lying on the ground. Six had taken head shots and were obviously already dead; the other five had chest or stomach wounds, which had been fatal for some who had already bled out, but not yet fatal for others as long as medical help arrived soon. I smelled the blood. After all the times I'd transformed into mist, I was getting a bit peckish, so the smell of blood caused my stomach to growl.

Other humans emerged from two booths at the far end of the dining room. A young woman probably in her twenties and two small children came out of one booth. The young woman saw one of the men wounded in the chest and dashed to him to hold him in her arms. An older woman, probably in her forties, crept out of a booth equally far away. She saw one of the men with a head shot. As she hurried to him, I shook my head and hoped I had a sad look on my face.

"The police are outside," I said. "One of you should run outside, tell them the gunman is dead, and that medical help is needed."

The young woman was weeping over her dying husband, so the older woman, who seemed relatively composed since her significant other lay dead in front of her, sighed, stood, and walked toward the front of the restaurant.

"Thank you so much," said the young woman. "If only my husband had been as wise as you."

I shrugged. "His attack on the gunman helped me kill the shooter. I'm sure if your husband had been carrying a gun he would have done the same."

The two children knelt next to their father as the woman smirked. "Keith doesn't believe in guns. I told him not to be brave, but..." Her voice died out.

The front door to the restaurant opened and closed, a voice shouted through a megaphone, then silence. *Good. That woman is safe.*

Walking over to the gunman, I stared down at him. One of his hands grabbed my ankle. His eyes met mine.

"Bloodsucker, you may have killed me—"

I shot him again in the head before he could continue.

Because, unfortunately, his shooting these humans is only part of the process.

XVI

Another Wild Party

Joe

Another night, another party. The party's location was again Dick and Shirley's hobby farm. Theresa had arranged this party with our host because it was to take place not long after their last party.

This time I arrived with company. I generally preferred to arrive at the Dick and Shirley parties alone, which gave me more freedom to explore. But I'd succeeded in getting into Theresa's pack, so I paid the consequences. I came dressed in a yellow shirt and brown slacks, the colors of our pack. One of the pack that was me. And I was happy to be since I was going to help expand the Koman pack. Then they'd appreciate me more. Then I'd stop their nefarious plot. Then Grant and I could party sometime soon.

I arrived with Ellen. Following the meeting, Ellen and I had continued the festivities at her place. Yeah, I know. She was one of the enemy. She was on my hit list once we figured out what this strange pack had planned. But a little rutting never hurt anyone. I'd rutted with female Wild Ones before and all had worked out fine. Sometimes even better than fine. More than once I'd convinced my rut buddy to join my cause. Being friendly never hurt anybody.

Theresa, Henry, and Victoria led the pack into the party; Ellen and I lagged behind, telling each other dirty jokes. Other packs ignored our entrance. That was the norm. A few packs watched for others because members from their pack always fought at every party. The Koman pack didn't have that tradition. *Time to have fun.* Drinking beer, wine, or hard liquor. Eating from the spread on the food table. Tonight, Dick and Shirley had an entire raw hog, ready for us to rip into using either our own claws or the large carving knife on the table. They had also set out chicken legs, pork ribs, steaks, and pork chops, all raw. A feast for a wolf.

As we passed the house, we gathered for a moment.

Theresa gazed at all of us. "Remember, tonight is for recruitment. We all know that means fights." She gave Henry a knowing look. "Henry, please do not fight. I told you that last time we were here and you didn't listen." She glanced at me. "No offense."

I shrugged. "None taken."

"You've been a good addition to our pack." She looked at Henry again, "Only if you think you can win a fight against your opponent, challenge or accept a challenge from that individual. We're better off without a pack than to be humiliated." She smiled at me. "Joe, I'm sure you'll be able to get at least one other pack to join, if not two or three."

Henry growled. Victoria grabbed his elbow.

"Victoria, make sure Henry doesn't do anything idiotic," our leader ordered.

Borman let his head sag. His angry eyes stared at me. Under his breath, he said, "Someday I'll get you."

I ignored his words.

"All right, split up."

And we dispersed into the partygoers. Ellen and I even went our separate ways. We both knew the other would get into a fight and win. Sexual prowess correlates well to fighting prowess.

My first contact was Vince.

"Looks like you're in the pack," he observed.

"Yeah, a good fight can accomplish a lot."

"Damn nice female with you."

"And a lot more," I said.

We both laughed. When we'd calmed down, I surveyed the party and the dispersion of my pack. "I need to get a fairly large pack to join Koman."

"How difficult do you want the fight to be?" Vince asked. He knew the specifics of all the packs that attended this party: which pack had the strongest members, which pack had the most members; which pack acted tough but wasn't; which pack had the most drunks; which pack came to spread its genes; which pack had the smartest members; and which pack was here only to cause trouble.

"I can fight someone lots tougher than Borman."

"The Sleshel pack has over twenty members. None are too tough. I think they frighten others only because of their numbers."

"Sounds like the pack I want."

"Is the Koman pack involved in something nasty?"

I smiled. "It's messy and I don't exactly understand it."

"Then good luck."

And Vince and I separated.

I went to the barn where I could see most of the packs. As I mentioned previously, some packs stayed together the whole time at the parties while others let their members roam freely.

I gazed over the crowd. Already, other members of Koman were interacting with other packs. Ellen was talking with a group of equally young females; Henry and Victoria with three other couples; Theresa with an older, more staid group of individuals I guessed were other pack leaders. Chuck, since he was wounded, hadn't come to the party because a wounded member is a liability when it comes to picking a fight. The other Koman members spread throughout the crowd.

Standing next to the meat table was a tall, black, muscular man about six feet tall, with broad shoulders, curly black hair, a scarred face, and huge hands. Definitely a Sleshel. After seeing him, I identified two others of his pack at the beverage table, gulping down some beers. *He's as good a Sleshel as any.* Theresa hadn't coordinated our attacks quite properly. If I'd have been in charge, I'd have assigned each of us a different pack. She hadn't done that. I guess she didn't worry that we might happen to overlap.

That way one of us can die, and we can still get the pack as an ally.

I took a deep breath and strode toward the tall man from the Sleshel pack. When I arrived at the food table, I grabbed a chicken leg and ripped away at it with my teeth.

The tall Sleshel was popping beef cubes and talking with a short, slim woman.

He made a comment, and she laughed far too uproariously for her response to be genuine. *I know what she wants.*

I stepped between the two.

"Hello," I said, without waiting for either to notice me. "I'm Joe Butler."

"Ryan Karr," said the man who loomed over me.

"Becky Douglas," said the woman.

"Another good party by Dick and Shirley," I observed.

"They always are," Ryan agreed.

"Especially the company," Becky said, giving Ryan a particularly happy smile.

Not far away, Ellen was arguing with one of the other females in her group. *Ellen should be fighting soon.*

The two I was talking to seemed content. I knew I might have a difficult time getting Ryan to fight me. *Of course, who says I have to fight him so he'll join our cause?*

"Yeah, I'm so glad they don't have any human pets here," I said.

Both Ryan and Becky studied me.

"Why would one of them be at this party?" asked Becky.

"That'd be majorly stupid," Ryan added.

Not far away, Theresa was in a cordial discussion with many of the other pack leaders. *Maybe she's trying a gentler, kinder approach as well.* Yeah, I like to transform into a wolf. Yeah, I like to fight as a wolf. But sometimes not being a wolf can be as productive. Sometimes personality can win the day.

"I wish we could kill them all," I said wistfully.

"Right," Ryan said sarcastically.

"Not going to happen," Becky put in.

"Well, it could," I said.

Ellen was shouting at one of the females in her group. That female was yelling at her. The other females backed away as Ellen and her opponent transformed into wolves.

Both Ryan and Becky noticed the fight about to begin then looked at me.

"Care to see the fight?" asked Becky.

"One wolf fight is like another," I said nonchalantly.

Ryan shook his head. "I find every fight has its own dimensions. The opponents are different. The goals of each vary. I enjoy studying werewolf kind."

Oh, my gosh. A philosophizing werewolf. I knew vampires were that way. They philosophized far too much. Take Sammy and his tale of our hunt of the vampwolf. Philosophy, philosophy, philosophy. I wanted to tell Ryan the best approach was learning by doing not by watching. But I needed to make friends. And friends don't like insults.

With his comment, Ryan walked toward the two fighting wolves. Not far away Henry and Victoria had both transformed into wolves and were preparing to fight. Theresa continued to talk with her fellow pack leaders.

"The natives are restless tonight," Becky commented.

"Makes for a better party," I said.

Ryan was in the circle watching Ellen fight her opponent. I saw another circle form around Henry and Victoria and their two opponents.

"Fighting's okay. But getting along is, too," I said as we both watched the fights from afar.

Becky raised her thick eyebrows. "That's not exactly in our nature. We belong to packs. Every pack wants to be dominant over every other pack. Each of us wants to be dominant in our pack. Fighting is part of who we are."

I had a difficult arguing with that logic.

"You know, that's part of our problem," I said. "If all of us true werewolves cooperated and didn't just fight for our pack, we could wipe out all the human pets."

Becky looked from me to the two fights. Ellen was doing a good job at defeating her rival. Victoria had already triumphed over hers. Henry was getting the hide whipped out of him. *Theresa won't like that.*

"All this fighting is good for the species."

"I guess," I said hesitantly. "Depends upon what our goals are."

As Ellen beat her opponent, Ryan walked back to the two of us. He sighed. "You could be correct."

"I probably am." Taking a compliment without gloating is often best.

Ryan smirked. "Some fights are similar to others." He motioned at Henry and his opponent, both of whom were transformed back into humans. "That same guy lost at the last party." Ryan laughed. "To you."

"Hey, some of us are really bad fighters."

Becky shook her head. "That guy sure is." She paused. "Ryan, this guy..." She nodded toward me. "...thinks that if we true werewolves cooperated we could kill off the pets."

"That's intriguing," he said.

Before he had a chance to comment further, a loud voice shouted, "Get ready for the human hunt! Get ready for the human hunt!"

Inwardly, I cringed. I like humans. I enjoy being with them. I enjoy having sex with them. I enjoy drinking with them. I enjoy dancing with them. Yeah, humans are a bit wimpy. But the good ones are always ready for a fun time. Like us werewolves.

At the last party, I'd finished my business before this event. Dick and Shirley always have at least one human hunt at a party. That's one activity that differentiates Wild Ones' parties from Friends of Humanity parties. Both of our parties have an assortment of booze and lots of different raw meats to snack on. That's all we have at FH parties. But Wild Ones are, as the name says, wild. And part of that wildness is hunting humans. To the death.

I hoped maybe I could avoid participating.

Ryan gazed at me. "That idea is fascinating. Let's make a wager."

I'm not gonna be able to avoid the hunt. Because I could guess the rival pack member's wager.

"Whoever comes closest to bringing down the human gets to tell the other one about his interesting idea."

"Do you have an idea, too?"

Ryan laughed. "I'll tell you if you lose." Then he gave me a menacing look. "If you win, I'll definitely listen to your idea and I'll share it with my pack."

I hate this. Humans should be treated with respect. Despite my revulsion of the hunt, I had to play along and win.

XVII

The Van People

Samuel

My cell phone rang. I shoved my pistol into its holster and grabbed the phone at my waist.

"This is Samuel."

"Ronald here. Two black vans have arrived. Two of what we believe to be aliens are coming out of each."

This news wasn't totally unexpected. Actually, I'd feared that one of my fellow special agents would have contacted me before I brought down the shooter. As I stared at the dead alien, I wondered whether killing it had been the best strategy. *I saved a few humans.* Okay, maybe that wasn't something to brag about. One human was just like another.

In any case, I said, "Let them come." I paused. "Well, make it difficult for them to come."

"I have another call," Ronald said. "I'll get right back to you."

He put me on hold as he took his other call. Ah, the miracles of technology. I stepped toward the young woman and her children.

"You'd be better off leaving," I advised.

"But my husband..." She wept.

"Other dangerous types are about to enter this dining room. If you value your children, you'd best leave."

The young woman looked from her children to her husband bleeding in her arms. Her husband whispered, "Yes, please go. Medical help will be here soon."

She kissed him passionately, gently laid him on the floor, and grabbed the hands of her children with her two own bloody hands. "Come, children. This nice man will make sure your daddy will be with us soon." She led them toward the door outside the dining room. I wished her statement was true. I didn't know how events would work out with the "medical staff" from the black van on their way.

"You there?" came from my cell phone.

"Yes," I replied.

"These medical people, or whatever term you want to use for them, aren't aliens. Ingrid checked their minds and they're pale, yellow spheres."

I knew what that meant.

For the uninformed, that is you humans and werewolves, we vampires can detect sentient life close to us. When we do such a search, we expand our minds and see the world as blackness. Within the blackness are spheres that indicate intelligent life close by. Humans appear as warm, yellow spheres; vampires as cold, black spheres; werewolves as very hot, red spheres; and aliens as green, slimy spheres.

I failed to mention the pale, yellow spheres or sometimes almost white spheres because these minds aren't the usual, run-of-the-mill. These minds belong to the clones or clones of clones created by aliens that I mentioned quite a while back. We consider them either clones or, my preferred term, pseudo-humans. Just to remind you, they're similar to real humans, except more focused on their jobs. In this case, the fake medics may only be concerned with picking up corpses and nothing else.

"I've encountered these beings before," I said.

"We'll do what we can to prevent all of them from getting into the dining room," Ronald said. "But we want a few to succeed in picking up some corpses, so we can follow them to their source."

"Correct."

Ronald hung up.

Then I walked over, picked up the shooter, and carried him to the beverage station where coffee machines, pitchers of water and iced tea sat on a counter, and water and wine glasses were in an open cupboard above them. I removed the shooter's rifle and strapped it over my shoulder. *Maybe I can get away with appearing to be an alien.* I walked to the center of the room where the pile of ash, the ten corpses, and the dying man lay. I heard the front door open and close, and I knew the survivors of the young family had left the building.

Toward the back of the building, I heard shouts and gunshots. *I didn't think the "medics" had pistols, or firearms of any sort.* Granted, the shots could have come from my fellow special agents. I'd worked with other special agents, at least tangentially, on another case not too long ago. Those agents had seemed to be competent. I wasn't so sure about the agents I was currently working with. I let my eyes drift around the floor close to me and saw the pile of ash that had been Hannah. *Why did she attack without first planning with me?* This batch was acting a bit impulsive almost like, dare I say, werewolves.

Two humans, wearing black uniforms and carrying black body bags, entered the room through the swinging kitchen doors. One stopped immediately, dropped to his knees, threw down one body bag, and pulled one of the corpses close to the kitchen doors into a body bag. The second "medic" strode into the room to meet me.

She was about five-seven with black hair in a bun behind her head, a black billed cap on her head, and sunglasses over her eyes. This woman wasn't overly muscular, but I thought for a human she might put up a good fight. *She's only a pseudo-human, so that might not be the case.* She stopped a few feet from me, scanned the corpses on the floor, then examined me.

"Why are you still here?" she asked. Her voice wasn't harsh or overly cold; she simply sounded matter-of-fact as if I should have left long before she came on the scene.

"I've bagged up both of these," said the male pseudo-human, "and I'm taking them out to the vehicle."

"Good," she said loudly back to him.

He threw one of the corpses in a body bag over his shoulder, grabbed the other bag, and exited through the kitchen doors.

She stared at me again, then pulled off her sunglasses so I could see her pale blue eyes. "You should be gone."

I gazed back determinedly. "Protocol is changing."

Her brow wrinkled.

I didn't like the look of that. *Where are the other two pseudo-humans?*

I continued, "I'm supposed to return with you."

She shrugged. "They didn't tell us."

I sneered. "Why should they? We're in charge." And by "we," I meant "us aliens."

"Then get out of my way," she ordered.

I stepped away from the corpses, including, I was in a way sorry to say, the young man who'd told his wife I would save him. *I've got other priorities.*

The kitchen doors opened again. William and Ingrid, wearing black medic uniforms that fit them poorly, entered carrying black body bags. Neither acknowledged my presence, which was just as well. I'd had a difficult enough time with this female pseudo-human who was kneeling and shoving one of the eleven corpses into a body bag. Having done so, she stood, threw the body bag over her shoulder, and exited out the kitchen doors. Ingrid and William walked up to me, knelt down, put the corpses into a body bag, then they, too, exited through the kitchen doors.

This procedure continued until the male and female pseudo-humans put the last two corpses into body bags and threw them over their shoulders.

"Coming?" asked the female.

"Of course," I replied.

I followed the two burdened pseudo-humans out of the dining room, through the kitchen and the storage room, and to the alley behind the restaurant. Once there, the pseudo-humans threw their burdens into the back of their van. I saw the second van parked behind the first and William and Ingrid in the front seats. Ingrid was driving and had already started the engine. *Where is Ronald? I hope he'll follow the vans.*

The two pseudo-humans climbed into the van, and I followed, climbing into the back seat, As I did so, the male gave me a quizzical look.

"It's new protocol," the female told him.

He cocked his head to one side. Since I sat behind him, I wasn't able to see her expression.

"They know best," the male said.

"That's what they tell us," she agreed.

The last pseudo-humans I met were more interesting than these two.

After starting the engine, the male turned the van around so it would emerge on the opposite side of the alley from the front of the restaurant. *Someone better be contacting WOVACOM out front.*

Another thought followed: *This operation will hopefully be less deadly than our last encounter with zombies.*

XVIII

Human Hunt

Joe

"Listen up!" came a shout from a megaphone. "Listen up!"

A silence fell over the party. We werewolves aren't known for being quiet. Most of us enjoy talking, laughing, shouting, and simply having a raucous time, especially at parties. But we also recognize when something is important. For these Wild Ones, listening to the rules of the human hunt qualified because the hunt was the highlight of the party.

Well, for everybody except for me.

Outside the house, both Dick and Shirley held megaphones. Not far behind them, three sets of two werewolves each led one human with a black bag over his head between them.

Our prey for the night.

Ryan looked at me and smiled maliciously. I gave back a devilish grin.

"All right," shouted Shirley. "We're dividing you into three groups. We have a human for each group. The first group to catch the human gets five points. The first group to kill the human gets ten. If the same group catches and kills the human, it gets twenty points. Prizes will be awarded."

Howls echoed through the farm. Loud, happy howls. Howls showing that we were ready and waiting for the hunt. The bloodlust of the hunt. The thrill of being wolves, hunting and killing. Our true nature.

"Listen up!" Dick yelled through his megaphone. "We want one group in front of the house, another group behind the barn, and the third group between the barn and the house."

Shirley added, "We assume you're smart enough to divide up into three equal groups."

I'd been to Wild One parties before at Dick and Shirley's, and once the group wasn't smart enough to split into two equal groups. (Fewer werewolves had attended that particular party.) Dick and Shirley had a fit. They'd yelled and screamed at us. One group was twice the size of the other. Certain packs wanted to stay together, and that was that. But that wasn't following the rules. That wasn't properly competitive.

If we werewolves aren't fair, we aren't anything. Surprisingly, that's true even with Wild Ones, who actually like to ignore lots of rules. But they don't like to break with werewolf tradition. And human hunts are very traditional. They go way back in time. So Dick and Shirley want the code followed appropriately. Thus, that one time when we didn't split up correctly, they threatened to call the whole thing off. Some packs then decided to split up because they'd come to the party for the hunt as much as anything.

Ryan looked at me. "Behind the barn?"

"Works for me."

And that's where we went. We and about fifteen to twenty others. A few were from the Koman pack, a fair number from the Schlessel pack, and lots from other packs. Dick strode around to the back of the barn with the two werewolves leading the human. Our host made a quick count, pulled out his cell phone, and called someone. They talked for a few minutes.

"Your group is a little bit low in numbers," Dick said seriously. "One group has five more than you do. Do you care?"

We're werewolves. Yeah, we want our hunts to be fair. Yeah, we easily get mad when we consider we've been cheated. Despite all that, we love challenges. We love to be the underdogs. Pun intended.

Almost as one, we shouted, "No! We want to hunt!"

Dick spoke quickly into his phone then hung up, keeping the phone in his hand.

Not too far away, we heard a similar shout from another group. *So another group might be short. Or maybe that's the group that has more partygoers than the rest.* A minute or two later, we heard a third group shout.

He told the two captors of the human to lead it in front of our group. He shouted in the megaphone, "Ready!"

All of us howled. Howls rang out from groups not too far away.

As the howls died, he shouted, "Set!"

This time we stood silently.

"Go!"

The two captors yanked the bag off the human's head. The human was a young male, probably in his twenties. He appeared to be well-fed and had a slim, athletic build. Glancing at the two werewolves in human form on either side, he stood still.

"Go!" shouted the captor to his right. "We explained what would happen. It will happen faster if you don't run."

Both captors pushed his back. He gazed at us. Then broke into a sprint. About twenty feet in front of him was a cornfield. Since late autumn had arrived, the cornstalks were at full height, making the field a very good place to hide. Or flee into. Or hunt in. As we watched, the human disappeared into the cornfield. Then we waited in silence.

For all good hunts, the prey needed some time to escape from the predators. If we pursued him too soon, the hunt wouldn't be as challenging as it should be. Of course, the hunt wasn't totally realistic. Our prey was unarmed.

A few minutes passed.

Dick again shouted in the megaphone, "Ready!"

Howls again broke out in our group, and other groups not too far away.

"Set!"

All the howling died as we knew we needed to ready ourselves for our transformation.

"Go!"

And we turned into wolves.

All around me wolves. Wolves smelling of other packs. Where's my pack? Why aren't they here? Why am I alone with all these foreign packs?

Don't care! Don't care! Time for a hunt.

Air smells of wolf musk. Members of Koman pack smell like wet socks. Members of Schlessel pack of decaying garbage. My own scent is lost among those.

Howl. [To glory!] Again and again. [To glory! To glory!]

Sniff the air. Smell a human. The sweat upon the human's frightened body. Yum. No. Humans are our friends.

Doesn't matter. Ryan. Huge black wolf beside me. Black wolf wants to catch and kill human before me.

Ha! As if I'll let that happen.

Almost as one, we wolves break into a run. The scent of the prey. The scent of all the wolves around me. Glorious! And in a hunt, too! Magnificent! Hunting. The way life should be.

Into the cornfield. Wolves in front of me. Behind me. In the rows on either side of me. Corn musk. Smell of dry leaves. Smell of damp dirt. Scent of wolves, wolves, wolves.

In the middle of the crowd. Not good. Not if I want to capture the human myself. I do! I do! Must show Ryan. Black wolf! Must show black wolf that smells of decaying garbage, damp fur, and whiskey.

Running faster. Leap. Over one wolf onto another. It wipes out. So do I. Stand, break into a dash. Growling behind me. [Enemy!]

Don't care! Don't care! Weave to right to another row. And another. No wolves ahead or behind me here.

Barking to my left. [Fight!] Lots of barking. [Fight! Fight! Fight!]

Sniffing as I run. Human, human, where are you? Come to wolfie. Come to me.

Notice others turning more to the right. Am I in the wrong place? Am I losing the hunt? Smell of decaying garbage, damp fur, and whiskey. Ryan is still close enough to me that I can smell him. Are we both on the wrong path? Smelling the wrong human?

Closer now, smell human. Human sweat. Human fear.

Can only see black and white. Black and white. Movement. If there is any. Far ahead! Movement.

More barking to my right. [Fight! Fight!]

Growls. [Enemy!]

Snarls. [Must die!]

Our group going after another's human. Naughty, naughty, naughty! Not in the rules. Happens sometimes. Happened once to me.

Remember. Running. Smelling. Smelling human fear. Suddenly, smell lots of wolves. Wolves charging at me. Charging at wolves. Human dashing out from between the two wolf groups. Fight! Fight! Fight!

No! No! No! Hunting now. Decaying garbage, damp fur, whiskey almost at my side. Don't look at him. Don't look. Must hunt. Must catch. Must avoid killing.

Cornfield breaks ahead of us. Opens up. No! Not open. Tall plants. Trees! Movement. Prey the size of a human. Trying to get higher.

Black wolf barks next to me. [Fight!]

Thinks he'll get there first.

Not if I can help it. I break into a sprint!

Leave decaying garbage, damp fur, whiskey smell behind. Still in cornfield. The small forest. To big forest. Human! Smell the human sweat. Smell the human fear. Smell the human flesh.

Yum! Yum! Live food. The best to eat.

No! No! Humans good. Not to kill.

But must. Must.

Very far away. Howling. [To glory!]

Growls. [Enemy!]

Snarls. [Must die!]

Barking. [Fight! Fight!]

Whimpers. [Help! Help!]

Large fight of wolves behind me and far to the right.

Ahead of me. Movement. Human trying to climb tree. Narrow tree. Branches up high. Human jumps, grabs branch, tries to pull himself up.

Leap into the air. Jaws open. Bite! Grab hard with teeth.

Human screams! Nothing quite like them. In human ears, don't mind. Wolf ears mind. Painful. Almost.

Let go. Jump again. Paws reach. Claws cut. Teeth bite. Human falls to ground. Screams! Screams!

Huge black wolf pushes me aside. Reluctantly, back away. Black wolf bites, claws, eats!

Must. Should. Don't want to. Can't blow cover. Rush forward. Bite leg. Chomp on flesh. Chew. Eat.

Both decaying garbage, damp fur, whiskey and I howl. Howl. Howl. [To glory! To glory! To glory!]

Loud human voices close to us.

And we transformed back into human form. Not too far away from us stood Dick, megaphone to mouth.

"We have two winners!" he shouted through the megaphone. "Two winners!"

I looked at Ryan who smiled with his bloody mouth, then let my eyes drop to the mangled body a few feet away from us. Ryan had eaten into the chest, but my bites on the leg were also visible. The young man's glazed eyes stared blankly forward.

Ryan stepped closer to me. "Now what was your idea about many packs joining forces?"

XIX

Ambush

Samuel

The male pseudo-human drove the black van out of the alley to the street behind the restaurant. I assumed Ronald—if nobody else—had contacted the police—hopefully all WOVACOM agents—to tell them we'd vacated the building. Between the two vans, we'd also left with all the corpses. A few families would be unhappy about that. Others might not care.

Riding in or following this van was a central part of this operation. Although we'd stopped the active shooter, learning the location where these vans went was equally important.

With the zombies increasing in number every night, Beryl thought discovering the origination place of the vans was vital in order to stop the zombie threat. He'd recruited VWW or Vampire Watchers of the World for this job. Typically, VWW helped VATE by detecting the alien presence in office buildings, restaurants, or other places where aliens worked. Normal VATE agents used this information to identify, hunt, and kill these aliens disguised as humans. For some reason, VWW had never detected aliens in residential buildings.

Regardless, for this operation, VWW had used its satellites and any other available technology to locate and follow these black vans. Unfortunately, all in vain. Although VWW was able to pinpoint where zombies were being released, when it came to tracking the vans, this organization simply lost sight of them. VWW theorized that that the vans had some piece of technology that kept them from being followed despite state-of-the art technology.

Thus, the value of this part of the operation.

We turned on one street, then another. The restaurant where the assault had occurred was a few miles north and west of downtown. Based on the direction we were traveling, I guessed we were heading toward downtown, or perhaps the east side of town. *This pseudo-human better be taking us to the location where the aliens are transforming corpses into zombies.*

The two pseudo-humans in the front seat said nothing. They didn't even look at each other or back at me. I really wanted to call the other special agents to discover what they'd heard from WOVACOM or Beryl. I hoped Beryl had contacted VATE to tell them we needed more agents on this assignment. The fact the two "medics" weren't saying anything bothered me. Although they were "pseudo," they were still humans and probably inclined to do moronic human stuff. Talking while I was in the backseat would qualify as being stupid—also being inquisitive and possibly giving me a clue as to where we were heading or if they were taking us into a trap or truly to the zombie factory.

Down one street. Turn. Down another. Stopping at traffic lights. Catching a green light. Getting stopped on a yellow. And so the journey went.

Until we entered an area of town with huge warehouses. Such buildings had been important in another recent case of mine, and I hoped would prove to be in this one as well. A large warehouse would certainly be a suitable zombie factory. Of course, the aliens might not be so obvious.

I gazed at the huge red brick buildings on either side of the street. All their windows were on the second floor, some the size of refrigerators, others merely narrow slits. A few metal doors opened on the ground floor, and most had at least one roll-up garage door also on the ground floor. Not far ahead of us, a roll-up garage door was rising to reveal the darkness inside the warehouse.

Our van turned at the drive to the building and went through the doorway. I glanced behind us to see the second black van follow. The door slid closed behind us after both vehicles entered. The two pseudo-humans in front of me stopped the van. William stopped the second van only a few feet behind ours.

I knew something was wrong. I'd been in traps before—okay, I'm usually fairly good at avoiding them, or if I encounter them, I plan to be taken in the trap—but this time I hadn't seen it coming. I don't know why I didn't. I should have. The two pseudo-humans hadn't questioned William and Ingrid replacing their fellow clones, and although they'd questioned me, I wondered if I'd been accepted too easily.

I noticed movement outside the van and heard the clicking noises of automatic weapons being cocked. The two pseudo-humans looked over the headrests and smiled at me. I didn't smile back.

Instead, I dissolved into a cloud of mist. Although I was mist, I could detect what was happening around me. And what was happening around me wasn't good at all. From both sides of the van, bullets broke windows, punched through the doors, splattered the blood of the two pseudo-humans in front all over the van, ripped apart their heads, tore the car seats, busted the dash, pounded into the engine, and so many other destructive works that, if I'd been in human form, I would have met a similar fate to the clones.

Being mist, I felt the bullets simply passing through me. Blood splattered through me as well. If I'd been in my human form, the blood might have tempted me because I'd done a fair amount of shape-shifting back when I was fighting the shooter and after a certain amount of transforming I tend to get hungry. Not that while our van was being pumped full of bullets was any time to pause and get a drink.

Finally, the bullets stopped riddling the van. I felt the front doors on either side of the van open. I floated through this empty space and over whoever had ambushed us. Since I wasn't in human form, I couldn't determine whether our ambushers had been werewolves, vampires, pseudo-humans, or aliens. Any of the four were possible. Not that it mattered. Because I wasn't about to re-humanize and find out.

I floated past the second van and wondered whether William and Ingrid had turned into either bats or clouds of mist before the bullets had inflicted too much harm. Again, I wasn't about to re-materialize into human—or even bat form for that matter—to find out.

I continued floating until I reached the door through which we'd entered and I slipped between the door and the cement beneath it. Rather like squeezing through a very small hole except that neither the cement nor metal door felt solid when I was in mist form. They felt more solid than carpeting or grass, but not as solid as if I'd been human.

Emerging from under the metal door, I floated a few yards along on the sidewalk that circled the building before transforming into a bat. I still didn't feel certain that I wasn't being watched. As a bat, I broke into flight and flew around the building to the narrow side where I detected a vehicle. As I landed next to the vehicle, I transformed back into a human. I was very hungry to say the least.

In the front seat of the vehicle, I saw Ronald who shook his head.

I climbed into the passenger's seat.

"A trap?" he asked.

"A bad one," I replied. "Have you seen William or Ingrid?"

"No." He gave me a wry smile. "But Ingrid was on the phone with me before I heard gunshots."

"So neither probably survived."

"Survival doesn't seem to be easy with this assignment," Ronald observed. "And we're no closer to figuring out where the zombies are created."

I snorted. He didn't need to tell me that.

Then he started the vehicle and sped away from the building. I yanked my cell phone off my belt and called Beryl. He wouldn't like what I had to report.

XX

Delivery Duty

Joe

Henry parked his large red SUV on a narrow street between two warehouses. He gave me a withering stare. Henry really didn't like me, but I couldn't blame him. I'd defeated him in single combat. I'd gotten Wild Ones' packs to join us with my helping Ryan kill the human in the hunt. And I'd volunteered to go on this assignment for our third party in our strange alliance. Nobody in the pack did that. Usually, Theresa told members that a particular night was theirs, and the persons forced to go would groan then give in because serving in this capacity was for the good of the pack.

Whatever was good for the pack was what should be done. Even if this action wasn't necessarily good for all of werewolf kind. We're pack creatures and loyalty to our pack supersedes all else.

Henry climbed from his vehicle. I followed.

"You're so smug," he said and growled at me. "Trying to get in good with Theresa."

"It's not too hard. At least compared to what you do," I shot back.

He growled louder. "Whatever. This is crap duty."

"All for the good of the pack."

Henry didn't respond to those words, but he continued to walk to the long side of the warehouse where a metal door was closed in front of us and not too far away was a metal roll-up garage door. I noticed a doorbell to the right of the metal door. Henry pressed the doorbell once for a few seconds, again very quickly, then again for a few seconds.

"That's the code," he replied to my unasked question.

I may be a werewolf, but I'm not stupid. You'd think I'd get some respect from a fellow werewolf. But this was Henry who wanted to kill me in the worst way.

The door swung open, and inside, in the dark, we spied two short women, wearing lab coats. One woman was about five-three, very slim, with bright red hair. The other woman was about five-two, a little bit plump, with black hair tied in a bun behind her head.

"Being dead is best in Des Moines," said the redhead.

"When the moon is full and the windows are painted black," Henry responded.

Neither woman smiled, but both backed away from the doorway so we could come in.

As we entered, the black-haired woman gazed at me, studying me from my feet to my head. "He's new," she commented.

"I wish," Henry muttered quietly. More loudly, he said, "He's okay. He's part of my pack."

Ah, Henry, I like you, too. Maybe we can get along. I certainly hoped we could. The women didn't seem to notice the discord between us werewolves, so they led us farther into the darkness. About ten feet from the roll-up garage door sat a row of four black vans. None currently were occupied.

Henry said, "One of those will be ours for the night."

"We certainly hope you won't be gone that long," said the redhead.

"Unless you're stopped by the vampire agents, we hope you will return once your cargo has been dropped off," the black-haired woman added.

Vampire agents? So our cargo is fighting Protectors.

"If our cargo is attacked, we don't need to help protect it, do we?" asked Henry.

Both women giggled.

The redhead answered, "No, we found that was a waste of resources."

That meant my wounded Wild One companions had been fighting VATE agents, too.

My colleague gave a sigh of relief and smiled at me. I wanted to wipe the smile off his face and punch his features into a bloody pulp. But I had a mission. I had to discover what the cargo was and the danger it carried for its deliverers. Although in that short conversation, I'd learned a lot.

The building was dimly lit. Despite that, I could see just fine. We werewolves have excellent night vision, which comes in handy for hunting at night. Also, good eyesight is useful at times when our assignments force us to be in the dark since our opponents often think that may hinder us.

As I said a while back, close to the roll-up garage door was a line of black vans. A puddle of green ooze about a foot in diameter lay on the roof of each van. On the narrow end of the building north of us was a wall broken by regular-sized doors. I counted seven and guessed each door led to a different office. On the narrow end of the building south of us was a wall broken only by one door.

I thought the arrangement was strange because if this building was used for the creation of our cargo I'd expect plenty of offices for the staff needed to create the cargo. Okay, yeah, a place had to exist to store the cargo as well. Maybe the southern blocked-off area was where that happened.

To our east was another large-walled off area with a few doors along it. To the north and south, those walled-off areas were only one story tall; above them was a platform with a railing around it. The walled-off area to our east was two stories tall. We stopped a few feet from one of the doors to this walled-off area.

"Wait here," ordered the redhead. "Once everyone has arrived, we'll disperse the cargo."

Henry whispered, "This always takes so fucking long."

"Wanting to get home to Victoria?" I asked.

My companion gave me a nasty stare.

The two women in lab coats returned to the door.

We waited for about ten minutes as other drivers arrived. First, came a pair of vampires whom I recognized as Troy and Dexter, both wearing black shirts and pants. The two women met them as they had us, then escorted them to stand beside us. Neither vampire acknowledged our existence as they came to stand about ten feet away. Next came two more werewolves, Melody and Leslie, both from Koman.

Henry whispered to me that Theresa had tried to get members of other packs to do this duty, but their leaders had refused, saying they'd help rid the world of pets but not aid in this pointless venture. Melody and Leslie joined the four of us already waiting. Leslie gave me a flirtatious smile. I gave one back to her. Melody looked enviously at the two of us. Finally, two more vampires were escorted in. I recognized them from the meeting as Lucille and Kelsey. Both of them ignored me, so I saw fit to do the same to them.

Does that mean the plan to destroy the good vampires and us Friends of Humanity is getting closer to coming true? I hope not. I don't want Sammy or anyone else I know to come to any harm.

Once the final team had joined us, the two women in lab coats led us to the door at the east end of the building.

"All right," said the redhead. "I want to be sure you understand your assignment—"

Kelsey snorted. "Of course, we do. We have done this before."

The redhead gave him a hateful look. "*You* may have," she said, "but not all of our workers are repeats." She searched our expressions to see whether anyone else was going to question her authority. When none of us did, she continued, "Your cargo is the same as it has been. Again, we will give each of your teams the locations where we want them dropped. Either drop them in that location, or if too many vampires are in the area watching for our cargo, return to this warehouse with the cargo still intact." She looked at us to see if we understood, then went on.

"Please drive a little way from the drop-off point and watch to see if the cargo encounters vampires. We want a report in terms of how well the vampires fight the cargo. We have been trying to improve the cargo to the point where two or more vampires are necessary to bring down one bit of cargo. If you see the cargo being destroyed, do not engage the vampires—"

Henry again sighed in relief. I rolled my eyes in shame. The other werewolves growled. Dexter whispered to Troy that he believed the two of them could easily take down those "human-loving idiots."

The redhead paused. "Are you done? We'll help your organizations destroy those troublesome human-friendlies of both your kinds, so we expect you to follow our instructions. As I said, do not engage the vampires. If the vampires detect your van and approach you, flee. If they follow you, contact us and we will instruct you what to do."

She again studied all of us. "Also, if you are to leave the van, say 'Thlothif.' If you don't return to the van in ten minutes, the van will self-destruct. If you do return, say 'Afdor.' That will keep the van intact." She paused. "Is all of that clear?"

"Yes," I said loudly. The other werewolves answered equally loudly and clearly. The vampires muttered their assent.

"Good," the redhead said. She gave an approving nod in my direction. "To have the cargo follow you to your van, say 'Althar di nokkin.' That command will get them to follow you, enter your van, and sit quietly until you command them to leave. That command is 'Harshish iv nazzle.' Do you understand?"

"Same as the last two nights," said Troy. He snorted again.

Shaking her head as if we were stupid, small children, the redhead turned to the brunette and said something in the strange language. The black-haired woman went to the closed door along the eastern wall as the redhead gave Lucille and Kelsey a set of car keys and ordered them to approach the same door.

Opening the door, the black-haired woman issued another command then backed away. Creatures emerged through the doorway. They were humanoid. I guessed they once were actually humans. Now they were human corpses, or more accurately reanimated corpses. *That's no way to treat humans. Dead or alive, humans should be treated with dignity.*

The creatures' skin was pale, paler than the skin color of vampires, well, at least Caucasian vampires. Most of their eyes were glazed as if covered by a film. A few had bright, clear eyes without the film. Their clothes were in relatively good shape, but I noticed a few items had bullet holes in them. Their arms hung loosely at their sides.

When I'd seen undead similar to these in movies, they tended to shamble along, often limping with one lame leg. These creatures strode along at a good pace. One or two even let their clear eyes flit from the back of the zombies in front of them to the two women we'd met here and the teams who would be transporting them into the environs of Des Moines. I counted six of the undead leaving the room.

Kelsey issued the command given by the women in lab coats. Lucille and Kelsey walked from close to where we stood to a black van that had its back doors open. The zombies climbed into it, and the vampires closed them in. Then the vampires slipped into the front seats. The roll-up garage door opened, and Lucille and Kelsey drove out. This routine continued with other partnerships until the redhead reached us and tossed Henry a set of keys for the remaining black van. She motioned for us to approach the brunette.

Henry nodded and approached the brunette who stood next to the open door again. One after another of the creatures strode from the room.

Loudly, my companion said, "Althar di nokkin." After saying these words, he turned and walked calmly to the remaining black van. I walked along at his side.

"We're delivering zombies," I whispered.

"Great deduction, Sherlock," Henry said sarcastically. He gave me a look that said that, at least this time, he had the upper hand.

He used the keys to open the doors to the back of the van, then hurried around the driver's side and scrambled in. Our "cargo" had slowly climbed in. I closed the back and stepped up into the passenger's side of the van and shut the door. The smell of decay and rot filled the van, but my companion left the windows closed.

"Isn't this bad, delivering these zombies to places in Des Moines?" I asked in a whisper.

"What happened to what's best for the pack?" Henry asked.

His phone buzzed. Sliding his hand across its surface, he nodded again. "Should be an easy drop."

The roll-up garage door raised up in front of us, and we left the warehouse.

We drove through town quickly. The smell of decay filled the van. It stank like garbage, like scraps of food that had been sitting out in the sun for five days. The scent was of putrefaction rather similar to rotten eggs, only more so. *Yeah, these could help wipe out human-friendly werewolves and vampires.*

In about ten minutes, we reached the western part of downtown Des Moines, close to the sculpture park. I think art is great. Yeah, though it has to be art that shows something, such as a painting of a landscape or person or a bust of someone famous. Modern art is beyond me. I liked some of the sculptures in the park, those that showed actual objects. The works of modern art can be left for others to enjoy.

Although the park was bordered by two of the busiest east-west streets in downtown, not too many vehicles got in our way. Lots of people in their teens or twenties scooped the loop. Such scooping meant going east on Locust, taking a side street, then driving west on Grand. Others often joined in minor parties—quite popular at the sculpture park. But none of them were doing their stuff on this particular night. Once or twice I saw a police car.

Henry didn't seem to care. He found a spot along the Grand side of the sculpture park, parked the van, opened the back doors, and gave the command, "Harshish iv nazzle."

The zombies exited the vehicle.

XXI

Zombies, Zombies, Zombies

Samuel

I was driving my car around yet again on zombie duty. I wasn't alone. After the beating Ernie and Mindy had taken, Beryl wouldn't let anyone go out to meet the zombies alone. Not only had he made that rule, but even as we'd been ambushed in the warehouse a bit south of downtown, my boss had been contacting higher-ups in VATE. The zombie case in Des Moines had become high priority.

What with the vampire/werewolf team in the black vans, the shooter and black vans working to kill people to create more zombies, and the trap that had been sprung on the two black vans this afternoon, higher-ups in VATE had recognized that a very large conspiracy was underway and that all the free agents—or even those working on cases of lesser importance—needed to come to Iowa to help thwart whatever this awful plot was.

Besides, every night the zombies were growing progressively stronger and smarter and were getting tougher to kill. I thought nostalgically of the days when I could easily kill one or more zombies by myself.

And that was less than a week ago.

So on this night, Ronald was my companion. He was more interesting as well as interested in this case than Ernie was. Of course, Ernie was dead. Mindy had been wounded severely, but had made a recovery and was on duty again tonight. At least one of the two agents who'd originally been sent to help me was in still commission. But William and Ingrid—as far as we knew—had been killed in the ambush. I was surprised they hadn't heard the automatic weapons being cocked as I had. Oh, well, stupidity happens to the best of us. It's just unfortunate when being idiotic results in your death.

Although VWW couldn't help with tracking the vans to their original locations, it could help to spot zombies being dropped off.

Beryl was worried that the sculpture park downtown might be hit again, so Ronald and I were circling close to that area with the idea we'd catch the zombies almost as soon as they exited the van. As another safety procedure, Beryl had arranged for VWW to shut off all the cameras in the area, so we wouldn't need interference by WOVACOM or VWW or VATE to eliminate an electronic record after the fact. Other vehicles were circling the park, but WOVACOM did its best to scare them off. Without humans hanging around the park and with the electronic surveillance shut down, our only concern would be killing the zombies.

Since we believed the zombie creators would soon drop off the zombies at the sculpture park, I pulled my car to the side of the road on the Locust Street side of the area, and after I parked, both Ronald and I got out. Tonight, we were armed with swords in their sheaths and shotguns holstered and on our backs. We expected the zombies to be tough.

My phone rang.

"This is Samuel."

"Samuel, this is Kristy from VWW."

I could have said "Nice to talk to you," or some such nonsense since I'd worked with her briefly on another case. But I knew she didn't like me and I certainly didn't like her, so I kept to formalities.

She continued, "We've just seen six zombies dropped off on the Grand side of the park."

"We'll take care of them."

In reply, she grunted. "Well, you should. It's your job." And she hung up.

I told Ronald the news from Kristy.

"Thanks to your parking, we can only see one side of the park," my companion said.

Sometimes, working alone seems like the only way to go. You can guess how I felt about this time.

I snorted and scanned the park. Ronald was correct. We stood close to some sculptures, but a hill sat between us and Grand Avenue. Of course, the logical thing was to move so we could see that side of the park, and that was what I proceeded to do. Ronald sighed and followed me. His sigh made me wonder how much he really wanted to fight the zombies.

Walking so we no longer had the hill between us and Grand Avenue, we saw nothing extraordinary on the north side of the park, and since we saw nothing, I knew we could proceed safely. With that in mind, I strode across the park, looking both to my right and left (or east and west) and kept my hand hovering over my sword in case I encountered the zombies unexpectedly. When I was halfway across the park, to the northeast I saw six zombies, moving quickly down the sidewalk still in a clump.

Not the way we want to fight them.

"That's bad," Ronald said, stating the obvious. So human of him.

"All we have to do is separate and destroy," I said. "I'll go to the west of the group while you go to the east. If we can each draw off one zombie at a time and dispose of it, we shouldn't have any problems."

Of course, I'd thought that about my last few encounters with the zombies. Each time the zombies had been more difficult to destroy than the time before, and tonight would probably follow the same pattern.

Ronald looked at me. But he didn't protest. Obviously, he lacked any better idea.

Simultaneously, we dashed in different directions. I sprinted northwest to be in front of the group and Ronald ran northeast to be behind the group. I skidded to a stop about ten feet in front of the zombies. The first zombie was a tall male, white as newly fallen snow—wearing clothes that hung loosely, but this particular undead didn't have a glaze over its eyes. Its eyes were as alert and as colorful as if the creature were alive. It was about five-ten and more muscular than me.

When it saw me, it moaned, "Kill vampire." That was the first time I'd heard understandable words from one of these creatures. Then it repeated itself.

I yanked out my shotgun and fired at the zombie's chest. Holes pockmarked the undead's chest and white pus flowed out. The zombie was unfazed by the wounds and walked toward me. I fired again, this time into its face. The shotgun blast obliterated a good portion of the face, including its eyes. Again, pus oozed from the wounds. Between the shotgun blast and the pus, the zombie's eyes were ruined. It groaned and moaned. It also continued walking toward me.

I jumped to one side, and the zombie continued its path although I was no longer in it. If that had been the only undead I had to worry about I would have been glad and probably proceeded to behead it.

Not too far to the east, I saw Ronald drawing off the closest zombie in the group, then a second behind the first.

Good luck, Ronald.

Not that I was one to talk. Although the first zombie was stumbling forward rather aimlessly, the second and third zombies, also both as pale as could be and both with bright, clear eyes advanced towards me.

"Bad vampire," said the second zombie, a petite female in a loose-fitting summer dress. "Zombie must kill."

The third zombie, a formerly young man wearing a loose t-shirt and baggy blue jeans, added, "Kill, kill, kill."

Then the second zombie dashed toward me. Yes, dashed. Not a walk. Not a stride. Certainly not an amble. It ran toward me.

I holstered my shotgun, yanked out my sword and plunged it into the zombie's abdomen. The undead continued to move even with the sword thrust through its body and pus oozing out. Both its hands grabbed my sword arm with a viselike grip. The third zombie went around the second and grabbed my other arm. Behind me I felt another zombie—the blind one?—grab my neck.

A few days before, I'd seen Ernie die when he was in a situation this. I wasn't about to let that happen to me. Luckily, I'd drunk plenty of blood before this encounter—Beryl had recommended we do so—yes, we might have been only fighting zombies but we needed full strength because we'd need to use all of our powers to survive.

I dissolved into a cloud of mist. Floating under the zombie behind me and noticing, as mist, that the undead froze for a moment in puzzlement, I re-materialized, yanked out my shotgun and blasted the back of the head of the zombie I'd blinded not too long before. Its head burst into a mess of pus and brains. The headless corpse collapsed to the ground. Seeing one of their comrades collapse to the ground, the other two jumped at me.

Not to grab me because again I'd dissolved into mist. I floated for a few moments as the two undead gazed around. Even as mist, I could feel another zombie join the first two.

Swell. What's Ronald doing? If I'd possessed a head at the time, I would have shaken it. Since I was only a cloud of mist, I couldn't.

Regardless, I found the zombie woman with the sword still in her chest and pus still flowing out. She was walking toward the statue of one black sphere atop a larger black sphere. Or maybe it was the statue with the small white sphere atop a larger white sphere. Both statues were about six feet tall. As if you care.

I re-materialized and yanked the sword from her body, causing a torrent of white pus to spew forth. As the one of the other zombies leaped toward me, again I dissolved into mist. *I'm going to be famished if I survive this.* I floated behind this zombie, re-materialized, and sliced off its head. Thus, another undead, the formerly young man in a t-shirt, fell to the ground, and melted into white pus.

Unfortunately, two zombies still threatened me. I looked beyond them to see Ronald trying to skewer the zombies close to him with his sword. The undead almost danced around him and chanted together, "Vampire must die. Vampire must die."

These zombies are thinking. Or the near equivalent thereof.

The two zombies close to me, the young woman undead with pus flowing out of her abdomen, and an older man wearing a button-down flannel shirt and brown corduroys, turned toward me.

"Bad vampire," said the woman.

"Killed zombie," said the older man.

Together, they leaped toward me. And not merely straight at me. One jumped to my right, the other to my left.

They're getting tactical. I hoped other VATE agents had less intelligent zombies to deal with than we did.

As for me, I dissolved yet again into mist. The two zombies smacked into each other as I floated behind older man zombie, re-materialized, and decapitated it. Another undead down. The young woman zombie stared at me.

"Why you kill?" she asked. "Why you kill?"

"Why do you?" I asked back.

The zombie looked at the ground, took a few steps away from me, and shook her head.

Was it having intelligible thought? I couldn't stop to care. Since she wasn't paying attention, I stepped forward, swung my sword and chopped off her head. Even as it fell to the ground, I dashed around it and beheaded one of the zombies Ronald still hadn't destroyed, making its head flop to the ground. The other undead attacking Ronald paused for a moment, long enough for Ronald to slice off its head.

He sighed heavily. "That was far harder than it should have been."

I chose not to reply.

Because if I had, I would have insulted my fellow VATE agent. *We're getting a lot of incompetents on this case.*

Of course, the answer also might have been that fighting zombies was much more difficult—especially if you didn't know how intelligent or strong the undead would be with each encounter—than fighting Evil Ones.

"Let's get back to headquarters," I said.

With all the special VATE agents coming to town, Beryl had established a headquarters at a local hotel instead of having us always returning to his house.

"Beryl won't like our report," I said.

I neglected to say that Beryl would be happy enough that we were reporting at all.

XXII

Returning the Van

Joe

Henry drove forward another block or two, then went around the block. As he approached Grand, he parked. We could see the zombies striding through the park.

I hope I don't see Sammy.

My companion was nonplussed. "This is the easy part," he said. "I wish I'd brought something to munch on."

"Yeah, meat's always a good thing." I lied. The smell of decay that still filled the van had killed my appetite.

"I'm glad we don't have to go out if the zombies do poorly."

I was glad of that, too. The last thing I wanted to do was to fight some vampires from VATE. We were on the same side, and I didn't want my being undercover to endanger Sammy or one of his friends. Yeah, I know. He probably didn't have any. Maybe me. Nah, I don't think we were ever friends. I tried. He didn't.

To make conversation, I asked, "Why do we have that green ooze on the roof?"

"To destroy the van if need be," Henry replied, proud that he had information I didn't. "Also, it keeps the human-loving vampires from following our vehicles with electronic surveillance."

These aliens were clever. I feared them even more for that.

Walking around a hill in front of us, beyond the zombies, were two tall men, both thin. Even in the streetlights I could see they were pale. Not as pale as the undead strolling along the sidewalk, but still very pale. We werewolves tended to have warm, pink or red cheeks, probably because of all the meat we eat.

One tall man motioned at the other. They exchanged a few words. I let my night vision kick in.

Whoa! That's Sammy! I had been afraid he might be involved in this "cargo" delivery mess, and I was right. *I'll have to tell Grant!*

The two vampires separated. Sammy went west of the zombies; the other vampire east. Yeah, I know. Sammy described what happened in other part of this narrative. I don't care! He was great. He was creative. Dissolving into mist. Using both his shotgun and his sword. He killed five of the six zombies. His partner only killed one. *Bet Sammy has nasty thoughts about that guy.* After reading his narrative about our earlier adventure together, I know he had nasty thoughts about me. Unjustified, I might add.

Henry whistled beside me as both of us watched Sammy do his stuff.

"I've seen that bloodsucker before. He's good."

"Yeah, that's for sure."

"That's why I was glad our third party didn't want us to fight if our cargo fought poorly."

"Or fought well but was outfought."

"I could kill him."

I laughed at that. "I'd like to see you try."

As we'd been talking, the two vampires had left the scene. After my last comment, Henry gave me an angry stare. He really didn't like me. He probably hated me. *Well, if all goes according to Grant's plan, maybe I can be done with him soon, too.*

My companion shrugged. "Okay, back to the warehouse."

When we arrived at the warehouse, Henry honked the horn once quickly, then pressed on it for about fifteen seconds, then gave the horn another quick punch. The metal door rolled up in front of us.

As we'd driven back, Henry told me that he wanted to do all the talking. Considering we had bad news to tell our third party associates, who had to be aliens, I agreed. Except for when Wild Ones had been forced to fight with the vampires, all from our pack had returned unharmed, so, unfortunately, Henry, even telling our "employers" bad news, would probably still live. A bad thing for werewolves around the world.

We drove in and saw that we were the second van to return. The first van was parked, and we didn't see any sign of its drivers. As we climbed out of the van, I smelled decay and rot. *Did that other van's zombies survive?* I hoped they didn't.

The two petite women in lab coats approached us.

"Please give us an update," said the redhead.

Henry did so. Both women frowned as my companion described the fight.

The redhead shook her head. "Although I'm glad to hear one bloodsucker was so incompetent, that other one we've heard about before."

The brunette agreed. "Too many times before. It was because of him that we decided your kind and his shouldn't engage in fights."

Henry nodded approvingly.

"Yes," said the redhead. "You should be glad you didn't engage him in battle. You'd be dead, too."

Henry growled. I put my hand on his shoulder to calm him. Instead, he growled even louder.

"No matter," said the brunette. "You did your job. Don't worry. We'll help in killing the human friendlies."

Then the two of them escorted us to the metal door through which we'd entered and let us out.

Henry sighed in relief. "That was close."

"Why?" I asked.

"Well, you never know what they might do."

Although I'd considered it before, now I knew beyond a reasonable doubt that not only was Henry a poor fighter, he was also a coward. I said nothing. I wanted to. Very badly. But I still said nothing.

"Luckily, we're done in time to make the meeting," Henry said.

Oh, yeah, that.

Between seeing Sammy fight and knowing the werewolf/vampire group plans, I had to let Grant know all that had and was going to transpire.

Because now we have to contact the vampires.

XXIII

VATE Meets WOOF

Samuel

Beryl and I met the werewolves at a coffeehouse. Yes, a coffeehouse. For those of you who read about my extremely unpleasant case where I was forced to work with a werewolf, you will realize the enormity of this statement. Werewolves don't like calm, contemplative settings. The wilder and rowdier, the better. I failed to understand what the werewolves wanted. Beryl was equally puzzled. But he'd been contacted by Grant, Joseph Butler's pack leader, and Grant had said we had to meet for a variety of reasons, not the least of which was the undead that kept appearing all over town. My boss agreed so fast to a meeting after that statement that neither of us could quite believe it.

We two entered the coffeehouse, located on Ingersoll Avenue, which had a narrow space with the coffee grinder and place for staff, coffee, and goodies on the west side and small, round tables with chairs along the east wall, which was adorned by paintings from local artists. Joseph and Grant sat at a table toward the back.

I recognized Joseph with his shoulder-length brown hair, beard, and mustache. He was wearing his bar attire—a plaid shirt, blue jeans, and cowboy boots. Grant, the other man at the table, had shoulder-length black hair in a ponytail behind his head and similar to Joseph a beard and a mustache. Those werewolves were always quite hairy. Joseph was five-eight; Grant was almost six feet tall with broad shoulders.

By the way, Beryl had told me I had to behave. Whatever these werewolves had to say was crucial to our zombie investigation.

Regardless, the two of us walked past the other patrons of the coffeehouse as Grant and Joseph stood. When we reached their table, the four of us stared at each other for a moment.

"Joseph," I said.

"Samuel," he said.

"Grant," Beryl said.

"Beryl," Grant said.

Then Beryl shook Grant's hand as I shook Joseph's, then I shook Grant's hand as Joseph shook Beryl's. Both Grant and Joseph gave firm, strong handshakes. I expected nothing less from werewolves.

"Care for a beverage?" asked Grant.

Beryl looked at me. I nodded.

"We'll be right back," my boss said.

We went to the counter where we ordered two hot teas—Darjeeling for Beryl and Earl Grey for me. I noticed the werewolves both had two cups of what I believed to be black coffee. Although I wanted to order a sweet pastry, a stern glance from Beryl caused me to decide otherwise. After Beryl paid for our beverages, and the barista said she'd bring them out to us, we walked back to the table and sat next to the werewolves.

"Nice afternoon," Grant said.

Beryl laughed softly. That wasn't good because that showed he was nervous, frustrated, or both.

"We're not here for chit-chat," my boss said.

Joseph rolled his eyes. I snorted. Both of us smiled at each other, because in our last encounter, each of us had performed that action in response to his partner quite a few times.

"These two have an understanding," the pack leader observed.

"Well, they had to work together more than we did," Beryl snapped back.

Luckily, at this point in the conversation, the barista brought out two small teapots in which our teabags were being steeped and a cup and saucer for each of us. Then she returned to her spot behind the counter.

"All right, I'll tell you the reason for our meeting," Grant said. Then he told us, well, you already know about it because you've been reading Joseph's account of his case up until now. I won't bore you with a rehash

Beryl and I listened in silence. Occasionally, one or the other of us would grunt approval or nod his head, but for most of the time, we kept silent. A few times, Joseph broke in and offered a correction or a comment about something his pack leader said.

When Grant finished his rather long monologue, Beryl commented, "That explains a great deal."

"And you can see why we had to contact you," Grant said.

I gave Joseph an approving nod. "So you'll help us hunt down and destroy the group creating the zombies?" I asked.

The pack leader smirked. "That's not your first priority." We both gazed at him. Okay, the threat from the Evil Ones was probably real, but certainly wasn't imminent. Grant continued, "The Evil Ones are planning to attack your group at the large meeting you're having at the hotel this evening."

Beryl had planned a large meeting of all the VATE agents who'd gathered in Des Moines to form a coherent strategy for destroying the zombies and to plan vehicle routes for the night. We were having the meeting at the hotel where most of the VATE agents were staying.

Despite my boss's no doubt best efforts, a look of horror momentarily crossed his face. "How do you know about that?"

Joseph shrugged. "At the meeting last night, Cecil said that's where they're going to attack you."

I shook my head. "We obviously have a mole."

We sat in silence for a few moments.

"How long have you been hearing about our plans?"

Joseph took a sip of coffee. "I think it's been happening since before I joined the Koman pack. I didn't figure it out until I went on the zombie run."

Beryl looked at me. "Do you have an idea?"

"Yes, and I don't like it," I said.

Grant cleared his throat. "The Wild Ones are also planning to attack a get-together we're having tonight."

And that was true as well. Many WOOF agents—I still can't keep from snickering even as I write that name—had come into town because of the threat of the Wild Ones. Grant had organized a meeting—more like a party from the pack leader's description—of these agents at a hobby farm outside the Des Moines city limits.

"I realize your mole is a problem. A bigger problem is that both Theresa and Cecil are probably aliens," Joseph said. "At that first meeting I went to and last night's, the werewolves and vampires would have fought each other to the death if those two weren't there. They get along almost as if they were brother and sister."

Beryl chuckled. "I'm sure we can deal with Cecil."

Grant, not to be outdone, said, "And we'll take care of Theresa." He paused. "Once we survive tonight, I'll let you have as many WOOF agents as you want to destroy the zombie menace."

I saw a pained look on Beryl's face.

My boss gave the pack leader a smile. "We'll need your help, but, as Evil Ones and Wild Ones worked better apart, we would be good to follow their example."

"I see your point," Grant said. Then he looked at Joseph and me. "Except for these two, of course."

Beryl smiled at that. "Yes, these two will definitely work together again."

I gave Joseph a suspicious stare. He gave me a happy grin.

My only comfort was we'd have to fight off Evil Ones tonight before our partnership—again?—resumed.

[The preceding is an accurate portrayal of Beryl's and my meeting with Joseph and Grant. I realize another narrative of this incident is also provided, but its many inaccuracies are too abundant to enumerate.]

XXIV

WOOF Meets VATE

Joe

Grant insisted that we meet Berry and Sammy at a coffeehouse. A coffeehouse! Can you believe it? What a dull place to meet. We werewolves prefer the chaos of a nightclub, especially the kind that's a meat—or meet—market. The wild lights. The loud noise. The crowds of people. My pack leader said we weren't meeting to bond with each other; we were meeting to exchange information. Yeah, whatever. Grant told me I had to be the respectable one between Sammy and me. That would be easy.

Grant and I arrived at the coffeehouse early. Since we'd called the meeting, my pack leader thought the vampires might take offense if we were late. I said it didn't matter if we were late or early, the vampires would take offense at simply meeting with us. Grant said he didn't like this meeting either. He still couldn't believe that Evil Ones and Wild Ones were cooperating. I had my own theory, but my pack leader didn't care about it.

Yeah, so we got there early. We sat at a table toward the back of the coffee house. Vampires might care some about what it looks like inside. I didn't. I wanted to meet at a bar and had dressed appropriately to do so. Grant had complained to me about that. I'd growled back.

We were drinking coffee, black, of course when Sammy and his boss Berry, as Grant liked to call him, arrived. Sammy was six feet tall, with short black hair, green eyes, and pale skin, although less pale than the undead. He wore a button-down cotton shirt, blue slacks, and leather shoes. His boss was taller than Sammy, had bright red hair, green eyes, and large ears. He looked tough, but he wore an outfit similar to what Sammy had on. Sammy said he respected his boss. With good reason, too.

As they walked past the other patrons, we stood.

"Yo, Joe," said Sammy.

"Yo, Sammy," I said.

"Yo, Grant," said Beryl.

"Yo, Berry," Grant said.

Then Grant and I both hugged our respective counterparts. I felt Sammy tense as tight as steel beneath my hug. I wondered if Berry was doing the same with Grant.

After we released them, Grant asked, "Getting something to drink?"

His boss looked at Sammy. My counterpart nodded. So they went to the counter and ordered a beverage, tea, if my hearing was correct. Sammy eyed the treats, but his boss gave him a stern look. Grant had done the same to me. Berry paid for their drinks and the two vampires returned to our table where they sat in the empty chairs.

"Nice afternoon," my pack leader said. I knew he was trying to relieve a bit of the tension that was palpable when our two guests sat down.

Berry chuckled. Sammy gave him a quick glance. *He knows that's a bad sign.*

"We're not here for banter," Berry said sternly.

I knew Grant wanted to growl at him. So did I. But we had to behave because we had important items to discuss with these vampires.

I rolled my eyes. Sammy snorted. We smiled at each other. *Yeah, we know the trials of trying to work with the other race. I know it far more than he does.*

"These two click," Grant said, ever so wisely.

"Well, they've got a working relationship." Berry sounded downright disgusted with the situation.

The barista brought the vampires their teapots and cups and saucers, then hurried back behind the counter. She gave us a frightened look. Fights aren't supposed to break out in coffeehouses.

I could see Grant wanted to be done with these bloodsuckers. "All right, here's why we're meeting." So he told about my investigation of the werewolf/vampire group, its desire to expand, its desire to kill the bands of human-friendly werewolves and vampires, and its plan to do so, and lastly, its delivery of the undead around town. (I know Sammy skipped this description, but I think it fits well into the course of the conversation.)

As my pack leader explained my adventures, the two vampires listened in silence except for occasionally giving a grunt or a nod of the head. Sammy was impressed. Berry not so much.

Berry gave a heavy sigh at the end of Grant's tale. "That explains a lot."

"So that's why we contacted you," Grant said.

Sammy gave me a knowing nod. That simply showed even more how impressed he was. Then he said, "So we'll work together to get the group making the zombies?"

I saw Grant cringe. Obviously, these vampires weren't as smart as they thought they were. He said, "We've got other worries now."

Berry and Sammy stared at my pack leader.

Grant continued, "The Evil Ones will attack your group at the large meeting at the hotel this evening."

Whoa! You should've seen the two vamps' faces. Yep, we knew they were planning a meeting of their VATE agents at a hotel that night. Berry had organized a large meeting to form a plan for destroying the zombies and confirm vehicle routes. The vampires had to plan stuff like that. We werewolves, especially if we're in the same pack, can just know how to work that out. Yeah, so they were having this meeting at a hotel where most of the out-of-town VATE agents were staying.

"How'd you know that?" asked Berry.

I shrugged. I really felt sorry for these guys. "At the meeting last night, Cecil said that was the plan."

Comprehension covered Sammy's face. He shook his head and said, "We've got a mole."

Grant didn't say anything, so I stayed quiet too.

"How long have you known?" asked Sammy.

I took a sip of coffee. "The Evil Ones mentioned at the first meeting I was at. They said that'd get more vampires in town for their attack."

Berry looked at Sammy. "Got an idea?"

Smart Sammy said, "Yep, but I don't like it."

I think Grant was feeling a bit left out. He cleared his throat. "We've got the same problem with Wild Ones."

My boss had organized a meeting—well, more like a party, because we prefer those to "meetings." The gathering was to be at a hobby farm outside of the Des Moines city limits, but not at Dick and Shirley's.

But I sympathized with the vampires, whether they deserved it or not. I said, "So you've got a mole. Worse is that both Theresa and Cecil are probably aliens. At that first meeting I went to and last night's, the werewolves and vampires woulda killed each other if those two weren't there. They're like brother and sister."

Berry laughed softly. "We'll get Cecil."

My pack leader gave me an indignant look before saying, "And we'll kill Theresa. After tonight, you can have the help of WOOF to destroy those zombies."

I thought Berry was going to vomit. Those vampires are so funny.

Berry said, "We'll need it, but we'd be better working apart."

I'm sure Grant thought that was nonsense. "Good point," he said. Then he looked at me and Sammy. "Except for these two, of course."

Berry smiled. "Yep, these two are definitely working together."

Sammy gave me a nasty stare. I smiled happily at him.

We get to work together again! It'll be so much fun! Maybe Sammy will even like me when we're done. Well, he could.

[The preceding is a truly factual narrative of Grant's and my meeting with Sammy and Berry. I know Sammy said otherwise at the end of his account, but Sammy lies, too.]

XXV

A Meeting at a Hotel

Samuel

For any observant reader, the VATE agent who was a mole for the Evil Ones is obvious. It's so obvious you werewolves and humans must have guessed as well. If you haven't, that's your problem, not mine.

The identity of the mole was clear to me even during our meeting with the werewolves. My mind still reeled in horror at the thought of joining with a group of werewolves. Conferring with two werewolves is one thing; assembling with ten to twelve—even if we had an equivalent number of vampires—was another. No wonder Cecil and Theresa had to keep the groups from fighting.

In any case, around 8 p.m. we VATE agents—mostly those from out of town who were staying at this particular hotel—gathered in a large conference room on the hotel's second floor. Toward the back of the room were two tables with carafes of blood, shot glasses, and mugs. The agents must have preferred bigger doses of blood because Beryl had ordered the same number of each, and more mugs were gone than shot glasses.

When Beryl had told his higher-ups that the zombie conspiracy was getting out of control and the details as to why, the higher-ups had responded appropriately. Thus, the many shot glasses and mugs, since a great number of us were gathering. All the special VATE agents also knew that we'd have to postpone our business until after we killed the Evil Ones attacking us. Only Beryl and I knew that Cecil was an alien.

Regardless, since we were going to be attacked, everyone was armed with either a battle-axe or a sword with the idea of beheading our opponents. Beryl guessed that the Evil Ones would be similarly armed.

By the way, although a large number of special VATE agents were in town, more were soon to follow to help eradicate the zombie menace.

Toward the front of the room were rows of ten chairs, five on each side of the aisle. We planned to use these chairs to brief the agents surviving the attack. I worried these chairs might impair our fighting space.

My boss and I had arrived a few minutes before eight—I because the last time I'd tried to socialize with VATE agents from other parts of the U.S., it had been a total bust, Beryl because he probably wanted make an entrance.

Other VATE agents of equivalent status to Beryl had come to Des Moines, so maybe Beryl simply didn't want to deal with them until he had to or maybe he'd already talked to them and knew they could keep this group in line before he arrived.

After we entered, we took shots of blood. Beryl then went to meet with his counterparts from other regions of the country, while I walked over to the group of agents who'd arrived in Iowa before the zombie case had become so huge.

Ronald and Mindy stood apart from the others. Both looked at me suspiciously. Each also carried a small mug of blood.

"What do you know about this attack?" Ronald asked.

"Enough to know that the Evil Ones may outnumber us," I replied.

Mindy snorted. "Why are we worried about Evil Ones? It's zombies that have been killing us."

I snorted in reply. "Don't you remember when you and Ernie were fighting zombies and I had to fight off Evil Ones and Wild Ones?"

She smirked. "We could have handled it."

Ronald gave me a smile. "And that's why Ernie is dead."

"All right, we needed his help," Mindy admitted.

"Thank you," I said.

Carrying a mug, a five-nine, thin vampire with very pale white skin—although again not as pale as any zombie's—stepped into our group. He gave us a conspiratorial grin. "I heard the source was a werewolf."

Mindy nearly spit out the blood she was drinking. "A werewolf!"

Ronald shook his head. "That's not possible. We don't talk to those kind. They're all wild, impulsive, and irrational."

All very true. I'd often said as much myself. *Better not to tell the truth.* I gave the new vampire a skeptical look. "Why would we listen to what a werewolf has to say?"

The other vampire laughed. "It's beyond me." He sipped his blood. "By the way, I'm Douglas King from Denver."

The three of us duly introduced ourselves.

Mindy sighed. "To think any vampire would work with werewolves. It's ludicrous."

"Insane is more like it," Ronald said.

Douglas shrugged. "Just telling you what I heard."

I gazed around the room suspiciously. "Who did you hear it from?"

The vampire from Denver stepped closer and whispered, "Supposedly, it was some of the locals. Rumor has it that these werewolves were investigating their own evil werewolves and somehow discovered a connection to this zombie conspiracy."

I smiled. "Ronald and Mindy are right. That doesn't make any sense."

Unfortunately, that was exactly what had happened. And I didn't like hearing this news from somebody besides Beryl. I excused myself and wandered throughout the room, listening to other conversations, most of which were about how we would fight the zombies, but a few discussions also disclosed rumors that VATE agents had been working with werewolves.

I sidled up to Beryl who was in a deep conversation with two female vampires. The talk concerned how to deal with employees and unruly agents, so I guessed they were in command positions similar to my boss.

"Hey," I whispered. "I have to talk with you."

Beryl gave me a nasty look, then laughed softly. "Please excuse me, ladies. My subordinate has an issue."

We stepped away from his group and from all the others and stood not far from a partitioned wall.

"Samuel, this better be good."

"Rumors are floating around that we received this lead from werewolves. People are not pleased."

Beryl gave me a quizzical look. "Well, it did come from werewolves."

"People don't like that it did."

My boss chuckled. "That's why I let it out. Hopefully, by the time we break it to all these agents that we'll have the help of werewolves in fighting zombies they'll be a bit more tolerant."

I snorted. *Couldn't have planned it better myself.* "Good job, Boss."

"My thoughts exactly." Beryl glanced around the room. "The Evil Ones will attack soon. You'd best be close to a certain someone."

We both knew who that "certain someone" was—or at least we guessed to be. Considering the mole was here, this vampire could hurt or kill fellow VATE agents as they fought the true Evil Ones. Beryl said my job was to kill or distract the mole once the fighting began.

"Right." I left my boss's side and slipped through the crowd of agents talking about former cases, Evil Ones, aliens, and, of course, most apropos, zombies—whether they were the threat

VATE said they were or whether they even existed. I was only about ten feet away from Mindy, Ronald, and Douglas when the lights went out.

I pulled my own sword from its scabbard. All around me I heard swords being drawn and battle-axes swinging experimentally.

Shouts came from all around us.

"Attack!"

"Kill the human-lovers!"

"Death to the stupid ones!"

And many, many more.

The Evil Ones had arrived.

XXVI

A Wild Party with Expected Consequences

Joe

I was attending another party at a hobby farm outside of Des Moines. I was especially excited about this party because sometime during the evening the Wild Ones would attack.

The hobby farm was about twenty minutes from Des Moines. It belonged to the Cummings family who ran an apple orchard. They made reasonable money with it, but similar to Wild Ones Dick and Shirley, they made even more money by letting werewolf packs have parties at their place. Also, similar to Dick and Shirley's, our vehicles were parked in a field between the highway and their house.

Unlike Dick and Shirley, though, the Cummings didn't allow partygoers to have sex in their house. They had a barn filled with a few horses, cattle, and hogs. The second floor was covered with hay. So werewolves desiring sex quite literally did it in the hay. Because the barn was more a place for lustful activities, the Cummings set up the party at the back of their house. Six picnic tables were covered with alcoholic beverages, soft drinks, platters of raw steaks, beef cubes, pork chops, and chicken legs. Raw chicken legs were quite popular but I preferred beef cubes. A bite full of raw meat goodness. Yum. Yum.

Since we were waiting for the Wild Ones to attack, all of us were armed with pistols, rifles, or shotguns filled with silver bullets. Yeah, it's more fun to wolf-out and fight as wolves. But we had to win this fight decisively. Kill them all. We didn't want any wounded ones getting away. (I'm sure the vampires were the same way with the Evil Ones who were also attacking them this night. Killing them all was the only way to leave this part of the case behind.) When the Wild Ones first arrived, all of us would shoot them with silver bullets. The idea was to wound or kill enough that we could mop up the rest while still having a few good fights.

Werewolves were here from all over the country. They were happy to be coming to Iowa to beat on some Wild Ones.

Grant and I arrived before any of the other werewolves because we wanted to greet them all. Other pack leaders of WOOF packs were attending, and Grant wanted to speak with them. I simply intended to meet and greet all the werewolves coming to our aid. In my WOOF experience, so far I've only helped around Iowa. I hope to be able to travel farther afield someday.

I roamed through the party. Like the Wild Ones' parties, some packs stayed together while other packs split up and talked to everybody. I was quite disappointed to see that my pack preferred to stay together. Well, most of it. Two females were out among the others, probably looking for a good time after we killed the Wild Ones. I know most of the guys and all of the gals in my pack trolled bars regularly to pick up humans. They succeeded too. Two guys each bedded down at least one new female a week. The two gals regularly bedded human males. One guy was gay and went to gay bars. He was usually successful, too.

Strolling up to my pack, I greeted them all. Melvin and Thelma. Peter and Pauline. Frank and Victor. Yep, the whole crowd was here. And everyone in my pack had a can of beer or a glass of wine.

"Joey, this is a great party!" Pauline exclaimed.

"Yeah," said Victor. "Wolves are here from both coasts."

Frank smiled. He winked at someone not too far away. "And I've got my eyes on a sweetie."

"You don't have much time," I warned. "The Wild Ones are coming soon."

Thelma sighed. "Ah, what a way to ruin a party."

Everyone else stared at her.

"What're you talking about?" asked Melvin. "This party couldn't be better. Yeah, wolfing-out and running through the field is great. But tonight we get to wolf-out and fight. Best party ever!"

A guy about five-ten with shaggy red hair stepped into our group. "Hey, I'm from Arizona. We've never had Wild Ones threaten us like this. It's exciting."

"And helping out vampires?" asked Thelma. She was the rather depressing one of the lot. Not a typical werewolf at all. She might get along with Sammy.

The red-haired guy laughed. "It'll be a hoot! I've always wanted to meet a bloodsucker. Working with them will be awesome."

Melvin gazed wistfully toward the orchard. On one side of the house was the orchard, on the other side a cornfield. Grant bet me the Wild Ones would come through the orchard because it provided better cover. I bet him that they'd come from both directions, forcing us to have a two-front battle. Melvin agreed with my theory. Thelma said they'd come from the highway. Peter and Pauline said they didn't care as long as we had a good fight.

A good fight. That's all a werewolf could want.

Howls echoed through the night. From the orchard. And from the cornfield.

The Wild Ones were going to put us in a two-front fight.

We all drew our weapons. Because before we transformed into wolves, we were going to inflict as much damage as possible.

XXVII

The Fight at the Hotel

Samuel

Evil Ones were stupid that way. That is, by announcing their presence when they attacked. Okay, some people might say they were being fair because they proclaimed their presence so those being attacked could be more prepared. I think that's an asinine argument. When I attacked someone by surprise, I made certain they didn't know what was coming. That gave me the advantage. Of course, maybe Evil Ones announced they were going to attack simply because they loved to talk. And talk. And talk. Joseph said they'd been far too talkative at both meetings he'd attended.

Regardless, even with the lights out, I saw the Evil Ones appearing all along the temporary wall that separated this room from other conference rooms. Each Evil One was dressed in black: black shirt, pants, shoes. Each held a battle-axe or long sword to attack us Protectors. The Evil Ones were being idiotic in other ways besides simply announcing their presence.

First, dousing the lights helped them not at all. If they'd been fighting humans, that might have been a good strategic move. We vampires can see better in the dark than in the light. Second, dressing all in black was another move that was pointless. Since we can see them in the dark, we can see them if they dress all in black. Stupid Evil Ones. Maybe they'd been around humans too long. Maybe they'd been around aliens too long and aliens were far more moronic than we'd ever imagined. In either case, the Evil Ones' idiocy was shining through. (Sorry, that was a cliché.)

I glanced behind me and saw Evil Ones also pouring through the door to this room. I wondered where Cecil was. My guess was he had come charging through the doorway. We didn't have any documented cases of aliens being able to transform into mist although they were able to transform into human bodies—and now we also knew vampire and werewolf bodies.

As I said, that wasn't my first concern. As I pushed my way through the crowd that was dispersing toward the sides of the room, I saw Mindy swinging her sword and beheading Ronald. *Yes, she's the spy all right.* Although nothing was "right" about it. She turned to decapitate Douglas who was fighting with an Evil One armed with a battle-axe.

"Mindy!" I shouted over the chatter of the Evil Ones.

Because they were still talking. Well, most of them. Saying how they were going to kill this, that, or the other Protector. Or how they thought we didn't know any better. Or how good blood tasted coming directly from a human. Or...well, whatever. Evil Ones would chatter for all of eternity if they didn't die of old age or weren't killed by us Protectors.

My early companion in the fight against zombies turned toward me.

"Killing Ronald wasn't nice," I said.

"It was not nice," she repeated sarcastically. "Are you a fool or an idiot? I have never been able to decide which..."

Even as she continued her statement, our swords clashed together.

"You're the one who's been telling where we were going to patrol for zombies," I interrupted her.

"So what if I am? These zombies were supposed to wipe out your kind. We certainly have not been able to devise a plot to do so..."

Slash. Feint. Parry. I knew I had to finish Mindy because other Evil Ones also needed to die.

"We should have been able to. We are smart enough. There are so many Elite organizations, well, and some Chosen organizations, but I do not understand the Chosen. They want to convert your kind. To what ends? Your kind loves humans..."

Throughout this monologue—unfortunately, similar to so many monologues, including not using contractions, another trait of Evil Ones, being spoken by our opponents within the room, well, until a Protector killed one of them and ended his or her endless talking—Mindy and I continued to fight. Slash. Feint. Thrust. Slice. Parry.

A voice behind her said, "Would you just shut up?"

Mindy paused in her monologue, turned her head, and saw Douglas who'd lightly tapped her shoulder with his battle-axe.

"I can talk—"

I sliced her head off. As head and body fell to the floor, they melted into ash.

"Thank you," I said.

"No problem," Douglas replied. "Her chattering behind me was proving to be a distraction."

Both of us broke through the crowd of VATE agents fighting off Evil Ones. By the way, prior to this meeting, Beryl had acquired photos of all the VATE agents who would be attending this meeting then distributed this list to all attendees. That way we knew the faces of our friends—well, except for Mindy—and if a face we encountered wasn't among the photos we all had memorized—because we can with our brilliant vampire minds— we knew that vampire should die.

All around us vampires, both Protectors and Evil Ones, were clanking swords against swords or swords against battle-axes or battle-axes against battle-axes as the Evil Ones kept up their obnoxious chatter. As well as simply fighting, others dissolved into mist then re-materialized in their human forms, often to surprise their opponents by slashing off their heads.

Others transformed into bats, either to flee the scene—I regret to say that I saw a few Protectors doing that—or re-humanizing behind unsuspecting Evil Ones. Others remained in their human forms and fought valiantly until killing their opponents or dying themselves.

Douglas gave me a grin to show me he was enjoying this fight.

If you're interested, I wasn't having a good time. Death isn't something to which I aspire, especially not in fighting Evil Ones who should have known to leave well enough alone. No, not them. They had to ally themselves with some crazy werewolves and both decide to kill off the human friendlies. Okay, aliens were probably behind it in the form of Cecil as a vampire and Theresa as a werewolf. But Evil Ones should be smart enough to know when they're being used by others.

All right, I'll stop with the philosophizing and get back to the fight.

I gave Douglas a shrug. He pushed his way toward the wall to join other Protectors fighting the Evil Ones. I paused and noticed that the Evil Ones were pressing into the room, leaving a space between them and the wall behind them. *Moronic Evil Ones.* My plan was obvious. I dissolved into a cloud of mist, floated among the fighting vampires feeling the swish of swords and battle-axes, the breath of those fighting, and the movement of the opponents in each fight. I re-humanized close to the wall partition and behind three Evil Ones. Protectors engaged in their fights saw me. One or two smiled. The rest continued concentrating on killing their opponents.

I stepped behind one, swung my sword and beheaded the Evil One. As head and body fell to the floor, both melted into ash. I stepped behind another Evil One, and did the same. Then I stepped behind a third and did likewise.

A few of the Protectors gave me angry stares. A vampire a bit taller than me with shaggy blond hair and blue eyes snorted in disgust. "I could've taken him."

I thought to remind him that our goal was greater than the triumph each of us would feel at killing our adversary in hand-to-hand combat, but then I looked across the room and discovered such a case was presenting itself.

Slashing their way through the crowd of Protectors—and by slashing, I mean wreaking damage upon anyone who stood in their way—was a wedge of Evil Ones, led by an almost seven-foot-tall black man armed with a sword. Two Evil Ones were behind him, backing up his every attack. Behind them were three more, with the one in the middle walking backward to fight off any Protectors who attempted to attack from behind.

Now here's a fun group to help fight.

"Well, you can kill the next one on your own," I said before I shrank into a bat and flew across the room.

Being a bat, as I've said previously, is strange because none of the human senses apply. Bats travel by radar and a bit by smell. My bat radar detected all the swinging and crashing of battle-axes and swords beneath me. At one point, I rose higher to miss a battle-axe swinging wildly. My goal was obvious. That wedge of Evil Ones. With Cecil in the lead. Before I took on Cecil, I wanted to eliminate the Evil Ones who would create difficulties for me in getting to him.

I flew around the head of the vampire in the middle of the second row. Even with my bat senses, I could hear her scream. I dived and bit at her skull and ripped at her hair. According to some not very smart humans, bats can land in a person's hair and get stuck. That might be the case with bats that are only bats, but I was a vampire and knew how to fly high enough above the head to avoid such entanglements.

Regardless, my interactions with the Evil One's hair were distracting enough that she failed to stay in line with the two on either side of her and also failed to properly defend herself. A nearby Protector sliced off her head, and she melted into ash.

I swooped over and did the same to the Evil One who'd been to her right. Again, another female vampire. And again, I dived and bit at her skull and ripped at her hair. She screamed as loudly as her compatriot had. Maybe louder. If aliens recruit Evil Ones in the future, they should find some who don't mind being bothered by flying bats. She turned away from the vampire she was fighting and swung her sword randomly at me. I simply flew higher and made my dives after her sword had slashed downward. Another Protector had the honor of decapitating her.

So I dived toward the third Evil One who'd been in the second row behind Cecil. This vampire was male with short hair whom I still could bug, but not nearly so well. Besides, he'd seen the fate of his fellow Evil Ones, so he ignored me and kept fighting with the Protectors who were slowly surrounding him. Even as a bat, I was able to determine that he broke off from the wedge, surrounded by my fellow VATE agents. As I flew away, I sensed him melting into ash.

This time, I dived toward the ground and re-humanized myself behind the two Evil Ones still fighting directly behind Cecil. Granted, decapitating a vampire is the quickest way to do one in, but sometimes merely stabbing one in the guts can be a good distraction. So I did that to the one behind and to the left of Cecil. I jabbed my sword through her back and yanked it out. Blood gushed out of both sides. She turned to face me, and I beheaded her.

The Evil One behind and to the right of Cecil, I decapitated before he even noticed me.

Not that any of this bothered Cecil. If anything, all this activity made Cecil even more deadly. I jumped back as the tall, black vampire swung his sword even faster, either decapitating or wounding nearly all the Protectors who sought to surround him. His speed increased and almost everyone who had stepped forward to attack him was either wounded or beheaded. As he finished his swing around, he paused when he saw me mere inches away from the span of his arm and sword.

"Hello," I said quietly.

A hush fell over the room. Even those Evil Ones still alive and fighting froze as did many of the Protectors who were close to where Cecil and I stood.

"Ah, Samuel," greeted Cecil. "I've heard so much about you. I'm glad that we finally meet."

XXVIII

The Wild Ones of the Night

Joe

The howls rang out on either side of us. The Friends of Humanity close to me were nearer to the apple orchard than the cornfield. I dropped down on one knee because I only had a pistol. I wanted to be out of the line of sight for those FHs with rifles and shotguns. Above me, shots rang out.

In the orchard in front of me, hundreds of huge wolf shadows bounded toward us. As the shots fired, yelps of pain filled the air, often followed by whimpers as the same wolves skidded to a stop still a long way from the farm. Others kept charging toward us, snarling as they prepared for battle. More shots rang out above and behind me; the second barrage of bullets.

I still hadn't fired because I wanted the Wild Ones to be as close as possible. When I shot, I wanted to kill my wolf targets. A hundred feet away, one wolf took a shot in the head. Another a shot in the leg. And still another a shot in the chest. And those were only what I saw. Many more collapsed long before they were close enough for wolf-to-wolf combat.

I gazed at the huge wolves attacking us. *The Koman Pack better be here.* I had some scores to settle. Yeah, I wanted to kill Henry once and for all. But Grant had other plans for that loser if Henry chose to fight me. *Bet he does. He really hates me.* I was a bit sorry we'd have to kill Chuck, Victoria, and Ellen. Especially Ellen. We'd had fun together. But Wild Ones had to die before we could continue this case.

And then Theresa came to mind. Grant and I had devised a special plan for her since she was probably an alien. That's why she could defeat other wolves so easily. Aliens are stronger and faster than us werewolves. Hell, they're stronger and faster than vampires. They're a threat to both of our species. And we werewolves became a target because I'd helped Sammy on a case not too many months ago.

Yeah, I know. Enough digressions (that's so Sammy of me). More about the fight.

Shots continued to echo above and around me. Finally, I saw the wolves were coming close enough for me to use my pistol. I fired once and hit a wolf between its eyes. It collapsed to the ground, transformed back into a human, covered in white fur. *Bye, bye, Wild One.* I shot again. And hit a wolf in the chest. It plopped to the ground, moaned, then resumed its charge. *Foolish Wild One. Sometimes fleeing is best.*

One more shot before I wolf-out. Another shot. Another hit between the eyes. *Two out of three. Good job!* But Theresa had hoped to have a two-to-one advantage over us Friends of Humanity. I didn't know the exact numbers, but she thought she was close. Yeah, I'd talked to Grant. Yeah, he made sure the Wild Ones' odds were less good.

Close enough!

Holstering my pistol, I jumped forward.

Wolves all around me. Know their smells. Grant gave to us a paper with the scents of all the FHs attending before the meeting. So we know the scent of good wolves and will only fight evil wolves. Ha ha ha! Fight. Fight against evil.

Lots of smells. Lots of wolves. Wolves charging toward us. One wolf sees me.

Howls. [To glory!] Growls. [Fight!]

Recognize! Good ol' Henry!

Smells of mold, antiseptic soap, and musty linen sheets. Bad smell. Bad wolf.

Henry. Small black wolf. Jumps at me.

Jump at him. Knock together. Claw. Bite. Bite him. Him not bite me.

Remember! The plan! The plan!

Let him push me to my back. Jumps on top of me. Growls. [Kill you. Kill you.]

I transformed into a human. The huge wolf stood above my prone body and stared at me. I drew my pistol, shot at Henry's back legs and hit the left one. The huge wolf howled. As it whimpered in pain, I holstered my pistol, yanked a silver chain out of my pocket, and whipped it around Henry's back legs. The wolf collapsed to the ground and transformed back into its human form. I wrapped another silver chain around him, binding his arms.

"You goddamn—"

I stood and picked him up as he shouted curses only a Wild One's mother could admire. Behind me stood two other Friends of Humanity in human form. I tossed Henry to them. "Keep him safe."

Before I had a chance to see what they did with poor Henry, more wolves charged us.

I leaped forward.

Wolves. Wolves. All smelling of the Koman pack. Smell of wet socks.

Want me. Want to kill me. See all. Victoria. Ellen. Sorry, girl, you bad now. She was bad earlier too. Good bad. Now bad bad.

Dodge Victoria's lunge. Jump on her back. Bite. Snap. Claw.

Victoria turns. Knocks me over. Another wolf pounces on her. Both roll away biting, clawing, snapping.

Ellen pounces toward me. I rear up. We meet.

Ellen: Whimper, whimper [Why? Why?]

Growl, bark once, twice. [It's war. Fight. Fight.]

Both of us barrel at each other. Roll on the ground, biting and clawing. Me more than her. Likes me still? Too bad. Wild Ones must die.

Roll her over on her back. Her paws claw at me. Bite one front leg then the other. Bones break. Crack. Ellen whimpers. [We were friends, lovers]. Bite her jugular. Blood, blood everywhere.

Ellen now dead in human form.

Growl behind me. Smell of decaying garbage, damp fur, and whiskey. Turn. See large black wolf. Ryan!

From human hunt! Recruited his pack to fight this battle. Ha ha ha!

Ryan growls, snarls. [Traitor. You must die.]

Growl. Bark twice. [Enemy. Fight. Fight!]

Pounce together. Bite. Chomp into flesh. Tries to claw me. Misses. Jump back. Pounce forward. Bite one leg. Crunch. Crack. Bad bone.

Ryan falls to ground. Growls. [Traitor] Barks. [Fight. Fight.] Howls. [To glory!]

Other wolves busy all around us. Fighting. Know by smells some FHs hurt, dead. Sad. Sad. Good WOOF fighters. Fight for honor. Fight for glory. Fight for life.

Pounce on Ryan. He flips over. Claw. Bite. Crunch. Another leg.

Ryan whimpers. [You recruited me] Growls. [Traitor.]

Growl myself. No need to explain. Chomp. Right through his jugular. Another dead Wild One. Human form. Covered in white fur.

Not far away, hear trouble. Great movement. Very visible. Even if all black and white.

Huge wolf. Angry wolf. Twice the size of all others. Nearly as big as a horse. Swipes claws. Shreds skin. Flesh. Cracks bones. One after another. FHs attack. Defeated. Wounded. Or killed.

Know this wolf. Has to be. Couldn't be any other.

I growl. Then bark, once, twice, three times. [Fight me! Fight me! Fight me!]

Theresa, the giant wolf, chomps another FH through the back, throws her away like garbage. Smell of algae, wet grass, and green pond scum. Yes, she's an alien.

Other wolves scatter. The giant wolf faces me and howls.

XXIX

An Alien in Vampire's Clothing

Samuel

"I hope all that you heard was good," I said in the silence of the room.

Cecil grimaced. "Hardly."

A few Protectors snickered at that remark. Their snickers died as the tall black man angrily scanned the room.

"We know about your exploits in destroying zombies as well as killing teams of vampires and werewolves," he continued.

"He should die for that!" screamed an Evil One.

Those were that vampire's last words because a Protector beheaded him while he was distracted.

Cecil shook his head sadly. "You bloodsuckers make for poor allies."

"We're better than those mutts!" shouted an Evil One. She tried to shove her way through, toward her leader, only to be decapitated by a Protector's battle-axe.

The alien gazed around the room, and my eyes followed his. I guessed about fifteen Evil Ones still lurked around the edges of this room and another thirty-five Protectors stood ready for combat. Over two to one in the favor of VATE agents. Cecil also seemed to be gauging the room.

Behind Cecil and about three layers of vampires back stood Beryl, sword in hand, carefully watching my confrontation with this alien.

Cecil shrugged. "I can't say." He let his eyes fall on me again. "Although no Hairy One thwarted our plans as well as you."

Then you don't know about Joseph. How will his fight with the Wild Ones go? I've only met Wild Ones in the two times I fought them in this case. Each time I was less than impressed. *I hope all the Wild Ones are like that.*

"Thank you," I said.

The alien groaned. Behind him, two VATE agents leaped forward, swords swinging. Although we vampires can be fast, aliens are faster. In mere moments, the tall black man turned, swung his sword, and decapitated both of his assailants.

"You're welcome," he said, as if the previous fight hadn't occurred. Despite all the Protectors he'd killed, Cecil hadn't sweated at all. *Must be an alien thing.*

He continued, "I'm certain you realize now that I'm an alien. Perhaps you did even before this conflict. You were obviously warned about it, and either I have a traitor among my followers or my werewolf counterpart did."

As Cecil made this little speech, some Protectors who'd scattered throughout the room dissolved into mist. I smiled.

Cecil hadn't observed the same activity I had, so he believed my smile was in reference to his words. "So you think my being an alien is amusing?"

"I always like when aliens reveal themselves. Saves me the trouble of thinking you might be some other kind of being." A few Protectors gave me a thumbs-up.

My experiences must not be atypical. Well, being special agents gets us in contact with aliens far more than we'd like.

The tall black man shook his head and snorted disgustedly. "For those of you who care, I am a warrior, the best at killing your kind."

A few seconds after these words, all those vampires who'd dissolved into mist re-humanized behind their intended victims—in about four cases, more than one Protector behind the same Evil One—and decapitated them. Three Protectors had to quickly jump behind another Evil One, so all were killed in this attack. Now most of the Evil Ones in the room were piles of ash.

"You're also a good distraction," a VATE agent standing in the circle around Cecil said. Others laughed.

"You bloodsuckers have no honor," the alien said. He turned to stare at me again. "This one has a bit of honor. He stands there in the midst of this circle, waiting for our fight to commence. He's willing to fight me hand to hand, alone, without the interference of any of the rest of you."

Actually, I was hoping that wouldn't be the case. As I mentioned, aliens are faster than vampires. They're also stronger. Many have the strength of three vampires. Their warrior class, of which Cecil claimed to be, might have the strength of four or more vampires. Not exactly someone I'd like to fight on my own.

Of course, the secret in defeating aliens is by surprising them. Since our speed and strength is less, to defeat these more powerful beings, we have to use our minds. Minds they tend to underestimate.

Cecil smiled at me. "That is a true statement, is it not?"

"I guess that's as good a way to kill you as any," I replied.

This time, the alien man laughed. "If I wanted, I could kill all you leeches in this room."

Among the crowd, I saw Beryl's face. My boss shook his head negatively. *Is Beryl indicating he doesn't believe Cecil or he doesn't want Cecil to try? If the latter, I know what needs to be done.*

I leaped toward Cecil, swinging my sword. He saw my movements and swung his sword to meet mine. Our swords clashed together. Cecil, with a longer reach and a stronger arm, pressed his sword against mine, and I felt myself giving way. *Not good.* And that meant I'd have to win this fight another way.

Cecil broke the lock and swung his sword at mine again. It didn't hit. Because I'd dissolved into a cloud of mist. Even as mist, I could feel Cecil laughing. He shouted something to the entire room. Not that I cared.

Nor did I remain where his swinging sword could harm me. Because once I'd dissolved into mist, the alien hadn't ceased his attack. In the air where I'd once stood, Cecil swung and slashed his sword, madly trying—quite in vain—to kill me or the essence of me or some misty aspect of me.

As a cloud of mist, I floated around behind the large alien. And re-humanized for a moment.

"Cecil, I'm—"

The tall alien pivoted, swinging his sword. Only to slice air. Or mist as the case may be. He shouted loudly again.

As Cecil swung his sword where I'd been, I floated to his right side. And re-humanized again.

"...over here."

The alien turned, his eyes blazing and his sword swinging. At a cloud of mist that I'd just dissolved into. This time I didn't feel the flailing of the sword. Instead, I guessed Cecil let it drop to his side.

Not that I was done. Because I floated to his left side. And re-humanized.

Before I could say a word, Cecil pivoted and swung his sword at me. I dissolved into mist before the sword sliced the air where I'd been standing.

All this transforming into mist and back to my human form was quite exhausting, and I wasn't done yet. Luckily, prior to this big meeting, I'd drunk a good quantity of blood, suspecting such an encounter with Cecil might occur.

To make life interesting, I re-humanized on the spot I'd stood before.

"Hi," I said before I dissolved again into mist and the alien again missed me.

I sensed other action occurring around me. Other VATE agents still fought the Evil Ones. A few agents were simply standing around, watching my fight with Cecil when they should have been making themselves more useful.

Well, the time had come to end this fight.

I floated beneath the tall alien and re-humanized lying on the floor between his legs.

"Here—" I said.

Cecil stared down at me and raised his sword. As the tip of the sword plummeted toward my head, I dissolved into mist again. The sword crashed through the wood floor.

I floated behind the tall alien and re-humanized to see Cecil standing, gazing at the sword stuck deep into the floor. I stabbed my sword through his back. Green ooze and red blood spattered from the wound.

The tall alien pivoted, yanking my sword from my hands. Before I had a chance to dissolve into mist, his hands grabbed me around the neck and hoisted me into the air. A smile spread across his face.

"Stupid, stupid Samuel," he said, his grip tightening around my throat.

Behind him, I saw Beryl raise his sword and swing. Cecil's head fell from his body and his grasp around my throat eased.

I fell to the floor at the same time as the tall alien's corpse.

A few Protectors applauded. Others continued to fight the few Evil Ones in the room.

"I knew you could be annoying, and I'm glad I'm not the only one," Beryl said.

Douglas stepped up to me. "You turned annoyance into an art form."

I shrugged. "I try."

Beryl stepped close enough to me and whispered so only I could hear, "And if the werewolves do their part, we'll only have the zombie problem to solve."

Oh, yeah, that. Well, I hoped Joseph had information that would help us track down the aliens better than we had so far.

XXX

Theresa, the Giant Wolf

Joe

I transformed into my human form. Yeah, I know. Sammy would say that was a stupid move on my part. 'Course, Sammy thinks all werewolves are stupid, so whatever we do is stupid. Anybody, including vampires, reading my part of this narrative knows better.

All around me were wolves, mostly Friends of Humanity whom I recognized in both wolf and human forms. Behind me, I still heard continued fighting.

The huge wolf that was Theresa growled at me, took a few steps forward, and transformed into human form as well.

"Hello Theresa," I said, greeting her.

"Joe, thank you for coming through for us."

I frowned. "You knew I was a spy?"

Theresa grinned. "We wanted lots of pets for this fight. You provided them and played the part of the mole perfectly."

Me? The mole?

"We had another to tell us of your activity. But you got all of these pets here to die."

Me? The mole? Anger filled me. "You goddamn fucking—"

I was angry enough that cursing alone wouldn't soothe the savage beast. But the wolf in me could. I leaped forward, transforming into a wolf.

Wolves all around. Except for one human. Not human. Fur erupts all over woman's body. Face expands to muzzle with sharp teeth. Feet and hands grow into paws. Instead of woman, a huge wolf the size of a horse faces me. Smells of algae, wet grass, and green pond scum. Bad wolf smell.

Other wolves back away from the two of us.

I want to kill, kill, kill, kill, kill!

I bark. [Fight!]

Huge wolf snarls. [Die!]

Leap at her. Giant teeth snap at me. Dodge. Snap at her fur.

Her huge body slams into mine. Fly through the air. Land on the ground.

Bark. Bark. [Fight! Fight!]

I charge again. Giant wolf slaps a huge paw the size of a platter against me. Again, fly through the air. Again, land roughly on the ground.

Howls all around us. [To glory!] Both FHs and Wild Ones watch. Stare silently at Theresa. She growls. [Fight] Then howls. [To glory!]

As she howls, again I charge. Huge jaws snap at me, grazing my back. Large paw slams into me and scratches my chest. Again, thrown to one side.

I transformed back into a human. Theresa did the same.

"What an idiot!" she exclaimed. "Even if this attack fails, the greater plan will proceed."

"You mean with the zombies?" I asked.

"I might," she replied coyly.

Fighting ceased around us. The wolves near me shifted their positions. Quite a few wolves from out-of-town packs had been fighting the Wild Ones prior to Theresa's transformation and mine. Many of these fights continued farther away. The other non-locals stealthily crept from where we stood to the south or east, depending on which battle they wanted to participate in. Theresa, if she noticed this action, ignored it, and if she didn't, she didn't care.

"Well, I do," I stated.

She smirked. "But you don't know what we have planned."

"You mean you aliens?" I asked.

"Who are they?"

"You and Cecil, to name two," I snapped back. "Werewolves don't work with vampires. Don't you know that? We would've killed each other if you hadn't been there."

Theresa shook her head. "More the fool is you. It doesn't matter. With our attacks tonight, we will have killed enough of both of your human-loving varieties that our plan will proceed."

"Your alien plot with the zombies."

"If that's what you care to call it," she said.

"I do," I said. "By the way, I knew you could transform into humans, but I didn't know you could switch to other forms as fast as werewolves and vampires."

"It takes practice," she admitted.

Being a werewolf, I knew that for us transforming into a wolf didn't take practice. Retaining your clothes and weapons while doing so, that took a bit of work. Now's not the time to explain how.

"Gotcha," I said.

She sighed. "Enough of this nonsense! Be a werewolf! Fight with honor!"

I transformed back into a wolf.

Wolves all around me. A human in front of me. No, not a human. An alien in human's clothing. Ha! Funny joke.

Again, Theresa transforms into the giant wolf.

Two wolves pounce on top of the huge wolf. Another two chomp into her rear legs. Another two bite down on her front legs. None of these four give any sign of letting go. Another two wolves jump on top of her, joining the two atop her, clawing and biting at her.

She shakes her massive body. Both top wolves fall, one smashed with a giant paw. She snaps her tremendous jaw at the two on her front legs. Crunch! One dead. Snap! The second dead, too. Quick turn. Crack! One on a rear leg gone. Others jump away as huge jaws snap.

Smile. Big happy smile. Her eyes bulge. She howls into the night. [To glory!]

And I transformed back into a human. I drew my pistol and fired between her eyes.

"Bet you think this is unfair," I said as I shot her.

With the first bullet, green ooze drizzled out. With the second, a gush of green ooze. With the third, red blood finally poured forth.

The huge wolf fell to the ground. It didn't transform back into human form, a human form covered by white fur.

"But you aren't a werewolf," I finished.

The wolves not from the local WOOF pack sprinted away to fight off other Wild Ones. All my fellow pack members transformed back into humans.

Grant walked up to me. *He must've been attacking Theresa, too.*

"We need to finish off the other Wild Ones," he said.

My fellow pack members transformed back into wolves. They sprinted off to fight the evil werewolves.

I remained where I stood.

Grant smiled. "All except you. You have a vampire to meet."

Sammy, here I come!

XXXI

I Am

Vod

I am....
    I am...
    I am Vod.

That name sounds strange. Not correct. My thoughts are sluggish. They move as if I am walking through mud up to my knees. Can I walk? What is walking?

I know the terms. I know these thoughts.

The name Vod is wrong. Vod. Vod. A very short and precise name. A name with no apparent meaning.

Vod. That's a name for an evil emperor of a galactic empire in some corny 1980s science fiction movie. That can't be my name.

But I know it is.

I open my eyes. I'm lying on a green leaf larger than I am and with green slime covering much of my body and the top of the leaf. I look down my body, my naked body that is as white as newly fallen snow. Or as white as the White House. Or as white as a piece of printer paper. None of these metaphors seems to ring true to me.

Close to me and licking up the green slime that covers the leaf and my body—but not my face—my face and the upper parts of my body feel rather sticky as if something had licked them dry—is a creature about the size of a Scottish terrier. But it's not a Scottish terrier. Nobody would say that. It's forest green with a long body rather similar to that of a dachshund. It has brown eyes that are occupied with looking at the green slime its huge tongue is lapping up as if it were water. It has short little legs with paws with tiny claws on them. Its mouth is toothless and constitutes most of the face. I don't see any ears or a nose. Is its sole purpose to lick up the green slime around my body?

A creature exists for that? Bizarre.

Well, I guess the name "Vod" is too.

The creature continues licking me. I assume it licked my face and some of my chest clean of the green slime.

As the tongue licks away, its sandpaper-like texture would have tickled me when I was... I don't know what. Whatever I was, what I am now doesn't like that creature licking me. Of course, I also don't like the green slime covering me which feels like gelatin.

"Yuck," I say in disgust.

Maybe I shouldn't look at the little creature. I look to my right and see a naked woman whose skin is as white as mine. She lies on a huge green leaf and is also covered in slime. A little green creature crawls on her abdomen and licks up the green slime that covers her in the same way the little green creature licks up the slime is covering me.

"What the hell?" I ask.

What is hell? I don't know. But I know that the term "hell" expresses my confusion about what is happening to me. So maybe "hell" is a bad thing. I shrug. Well, at least I'm alive.

The clicking of wood against the floor approaches me. Two pairs of small feet in black pumps stand between me and the naked woman. One woman wearing blue slacks, the other black slacks. Both kneel down and I see they're also wearing white lab coats. One woman is very slim with bright red hair; the other is a bit chubby with black hair. The redhead bends down over me, pushes up one of my eyelids and flashes a light in that eye. I want to grab her to make her stop, but my arms feel as heavy as cement.

That's heavy. She moves quickly and pushes up the eyelid of the other eye and flashes a light in that eye.

"Hey!" I shout.

Both women jump away.

"He's got great responses," says the redhead.

"He's one of the most vocal we've ever had at this stage," says the brunette.

"We want them to be self-aware," says Redhead.

"That black man two rows down is having similar reactions," says Brunette.

Black? Black? That doesn't make sense. We're all as white as newly cleaned sheets. How can any of us be black? I don't know the answer. My thoughts are still sluggish, and so many of them don't make any sense at all. For that matter, what is "sense"? Or cents. I remember something about "cents." They're small copper coins with the face of a president on them. They are worth less than it costs to create them. *Well, that's stupid.* I enjoy some of my thoughts. That's one of them.

I giggle to myself. I guess I do that out loud because the two women look at me again.

"He's capable of making jokes to himself," says Redhead.

"Very promising," says Brunette.

A strange thought comes to mind. *Vampires are bad. I must kill vampires.* Those thoughts are silly. *Vampires don't exist. So why do I care? And I certainly can't kill them if they don't exist.* This time I laugh loudly.

Brunette bends over my head and gives me a concerned look.

"Are you sure we want them this intelligent?" she asks.

Redhead bends down, holding a tablet. *Using for notes? Why take notes about me?* I am Vod, Evil Emperor of the Galaxy. I laugh at that too.

Both women stand. As they do so, I see both shake their heads. I want to apologize but I don't know for what or why.

XXXII

The Warehouse and the Werewolf

Samuel

All right, I admit it. My last narrative about my adventure with Joseph had its inaccuracies. The foremost one being the names we called each other. In my narrative, I always called him "Joseph" and he always called me "Samuel." That isn't exactly true. Since I insisted on calling him "Joseph," he referred to me as "Sammy." Yes, Sammy. Even writing these words cause me to cringe.

These naming conventions and our arguments concerning them were unnecessary to that other tale, but since Joseph, or Joe, will read this one before I can publish it, I thought I should set the record straight. When we began working together this time around, I agreed to call him "Joe" if he agreed to call me "Samuel." Yes, I gave in to a werewolf. To my vampire readers, I apologize in advance. To my werewolf readers, don't think you can win every battle of words with vampires just because Joseph won this one.

I parked my car around the corner from the long side of the warehouse where we VATE agents had been ambushed. Since the ambush, and since learning about the warehouse where Joseph and Henry had picked up the zombies, VWW (Vampires

Watchers of the World) had been investigating the owners of these warehouses and possibly other warehouses in this same district of Des Moines.

A side note before I continue: As you noticed—and as Joseph probably also noticed, in the last paragraph I referred to my werewolf partner as "Joseph." I may have agreed to call him "Joe" when we talked, but in my narrative, he will remain "Joseph."

In any case, VWW hadn't detected the aliens. Sure, VWW could detect aliens in an office building or restaurant, but it hadn't detected the many aliens behind this zombie plot. For example, it hadn't known of the two who'd given Joseph and Henry their zombie cargo for the evening. Higher-ups in VATE were suspicious that the aliens had figured out our methods and had made efforts to become invisible to them. But I digress.

VWW, being the most technologically astute of our vampire organizations, was hacking companies in an effort to discover who owned both or either of these two aforementioned warehouses. So far VWW had uncovered a series of shell corporations and were still in search of the true owners.

Joseph and I exited my car. We were both armed with automatic rifles and swords. Okay, not exactly a set of weapons that a typical fighter would have. However, we wanted to be prepared for any eventuality. I'd insisted on the rifles. Joseph on the swords. (Maybe he thought more Evil Ones were waiting for us? I don't know. I didn't ask.)

"I still say we should have gone to the warehouse where Henry and I picked up the zombies," my werewolf partner said. "We know they have a zombie operation going there."

I gave him a grim look.

"That's our next stop," I said.

"But we know zombie operations must be in that building," Joseph continued. "Henry said he went to that building for every delivery."

A true fact. At least according to our werewolf sources. That didn't negate that good VATE agents had died in this building, and we needed to clear out the scum who'd done it if they were still here.

As we talked, we also walked from the car to the corner of the building.

Joseph rolled his eyes. He does that when I say stuff, he thinks is nonsense. I usually snort when he says stuff, I think is stupid.

"I'm just saying—"

I sighed. "I know what you're saying. We're not only going to the building to find intel. We're also going to avenge the deaths of my comrades."

"Oh," Joseph said. Then he smiled. He smiled a malicious smile. Maybe werewolves are even more into revenge than us vampires. Beryl said we could skip this building, although his sentiments were the same as mine. My partner continued, "So your kind isn't as emotionless as you claim."

All right, I wanted to give a sardonic remark. Luckily, we'd reached the door under which I'd escaped as mist in my last encounter here. My car was parked approximately where Ronald's car had been. I didn't feel bad about the deaths of William and Ingrid—she was rather a bitch—but I did feel the loss of VATE agents. Especially since this zombie thing was beginning to decay out of control—get it? Zombies, decay.

Following our fight at the hotel and the werewolves' fight at the farm, about twenty zombies had been released. Five had killed some humans. The rest wandered about, unhindered by either vampire or werewolf kind, then were picked up by black vans. In some cases, we saw these actions on camera; in others instances, we merely guessed.

And how many will be released tonight?

I noticed a doorbell to the right of the door. Joseph reached toward it.

I grabbed his hand. "No."

He growled as my hand grabbed his. "I know the code. Or at least the code for the other warehouse."

Letting go of his hand, I said, "Then we can use it there. We don't want to warn anybody inside that we're coming."

Joseph rolled his eyes again. "Okay. But I want lead at the next building."

"My pleasure," I lied. I didn't think werewolves should ever be the lead. Although after our last mission together, I knew werewolves were far more devious than we'd imagined.

I knelt down, removed some lock picking tools from my side pocket, and began attacking the lock. Joseph stood uneasily, flipping the safety of his rifle on and off and on and off. I would have snapped at him that such actions were disturbing my concentration, but appealing to a werewolf's sense of consideration rarely worked.

Both of us heard the sound of the lock opening. I stood, put away my lock picking tools, grabbed the doorknob, and opened the door. Joseph walked in first, and I followed.

Upon entering the building, I slowly and quietly closed the door. To our right were the two destroyed black vans. I found that surprising. I'd thought the aliens would have removed their handiwork since the ambush had occurred a few days before. I couldn't interpret whether that was a good or a bad sign. Maybe that meant the aliens didn't think we'd be back. Maybe that meant that the aliens thought we'd be back and wanted to remind us of a past defeat. Maybe that meant simply that the aliens were lazy and had other concerns.

Joseph gazed at the two vans, the cabs of each pockmarked by hundreds of bullet holes on this side alone. The storage parts of the vans were unharmed. *So they wanted to keep the corpses intact to turn into zombies.*

"You survived that?" he asked in wonder.

I smiled this time. "Turned into mist. Bullets passed right through me."

My partner grimaced. "That's right. You vampires have various ways of cheating death."

"Your kind are difficult to kill as well."

"Yeah, but we can't simply dematerialize if events are getting deadly."

Still in the dark, I surveyed the rest of the warehouse. At the time, I didn't know that this warehouse setup was similar to the warehouse where Joseph and Henry had picked up the zombies. On the narrow end of the building north of us was a wall broken by seven regular-sized doors through which were probably different rooms. The walled areas to the north and south were only one story tall. On the narrow end of the building south of us was a wall broken only by one door. Directly in front of us—to our east—was a large walled-off area that was two stories high and had a few doors in it.

"This looks very familiar," Joseph remarked.

"At least to you."

My partner ignored my obnoxious comment. Instead, he said, "You know, those zombies stink."

I understood. "You're right about that. They're intelligent, strong, and hard to kill."

Joseph stared at me. "No, I mean they literally stink. You know, smell bad?"

I didn't see the relevance to our situation. I did know that we should be investigating further because we had yet to check out where the various doors led in this warehouse.

"Henry and I had to deliver some, and I thought I'd puke from their bad scent," Joseph continued.

"Whatever," I said noncommittally.

One of the doors on the east wall opposite us opened, and five creatures exited wearing clothes that fit them loosely and with skin the color of clean white sheets. Each carried an automatic rifle.

"And I smell them right now!"

I'd seen them before Joseph's comment. As the zombies began shooting at us, both of us simultaneously dived to the ground. My partner started shooting almost as soon as he hit the floor. I had to pull my rifle into position.

Luckily, the zombies were extremely poor shots rather like in some science fiction movies where the heroes are being chased by hordes of bad guys with laser rifles while the heroes have a few little pistols. The bad guys shoot and shoot and can't hit the broad side of an asteroid to save their lives, while the good guys take very few shots, and kill the bad guys every time. This time I was glad the reality was imitating fiction.

Joseph sprayed the five zombies with bullets, the bullets splattering against their chests from which that ever-present white pus oozed. I took a more focused approach. I shot repeatedly at the head of one until that zombie decayed into a pile of ooze. Then I did the same with the next. And the next. The zombies continued to approach and continued to fire far above our heads.

When the last zombie collapsed into white pus, we both stood.

"Feel better?" asked Joseph.

I guess that was in reference to our coming here for revenge.

"Lots," I lied. Actually, I didn't feel a thing. *Joseph was right. This was a waste of time.* We still had to search the place, but I had a feeling we wouldn't find anything helpful in our search for the alien hideout.

This endeavor had been a waste of time because (1) obviously the zombies who'd just attacked us hadn't been responsible for the ambush in which my colleagues were killed and (2) the perpetrators of the ambush were still at large to do further harm to vampires.

XXXIII

The Women in the Warehouse

Joe

Yeah, I know. I made a deal with Sammy. I'd call him "Samuel" if he called me "Joe." He made some snide remark in his part of this narrative that vampires shouldn't make any agreements with us werewolves. Don't vampires understand compromise? Yeah, we werewolves sometimes don't either. Because in my narrative, he'll always be "Sammy."

We stood in front of the door Henry and I had used when coming to pick up the "cargo." Sammy had parked his car around the corner in almost the same place he had at the warehouse where we'd been ambushed. What a thrill! Getting caught in an ambush. Being attacked by zombie fighters. Destroying the zombies in a team effort. In the end, they were pools of white pus with their clothes and weapons lying in the stuff. It stank something fierce.

I think Sammy was disgusted that during our search of that building we found nothing interesting. All seven office-type rooms were empty. Completely. Nothing in them at all. No sign of any occupation. The door on the opposite wall revealed a larger room, equally empty. Now the back room was a bit different. Its floor was covered with what appeared to be the remains of huge, wide leaves or, as Sammy said human-sized husks of corn, without the cobs. Leave it to a vampire to think up a vegetarian solution.

By the way, driving around in downtown Des Moines wasn't easy. News trucks from every one of the national news networks were parked all around the Civic Center, a theater where the Des Moines Symphony performs and off-Broadway shows are presented. A presidential debate was to be held there later this week. Iowa has the first in the nation presidential caucuses. That's one reason why the debate was being held here. Although most of the news vehicles were around the Civic Center, other news trucks were parked in random locations throughout downtown Des Moines, making it that much more difficult to get around.

I think it's great that Iowa has the first in the nation presidential caucuses, because we get to meet all of the presidential candidates ourselves and ask all kinds of questions. I've been to a fair number of events where the candidates gave talks. I've shaken hands with a few candidates as well. None are werewolves. Someday. Someday. When the USA has a president who's a werewolf, American life will become near perfection.

Yeah, I'm writing like Sammy with his digressions. Well, that was mine. But mine was better than any of his.

Standing in front of the door, Sammy stared at me.

"Are you going to ring the doorbell?" he asked.

Sammy is sometimes so obnoxious. But we'd previously had a good adventure together, so I was willing to forgive him. Even if he said something that any werewolf would know the answer to. (I don't like to call people "stupid." That includes vampires.)

"Better not. That might give them too much warning," I said.

Sammy snorted. He enjoys doing that. I think it's a vampire thing. Then he pulled out his lock picking tools and went to work. In less than two minutes, he'd picked the lock, stood, put away his gear, and gave me a smug smile. There's that vampire arrogance. Gotta love it. He opened the door. I went in, and Sammy followed, then carefully and quietly closed the door behind him.

Entering the warehouse, I was a bit disappointed. Yeah, I had the thrill of knowing this warehouse could hold an ambush, too, if we could only be so lucky. I was sad not to see a line of black vans in front of us the way they'd been when Henry and I had been in this same warehouse a few nights before. *Henry, what a loser.* And he really has to be one for a werewolf like me to say that. Our kind is always looking for the best in people and other werewolves.

Unlike in the first warehouse, all the lights were on. The lights had brightly illuminated this huge area when Henry and I had been here. We werewolves don't need any light to see and vampires are the same way. There you go. That's something our two species share. We have that in common, and humans don't. See? We should get along because we have similarities our human cousins don't.

I didn't say that to Sammy. From the look on his face, I could tell he wasn't happy. *Well, be a glum ol' vampire if you want.*

"I don't see any vans," he said, stating the obvious.

"Yeah, no kidding," I said. Yeah, that was a sarcastic remark. Grant told me I had to be the peacemaker since my partner wouldn't.

"But there's more to this warehouse," I continued.

Sammy glanced around. By the glint in his eyes, I knew he recognized the setup.

"This warehouse has exactly the same floor plan as the one where we were ambushed."

Ding ding ding! We have a winner! I was so proud of Sammy when he saw the obvious. Besides, at the last warehouse, I'd told him as much. Guess he didn't believe me.

"So are we going to search all the rooms the way we did in the last warehouse?" he asked.

He really was giving me the lead on this one. *Good Sammy.*

"No, I think we should go to that door opposite us and enter there," I replied. "That's where the doctor types brought out the zombies." I glanced at my partner. *He's thinking something sarcastic.* "Once we know it's empty, we should check out the other rooms."

The two of us strode across the open area of the warehouse to the single door on the wall opposite the entry. I wanted the glory in this encounter, so I tried the door. It was unlocked.

"Let's check it out."

"My pleasure," said Sammy.

I opened the door and walked in. Sammy followed and closed the door.

What we saw wasn't what I expected at all. Sammy's eyes widened. I could see I wasn't alone in my bewilderment. Bright neon lights illuminated this chamber even more so than the previous room. The room was filled with plants three feet in diameter with a circle of black substance beneath them. These plants had foot-wide leaves that coiled around each other and were shaped like aspirin tablets with a green stub in the middle growing from among the leaves. Each plant pulsed rhythmically, similar to the way a heart pumped blood. Each plant pulsed to a different beat. I guessed about ten seconds elapsed between each pump.

The rows upon rows of plants began five feet in front of us. Each plant was about ten feet away from the other. Each row was about ten feet apart. Amazing stuff! I wanted to take a photo. *If I do that, Sammy will slap me.* (He says he's cold and calculating, but he can become very angry.)

I had a second reason for not yanking out my phone and snapping photos of these strange plants. The plants weren't the only things in this chamber. The two "scientists" who'd arranged the zombie deliveries stood among these strange plants, and both held tablets on which they were either typing or drawing designs. One woman was very slim with bright red hair; the other was a bit chubby with black hair. They continued their work despite our entrance until they finally saw the two of us.

The redhead threw her tablet toward me as if it were a frisbee and the brunette did the same to Sammy. Both of us jumped in opposite directions to avoid these makeshift weapons. Dodging the tablets was one thing; avoiding the attacks of the two women was another. They sprinted across the room so rapidly they were almost a blur.

The redhead kicked me in the chest, and I flew through the air to smash against the wall behind me. *These aliens are fast. And these two are scientist types.* I knew what I needed to do.

A black and white world. Lots of movement. To my south, movement of two human figures. The short one yanks the rifle away from the taller one. Fight, Sammy, fight!

Taller one jumps back. Shorter aims rifle at him.

Hear scream behind me.

Ignore it. Leap at woman with rifle. Land upon her, smashing her into the floor and into one of the plants. Green ooze splatters us both.

Feel another person on top of me. She hits my head and yanks at my fur.

I roll upon the floor, releasing the other short woman from beneath me. I whimper from the pain. Then roll on my back, taking the woman with me. As I roll, we splat into another plant. Green ooze splats on each of us. Tastes horrible. Like algae. Or very sweet green gelatin. Spit it out.

Woman loses her hold. Slips away. Look to see Sammy disappear from sight.

See? He turns into mist when he's afraid. Not an option for me.

Both women slip and slide around since they're covered in green ooze same as me. The closer woman takes a few steps toward me then falls to the floor. The second woman raises the rifle, only to have it slip from her ooze-covered hands. She yanks out a small device. A cell phone!

Before she can use it, Sammy reappears behind her, sword in hand. Slice! Off goes her head.

So much for that phone call.

I leap on back of the other woman on the floor. She pushes herself up. I chomp down on her shoulder. Yuck! The green ooze in her body tastes like old motor oil. Rip off her shoulder. She screams.

Sammy sprints to me, but she kicks him in the groin and he flies away.

But she's distracted. I leap up and bite her neck. Crunch! Lots of blood and lots of ooze.

I stood as a human again. The redhead lay on the floor with her neck broken. For good measure, I yanked out my rifle and shot her in the head a few times.

Sammy walked up to me.

"Good fight," he said.

I thought I almost heard a "but." Yeah, I know. Sometimes, I'm a bit too quick to wolf-out. Hey, I'm a werewolf. It's only natural.

"I'll call some VATE agents to check out these growths before we destroy them."

"I'm not sure WOOF will care." I wasn't either. Aliens aren't our enemies. Okay, maybe after the last few days, they are.

"But we still don't know more about the zombie plot," Sammy said.

I gave him a malicious smile. "Right. But I think WOOF has someone in captivity who does."

XXXIV

We Are

Vod

I am...

I am not alone. Yes, a naked female lies on the floor to my right. I also see a naked, chubby male to my left. Both women in lab coats look at them as well. Redhead and Brunette kneel by each of them, too. Neither react as much as I do.

All time seems to be as if it is now. All memories are as if they are now. At least the memories since I awoke on this large green leaf. I am living in the eternal now. That's important. I think I should capitalize it—The Eternal Now.

Redhead and Brunette return to me. Brunette is carrying a bag. Yes, it is a bag. Not a purse. Women carry purses. I know that. Because I have memories of a woman, I know...I care about... Not me, but somebody like me cares about. I don't care about Brunette because I don't know her.

My thoughts are so confusing. They're so jumbled. As if somebody takes my brain, no, my mind, that is a better way to say it. As if somebody puts my mind in a blender. Before they place my mind in a blender, my mind is organized so I can find what I want. After they mix it in the blender, I can still find items in my mind, but not where they belong.

That is a confusing mess of a thought. I'm narrating this into a recorder, so I don't know what is made a paragraph, and what isn't. But that last bit sounds as if it is a nice, short paragraph.

My thoughts are still slow sometimes. I am alert enough, oh, and I am talking about being alert as I still lie on the floor, not as I make this recording—though both time periods seem the same time to me. I know. What I'm saying makes sense to me, maybe not to you, my listener—or reader, if this recording is ever transcribed.

Anyway, Brunette removes a syringe and a vial from her bag. She pokes the needle of the syringe into the whiteness of my arm. I feel no pain. I laugh, but Redhead presses down on my arm, so my laughter doesn't stop Brunette from sucking whatever it is she wants to suck out of my body. I see the vial fill with a white liquid. That ain't no blood! If I'm capable of feeling nauseated, I am. But my stomach remains perfectly fine. Brunette pulls out the needle. Neither woman puts a hand or a gauze pad over the puncture point. I gaze at it. A bit more white pus flows from it, then a white scab forms over the wound.

The two stand and do the same to the woman beside me. I watch as they continue to do the same to all of the white humans—that term doesn't seem quite right—lying on the floor with me. To watch, I sit up and discover that many of the others, white as a sheet like me, are doing the same. Some sit quietly with glazed eyes that are like the eyes of blind people. Others have eyes similar to mine that dart back and forth, and when they see eyes meeting theirs, they look at them, or wink, or turn away.

My thoughts are still so slow. I watch as Brunette takes other syringes and vials and sucks out white liquid from all the other white beings around me. What are we? We're alive. We can sit up. I can speak. I hear many others simply moaning. Although they moan, I can understand them. The chubby naked man to my left moans, and I know he's saying, "Where are we? Who am I? I remember. No, I don't. Do I?"

In my messed-up mind, I have memories, memories that don't seem to belong to me. I remember lying on the floor. My wife? What I am now can't be married. I can't have sex either. Can I? Two children and my wife kneel beside me. She weeps. The children appear scared. Their huge eyes look down at me. A tall, thin man in a cotton shirt and jeans stands over them and me. He's pale, but not as pale as I am not. He's armed with a sword and a pistol.

The woman says, "Thank you so much. If only my husband had been as wise as you."

The tall man shrugs. "His attack on the gunman helped me kill the shooter. I'm sure if your husband had been carrying a gun, he would have done the same."

The woman says, "Keith doesn't believe in guns. I told him to be brave, but..."

The image fades away.

Keith. Who the hell is Keith? I'm Vod. Emperor of the Galaxy Vod. I laugh. All my nearby pale creatures stare at me. I laugh for a few minutes until my laughter seems to be nonsense. Many of the others are moaning and saying, "He's weird. I'm not. He's weird. I'm not." None of them realize they are simply moaning and not saying any real words.

A pale African American who sits three rows from me says, "They don't know that they aren't speaking." This man is only about five-three with a paunchy belly.

"You just did," I say, stating the obvious.

We both laugh.

Brunette walks over to the African American; Redhead comes to me.

Redhead says, "Please don't speak. You're disturbing the others."

Brunette says much the same thing to the African American.

Both women stand. Brunette shouts, "Bring out their clothes. You know the routine!"

We have clothes? I think being naked is my state of being. Surely, we're normal because we don't wear clothing. How do I know Redhead and Brunette are wearing clothing? The same way I know that my fellow pale people who moan aren't talking properly. When you talk, you use words—in a way like the African American man and me.

Five people wearing shirts and pants carry plastic bags, each marked with a sticky note and a number, and give them to each of us sitting—well, some are still lying on the floor, and most of them are Moaners. Although five people are doing this—these people aren't white like printer paper, or clean white sheets, they have some color to their faces and hands. A man wearing a plaid shirt and blue jeans gives me a plastic bag with the number 18 on it.

"Urkil na zazlip!" shouts Redhead.

I never heard that language before. I don't understand. Yes, I do. Although I don't want to put on these clothes in this bag, Redhead's words compel me to do so. *She has a magical power over me!* I don't know too much in the world, but I know I don't like that at all.

I'm thinking...something or other. I don't know what to call myself. I know I'm different from Redhead and Brunette and also different from the people who distributed these plastic bags of clothes. Redhead and Brunette are different from the delivery people. Why I know this is beyond me. Beyond me. I laugh at the idea.

But I laugh as I put on the plaid shirt, blue jeans, a leather belt, white socks, and athletic shoes. The shirt is too big for me and has two or three holes in it. I feel as if I'm wearing a tent. If I don't have a belt, the pants fall from my waist. I have to tie the shoes very tight for them to fit.

From somewhere in my mind, I know clothes should fit as though they were made for me or I should buy different ones from a store that sells clothes. An amazing idea!

"Please follow these people out of the building," Redhead orders.

The man who gave me my clothes opens a door on one side of this chamber and holds it open as the other people similar to him walk through it. The Moaners are quick to follow. I hang back until the African American man—if that's the correct term—catches up with me.

"I'm Vod," I say.

"I'm Modod," he says. "Do you know what's going on?"

"No. I wake up and here I am."

"I feel the same."

We quickly join the herd of some forty individuals—all white, similar to ourselves. If you can say a black man is white. Black is white. I think that's funny and laugh.

"What's the joke?" asks Modod.

"Black is white," I reply.

He stares at me blankly. "No, you mean white is black." And he laughs.

We follow the others across an even larger chamber than the one in which we awake—again, they are mostly Moaners but I hear a few others talking in a way similar to Modod and me. A door large enough for a car to drive through—a car? I know what that must be, although I'm not seeing one since I awake, and that is the beginning of my life. My life as Vod—begins with an open door, and all of us are walking through it. We emerge into a world that is bigger than anything I've ever seen. I examine the blue sky, the sun, and all the buildings around us.

In front of the building we exit stands a line of black vans with their doors open.

Redhead shouts behind us, "Althar di nokkin!"

And I feel compelled to climb into a van. Modod looks at me.

"Into a van?" he asks.

"Into a van," I reply.

XXXV

An Evil Werewolf

Samuel

We stood in the basement of the WOOF headquarters. The room had black cement walls and was to the right of a hallway with a staircase that led to the first floor. The hall beyond this room led to a steel door, usually locked, that opened to the hall filled with cells where WOOF kept prisoners. Each cell also had a steel door and bright neon lights that shone at all times—a method of torture according to Joseph.

On the night of the Wild Ones' attack, WOOF agents had captured a few of their evil counterparts—for information and rehabilitation, or so Joseph said. One of their captives was Henry Borman, a medium-built man with shoulder-length black hair and a very bushy beard, but no mustache—Joseph said that was unusual for werewolf males. He wore a torn yellow shirt and dirt-smudged brown pants—the colors of the Koman pack. Henry stared at us defiantly, but couldn't do much else because he was tied to a metal chair with silver chains.

Yes, WOOF has a headquarters in Des Moines. I've written that name four times and resisted breaking out in laughter. Maybe I'm becoming more tolerant. Maybe it's because I'm numb after writing the name so many times.

Still, I think life is unfair in that WOOF has a headquarters and VATE doesn't. Okay, WOOF's headquarters isn't that great. It's in a strip mall on a street leading into downtown but not in downtown proper. I swore to Joseph—and more importantly, Grant, his pack leader—that I wouldn't disclose its exact location. That's for you humans reading this. WOOF doesn't want every curious human dropping by to see what werewolves do. Not that they do anything too exciting.

The first floor of the office mostly has cubes where werewolves perform office work keeping track of WOOF agent assignments and the prisoners in the cells in the basement. Those office people must have been very busy after last night's fight. As a VATE agent, I think keeping prisoners is nonsense. When we VATE agents encounter Evil Ones, we kill them. No prisoners. Evil Ones treat us the same. Werewolves must believe that good can come out of evil. *Foolish werewolves.*

Regardless, when I see Beryl again, I'll complain about the inequality of this situation. For our local VATE chapter, Beryl's house is as close as we come to having a headquarters. That's why all the visiting VATE agents are staying at hotels. Joseph says all the visiting WOOF agents are staying with werewolves in town. VATE should have a headquarters. VWW has one. VBS—Vampire Blood Supply, the blood bank that provides all of us Protectors with blood—has an office of its own. The local High Ruling Council or HRC, that institution that provides us Protectors with the special laws and rules we live by in addition to those humans have to follow, also has its own building. (HRCs also exist at the state and federal levels. The state HRC building puts our local HRC building to shame.) In any case, I'll propose to Beryl that VATE get a local headquarters. I've heard rumors that VATE in larger cities at least have some rented office space.

But I digress because I didn't want to describe this horrible scene.

This horrible scene where Henry was proving that werewolves are wild, impulsive, irrational, and stupid—yes, even with what has occurred in this case, I still rank werewolves with humans.

Not only was he staring at us, he was shouting. "You fucking traitor! You're a goddamned human pet! You humiliated me in front of my pack! And you're a damned pet! You humiliated me in front of Victoria! She's the love and lust of my life! And you made her ridicule me! And made me look like a fool in front of Theresa! She's my pack leader! If I hadn't done cargo runs, she'd have thrown me out of the pack! And you're with a bloodsucker! You dumb, fucking traitor!"

As Henry carried on, Joseph occasionally said, "Now, now, watch your language. We have a guest here."

Such soothing words did little to quiet Henry.

"I hate you! I hate you! I hate you! You fucking traitor! You fucking traitor! The Koman pack is great! We're the best pack around! We could rule this whole fucking town!"

Joseph rolled his eyes and shook his head.

I snorted.

My werewolf partner must have had enough because he slapped Henry on one cheek then the other. Henry snapped at Joseph's withdrawing hand then growled at us.

Of course, this interrogation wouldn't have been necessary if we'd discovered any decent leads at the second warehouse where we'd encountered the two female scientists. Granted, we couldn't coax any information from the scientists—who, as the observant reader guessed, were aliens—because they were dead. We also couldn't acquire any clues from their tablets because when the tablets smashed against the wall they shattered. The aliens' cell phones were locked. We'd taken them to VWW—our tech savvy vampires—who so far hadn't cracked the phones. Joseph suggested we might be able to obtain some information from WOOF captives. So here we were.

Since we had a moment of silence, I said, "We vampires don't take prisoners. Evil vampires can't be rehabilitated."

Henry gave me an angry stare. Then he smiled. "Yes, that's better than this. Go ahead, kill me. I would have more dignity."

I glanced at Joseph. "Sounds like he has some self-respect."

My partner rolled his eyes. Then he yanked a pistol from a holster at his side. "Hey, Henry, if that's what you want." He aimed the pistol at the evil werewolf's heart. "This Glock is filled with silver bullets, so your death should be quick."

Henry's mouth dropped open. His eyes widened. "I didn't think—"

I interrupted him, "You're a werewolf. Your kind never thinks about anything." I glanced at Joseph. "Well," I added, "present company excluded."

My partner shook his head. "I thought we could come to some arrangement. We werewolves attempt to be more merciful than vampires, but if you want to follow the vampire example, it's fine with me." He cocked the gun.

"No!" screamed Henry. "No! No! No! Don't kill me! Don't kill me! Don't kill me!" Tears streamed down his face as he wept and howled.

This display of sheer cowardice provided proof that my partner had been telling the truth when he'd told me Henry was a loser and a wimp. In fact, Joseph had understated the truth significantly.

"Please don't kill me," Henry wept. "Please don't kill me. I'll tell you whatever you want. I'll tell you anything you want to know."

I shook my head. Joseph holstered his pistol.

"Okay," Joseph said. "That's more like it."

When will my partner tell Henry everyone in his pack is dead and its leader was an alien from another planet? That would break this fool.

Joseph took another course.

"I know you were one of Theresa's favorites," my partner said. He left out the *but I don't understand why because you're such a wimp.* Yet I knew Joseph was thinking that. "That's why she took

191

such offense when I defeated you at the party. That's why she kept you around, despite you being such a pitifully poor fighter."

Henry snickered. "I really am bad. I need to fight a crippled wolf to win."

Probably true. I remained silent. *I don't understand werewolves, but let's see where Joseph is taking this interrogation.*

"And you brownnosed her—"

A truly accurate term for werewolves since in wolf form they do enjoy sniffing each other's butts.

"Especially by participating in all those cargo delivery missions. You went on more than any other member of the Koman pack."

"Yes, yes, I did," Henry agreed enthusiastically.

"So she must have thought you were special," Joseph said.

Henry shrugged. "I wouldn't say that. She did think I was worthwhile to have around even if I was a terribly poor fighter."

"Did she let you participate in any other activities that others in the pack didn't?"

The Wild One grinned. "Yeah, she did," he whispered.

I thought such whispering unnecessary. I said as much. "You don't need to whisper. None of your pack will hear you." A far truer fact than Henry could know.

He laughed as his eyes widened and flared sickeningly.

Definitely a psycho. One minute he's begging for his life, the next he's laughing insanely.

"How right you are!" Henry exclaimed. "I can tell you whatever I want because nobody else will know." He laughed again.

Joseph raised his eyebrows.

The Wild One continued, "Theresa treated me in all kinds of ways she didn't treat others in our pack." He paused. "You weren't there long enough to know it. Like I went to two of her meetings with Cecil. Yeah, I did."

We both stared at the captive.

He sighed. "All right. I had to wait in the hallway while they talked. I waited with one of Cecil's vampires. We nearly got into a fight, but I backed down at the last minute because he would've killed me for sure."

Henry has some smarts. Granted, not many, but a few.

"No, really I went to two of their meetings. The first I waited with a vampire, but I tried to talk to him so he might like me. He didn't. He said I was a wimp. I think he wanted to fight me, but I didn't take the bait."

We waited.

"At the second meeting, Cecil and Theresa met in a back room of a restaurant, so I sat at one table and a vampire sat at another. Theresa said that was because I couldn't behave at the first meeting."

We still waited.

Henry shook his head irritably. "Well, that was special."

"Yes," Joseph admitted. "It was. Anything else?"

The Wild One thought for a moment. "Oh, yeah! One time we went to an office building. It didn't have any werewolves or vampires. I can smell both." He sniffed the air. "You smell so much like a bloodsucker."

"I am. So it fits," I said.

Henry blushed. "Anyway, we went to the office building. I was stuck waiting by the receptionist, but Theresa went right in. She talked for about fifteen minutes. Then she left. As we were leaving the building, Cecil and that same vampire I'd nearly fought were entering."

Joseph smiled. "That's the information we're looking for. There's hope for you yet, Henry. Tell us its location."

The Wild One did.

XXXVI

A Dangerous Office

Joe

Sammy stopped his car in a parking spot in front of a small office building. I read the sign *AO Companies Inc.* Henry and Theresa had visited this place a few weeks before when they had avoided meeting Cecil and his goon. And now Sammy and I were here. I thought the name of the company left little to the imagination. "AO." Both Sammy and I knew that stood for "Alien Operations."

Both of us wore suits and ties. For many of his assignments, Sammy had pretended to be an FBI agent. I had, too, so both of us knew the routine. Each of us was also armed with only a Glock pistol. Yeah, I know. It can pack a punch. But these were aliens we had to deal with. I'd dealt with one in the past, and she was far stronger and quicker than she looked. Hell, even those two "scientists" were decent fighters. Though Sammy and I were better. Well, naturally. But the alien scientists gave us a good fight.

Speaking of which, vampires went to that warehouse where they burned most of those strange plants and took one to some special vampire lab. Sammy didn't know the details. He acts smart and in the know about everything, but his fellow vampires hide certain details from him, in a similar manner to certain werewolves withholding information from me.

See? As in the beginning of this part of the narrative, Sammy and I have lots of things in common. We both play fake FBI agents and both of us have others of our kind who keep secrets from us. Of course, we should be able to get along.

We climbed out of the car and walked up to the entrance.

"Shouldn't we have backup?" I asked.

Sammy gave me a skeptical look. (He's good at that.) "We're simply checking out Ms. Wakowski. If she gives us suspicious answers, we'll get out fast and call for backup then."

Ms. Wakowski was the CEO of AO Company, Inc.

"Okay," I said hesitantly.

I would have called for backup. We'd met those two scientist aliens in one warehouse and a bunch of zombies at the other. *These aliens have a complicated operation. We should act as if they're going to be suspicious of us, not the other way around.*

Yeah, I know. I was letting Sammy take lead, so I followed like an obedient dog. Ha ha.

Sammy held the door for me. I nodded acknowledgement. He snorted. I walked through the door, then through an inner door into the office, followed by my vampire partner.

We entered a reception area with a wall and a closed door behind the receptionist's desk. Couches and a few end tables with magazines that were out of date were positioned around the room. Just like going to a doctor's office. Even werewolf doctors have out-of-date magazines for entertainment.

Behind the desk sat a young woman in a blue dress with a modest cut. She sat, typing fitfully, then sighing and continuing. Her desk had the PC, a phone, a desk calendar, and an assortment of photos of her friends and family.

Sammy and I walked up to the desk, yanked out our badges, and flashed them at the receptionist.

"Agent Simon Jackson," said Sammy.

"Agent Jacob Barker," I said.

The receptionist gazed up at both of us. I swore I saw recognition in her eyes.

"We'd like to see Ms. Wakowski," my partner said authoritatively.

The receptionist smiled. "Just a minute." She picked up the phone and made a call. "Two FBI agents are here to see you," she said. Pause. "Yes." Another pause. "Yes." A third pause. "Of course." She hung up and looked at us. "I'll take you to Ms. Wakowski myself."

I glanced at Sammy. *This is too easy.* My partner snorted as if in response to my thought.

The receptionist led us through the door into a large room. It was filled with cubes with an aisle that went straight from the door we'd entered to another across from it. Other cubes made a maze on either side. This room lacked any windows. The people, all dressed in formal business wear, talked on the phones or typed furiously on their keyboards. One or two glanced up to see us pass by to a door at the other end of this work pen.

Again, the receptionist opened the door and held it open for the two of us. She didn't enter. Our business must have been none of hers.

We walked into a room also without any windows. *Couldn't work here.* Two goons stood on either side of the door with their backs to the wall. The term "goons" is accurate. Both were about six and a half feet tall with huge shoulders and probably weighed about three hundred fifty pounds. One had messy brown hair; the other had short, black hair. Both had hands almost as big as my head. If these two were aliens, I didn't want to fight them.

Paintings of the Des Moines area adorned the other walls. Two potted plants stood in the corners on either side of the desk. A wooden desk with only a PC and a phone as decorations was in the back center of the room. The PC wasn't on. A petite woman with short blonde hair, dark-green eyes, and a small nose and mouth sat behind the desk. She wore a dark blue business suit. Two cushioned chairs stood between the goons and the desk.

We introduced ourselves again.

The woman nodded in acknowledgement. "Please sit," she said in greeting.

We sat. I didn't sit comfortably because of the two goons behind us. Sammy even glanced back at them.

"I'd like you to meet my associates." She said, motioning at the goons behind us. "Mr. Brown..." She pointed at the goon with the brown hair. "And Mr. Black..." She indicated the goon with the black hair. As she made these introductions, we both glanced over our shoulders at the respective goon. Each nodded in turn.

When we returned our focus to Ms. Wakowski, she said, "I'm glad I finally get to meet you."

My wolf instincts kicked in. *Run, run, run. It's a trap.* Sammy sat calmly, but he raised his eyebrows.

Ms. Wakowski considered me. "You aren't Jacob Barker, but Joe Butler." She stared at Sammy. "You aren't Simon Jackson, but rather Samuel Johnson."

My vampire partner shook his head. "I neither deny nor confirm that allegation," he said.

The woman smiled. "You have caused us a great deal of difficulty in this operation."

"Ditto," I said.

I again felt my panic instincts kick in. *I hope she isn't about to reveal the whole plan to us.* And I had good reasons for that.

"However, that is inconsequential now." She drummed her long fingernails on her desk. The goons shifted nervously behind us.

"I must congratulate both of you and your kinds on surviving the struggle with your respective evil counterparts," Wakowski continued calmly. "Although that was part of our plan. We hoped both of your kinds would gather many more powerful warriors to combat the evil of your kind." She gazed at Sammy. "Your group had a mole from the beginning urging you to get more agents here. She was quite successful—"

"And she died quickly in the fight," my partner interrupted.

Wakowski waved her right hand dismissively. "Irrelevant. I'm sure your boss arranged for even more agents to come to make up for the losses in the struggle last night."

I glanced at Sammy. He looked impassively at our hostess.

"Your lack of reply is confirmation enough for me." She smiled, then turned her attention to me. "And you must be Joe Butler. You proved to be a good mole for us with your human-friendly werewolves. We had another werewolf to tell us of your group's plans, but you were the one who gathered so many warriors for the fight last night and beyond."

When I'd learned this from Theresa, I was angry as all my readers know. (Look, I copied a move Sammy makes with his writing in citing the readers' knowledge.) Now I only shrugged. Sammy chuckled.

"But the struggles of last night were merely foreplay in the grand scheme of things," Ms. Wakowski continued. "The final part of our plan will reach fruition tonight. With all the national networks in town for the presidential debate, they will appreciate a diversion of our making."

"I'm excited to see the debate," I cut in. "I always like to see what the candidates have to say. I want to vote for the best one at the caucuses." I really do like that Iowa plays such a special role in the choosing of presidential nominees.

Sammy shook his head. Ms. Wakowski grinned. Both seemed disgusted with what I'd said. *Yeah, but it's true.*

"Hardly the point, Mr. Butler," the CEO of AO Company, Inc. said. "We timed the finale of our operation to coincide with when they were in town."

"So all the zombies appearing around town have been a prelude to tonight?" asked Sammy.

"Exactly," Ms. Wakowski replied. "And an effort to draw more of your kind to this fair city, an effort that has met with great success. In a way, you might say, your defeating the others of your kind so successfully leaves more for the main show tonight."

"My kind did well against the Wild Ones you had fight us!" I exclaimed.

Again, both Sammy and Wakowski gave sounds of exasperation.

"Hey, I've helped a lot in foiling this plot," I continued.

Wakowski smiled. "But not nearly good enough." She took in Sammy. "Nor have you, Mr. Johnson."

I knew what was about to come. She was about to reveal the real purpose of this plot and its details. *And if she's telling us, she believes we won't live to tell anybody else.* I maintained a calm face. *Sammy and I can fight this alien woman and her goons. We'll kick some alien butt.*

"You see, tonight we're going to release between one hundred and fifty and two hundred zombies into the city. All at once. All in the same location. Such a mass of zombies will require all of the agents of both of your kinds to fight it. Not only will this situation require all of your available agents to fight them, you will need to resort to using your special powers."

She flicked a hand toward Sammy. "Your kind will transform into mist and bats." She nodded at me. "And your kind will transform into wolves." She laughed. "But before you arrive, we'll have the national and local media covering the zombies. So when you both use your supernatural powers, the whole world will see, and when humanity sees the presence of such supernatural beings, of course, it will again hunt down and kill all of both of your kinds."

Sammy stood. I quickly hopped to my feet.

"Not if we warn them first!" I shouted.

My partner gave me an angry stare.

That amounted to nothing because each goon stepped behind each of us, poked a syringe into our necks, and shot us full of some sort of chemical.

A chemical that had an almost immediate effect.

As I felt myself falling to the floor, everything went black.

XXXVII

Where Are We

Vod

Where are we? In a warehouse again. We must be the Warehouse People. That must be what's special about us. We live in warehouses. If "living" is what we're doing.

In my memories from the person named Keith, I see that he lives in a house with a two-car garage, a backyard that he mows in the spring, summer, and fall; and a front yard always being invaded by dandelions from his neighbors. He sleeps in a bed in the master bedroom with his wife, and his two daughters live in another bedroom. Each bedroom has its own bathroom where each person brushes his or her teeth, takes showers or baths, and does something I find extremely repulsive. On a weekly basis, he goes to a place called a grocery store where he buys food to bring back to his house—steaks, cereal, apples, lettuce, milk, and so much more.

If the memories of Keith are correct, then the term "living" doesn't apply to us Warehouse People. We don't have houses. We don't have yards with grass. We don't have bedrooms or bathrooms. Without bathrooms, we have nowhere to shower or brush our teeth. We don't go to the store. No, we simply are born in one warehouse, then people, not "Masters," take us in black vans from one warehouse to another.

Some of us explore the warehouse, which has lots of nothing. The floor is cement. The walls are drywall. A few doors are in the walls, but they are locked. Modod wants to see what is behind one of these locked doors. He rips it off its hinges. Only to find a room with a cement floor and drywall. Modod and I explore much of the warehouse and find a steel door leading outside as well as the roll-up garage door that is raised when we enter. The huge door rolls up toward the ceiling when opening and down to the ground when closing. Both are locked. We fear the outside, so we don't break them open.

Another thing Keith has that we don't. Food. I'm hungry, but I can't tell you for what. I know I'm telling this all in the present tense—a way of describing language I know from my Keith memories—but like I say, I live in the Eternal Now.

We Warehouse People are many. Modod and I count and discover almost two hundred of us are gathered here. We Warehouse People aren't all the same. Modod and I divide us into three groups: Moaners, Tweeners, and Talkers. Both Modod and I are Talkers.

Talkers speak real words and sentences and can communicate with other people who aren't of the Warehouse variety, such as the two women scientists, who are also Masters. We Talkers don't worship the Masters. When the Masters say certain commands in a strange language, which is not English, the language we speak and think in, we have a compulsion to obey whether we want to or not. When Modod and I arrive in this warehouse, we find other Talkers. Modod, Voov, Moom, Kalp, and I from the last group to arrive are the leaders of the Talkers. We are also the most fluent. We count about twenty Talkers.

Moaners are the largest category of Warehouse People. To communicate, they moan. Now we all understand what they're saying when they moan and they understand each other. They moan stuff like "I'm hungry..." "Kill, kill, kill..." "Who am I?" "What the hell..." "Kill vampires..." (I laugh when I hear that one. Vampires don't exist. Why do we want to kill something that isn't real?) One Moaner woman sits on the floor and says, "Babies, babies, babies..." A large, fat Moaner man wanders around in circles and says, "A dog, a dog, a dog..." Many Moaners say the same things over and over and over and over. You get the idea? Sometimes, Moaners simply become quiet, stand in one place, and drool. Luckily, if we Talkers give them a command, they obey it. Unluckily, if the Masters give them an order, Moaners follow that command faster than when we Talkers give one.

Tweeners are more numerous than Talkers, but less numerous than Moaners. Tweeners moan most of the time, but sometimes say a few coherent words or sentences. When they moan, they talk to each other. They ask how another Moaner or Tweener feels, where they want to go, or what they want to eat. (Their answer is usually "brains.") When Tweeners talk coherently, more times than not, they say "Kill vampires. Kill vampires..." or simply "Kill, kill, kill..." Similar to Moaners, they quickly obey the Masters, or the Masters' cronies such as the ones who drive us here. They also obey Talkers when no Master or crony is around.

Modod and I are talking.

"I'm not sure I enjoy being a Warehouse Person," says Modod.

I say, "I don't think it's bad. We have space to wander around and nobody keeps us from talking to each other."

"There must be more to life than warehouses."

"We know there are vans and the great world outside."

Modod spits some drool on the floor. "Yes, why didn't they let us stay outside?"

"You mean the Masters?" I ask.

Modod laughs. "And those other people."

So far, we call the other people Non-Masters. Not a very good term. These Non-Masters obey the Masters, too. We try to talk to the Non-Masters as they drive the vans to this warehouse. The Non-Masters laugh at and ridicule us. We moan to each other so they don't understand us.

"Hey, look," says Modod. He points at the people-sized door leading outside.

The door opens. Two huge people enter. Even from here, I know they are Masters. They are six and a half feet tall with wide shoulders. Each carries a chair. They deposit the chairs, then leave.

"We can use some chairs to sit on," Modod says.

"Yes," I agree. "That is better than sitting on the floor."

The door opens again. The two Masters return, each carrying a limp body. Each Master ties the body he's carrying to a chair. We have good eyesight. I can see one has a stake sticking out of its chest.

The door closes, and the Masters don't come back.

The Moaners sniff the air. They moan loudly. Most moan, "Food. Food. Food." The Tweeners also sniff the air and say, in real words, "Food. Food. Food."

I call to the other Talkers who come quickly while the Moaners and Tweeners wander aimlessly rather than toward the two "others" (because I know they aren't Masters nor Non-Masters). I tell the Talkers to keep the Moaners and Tweeners here, far away from these two people tied to the chairs.

"These people may help us," I say.

"Or be food for us," adds Modod.

"But we need to talk to them and see how they treat us," I say.

"Okay," say many of the Talkers. "We'll keep the Moaners and Tweeners here."

Modod and I walk across the floor toward the two beings tied to the chairs.

XXXVIII

Joseph, Zombies, and Me

Samuel

Even with my eyes closed, I could feel my arms and legs tied to a chair and a sharp pain in my chest. I sighed heavily. *Not again.* The last time I'd worked with Joseph, the two of us had found ourselves tied up, and I'd had a wooden stake in my heart. *I have to stop working with werewolves.*

As we'd sat in Wakowski's office, I thought the two goons would walk up behind us and strike us on the back of our heads. I have the ability to feign being unconscious, so I'd decided the moment before the goon hit me, I'd collapse as if unconscious. That way, when one of them tried to put a stake in my heart, I'd dissolve into mist and escape. But, no, they had to use syringes with some knock-out chemical in them. *How do the aliens know what can knock out a vampire?*

I opened my eyes and gazed down at my chest. Indeed, a wooden stake stuck out of it. My arms and my legs were tied to the chair with ropes. Although I could feel my limbs, I couldn't move them. Since I had a stake in my heart, I was paralyzed from the neck down. A highly efficient way of disabling a vampire. I glanced both to my left and to my right.

To my right was Joseph, similarly bound to a chair, but he was tied up with chains.

"They're silver," he said to my unanswered question. "I see you've got a stake in your heart again."

I snorted in disgust.

My partner snickered at my reaction.

Before continuing, I should say both of us were sitting in the dark not too far away from a closed steel door and a roll-up garage steel door both of which presumably led outside.

In any case, I closed my eyes. When we'd been in this situation before, I'd been able to perform some tricks to help us escape. I hoped to do so again. As mentioned quite a while ago, I have the ability to detect sentient life—the intelligent reader will remember how each type of being appears to us. I let my mind expand. First, I found the fiery hot, orange sphere that was my partner. My mind continued to expand. I let it fill a bit of the warehouse, but I assumed the warehouse was empty besides Joseph and me, so instead, I let my mind slip outside the warehouse where I found two pale, yellow spheres.

These pseudo-humans were similar to the ones who'd stolen the corpses. I attempted to dive into their minds and was bounced back.

I've done numerous mind attacks on humans. A few times I've done them on these pseudo-humans. So my attempt should have worked. It didn't.

I opened my eyes again.

"Any good mind tricks?" asked Joseph.

I shook my head. "Not this time."

"You know," my partner said.

Have I told you I hate that expression? No, well, I do. I don't care who uses it. Joseph did, so I wanted to make a snide remark—okay, I would have resisted because that move would have gotten me in trouble with Beryl.

Before I said anything, Joseph continued, "It really stinks in here. It smells as if hundreds of zombies are nearby."

I sniffed the air. I detected a scent like that of rotten garbage, but figured that was simply warehouse smell. Then I studied the darkness.

The warehouse—where I presumed we were trapped because the room in which we sat was far larger than found in most homes or offices—had its lights turned off and was only one story tall. As the alert reader knows, darkness isn't a hindrance for vampires like me. I assume werewolves have the same ability to see in the dark. Of course, I hadn't asked my partner nor was I about to. Regardless, being in the dark wasn't a frightening experience.

As I studied the other end of the warehouse, the darkness became a scarier thing because of other beings who were with us. Far away from us, I saw humanoid figures. I use the term "humanoid" because I recognized that they weren't human, at least not living ones.

These beings, most as white as newly fallen snow and wearing clothes that fit each of them loosely, wandered around, sat against a wall, or stood quietly and drooled. Many of them moaned, almost non-stop. Others said words I could understand—using my excellent vampire super hearing—although not necessarily coherent. A few incoherent sayings I heard were: "Go, go, go...." "Up and down and up and down..." "Eggs, we need to fix the eggs!"

One coherent undead was saying, "Go there. No, here. No, there..." Others were saying, "It's important that you stay here. Yes, it is. Yes, you, too." About ten to fifteen were saying that or a phrase similar to that to many of the others. Mostly to the ones who only moaned.

I decided to ignore the specific activities of creatures I could identify and instead to focus on the group, or, more accurately, to count the group. Although some continued ambling about, I was still able to reach a decent count. *One hundred eighty-five. This is the group of zombies Wakowski plans to release in Des Moines. The group that will be destroyed or kill all the vampires and werewolves who come to fight it.*

"There's almost two hundred zombies in this building with us," said Joseph, who had obviously been observing the undead the same as I had.

"And it's probably the group the aliens are planning to use to lure out our races," I added.

After my words, Joseph struggled pointlessly against his bonds. Silver weakens werewolves regardless of whether it binds them or is shot into them. I chose not to discuss his problems at trying to escape. He wasn't going to be able to move until his bonds were broken, and I wasn't until the stake was removed from my heart.

Two zombies emerged from the group and walked toward us. One of them was a presumably young man, perhaps in his twenties with black hair, a small mustache, and green eyes. He wore a plaid shirt and blue jeans, neither of which fit him well. The second was an older—perhaps in his forties—African American who was five-three, plump, and had dark brown eyes. He wore a black t-shirt and corduroys. The clothes fit each of them very loosely.

At least only two are coming to see us. We might survive this yet.

These two walked until they were within five feet of us. They stared at us. We gazed at them. I knew I should think of a good opening line.

Unfortunately, the more extroverted of us spoke first.

"Hi, I'm Joe," the werewolf said.

"I'm Vod," said the white young man.

"I'm Modod," said the African American.

Not wanting to be left out, I said, "I'm Samuel."

I recognized "Vod" as Keith, whom I'd let die in the shooter incident that had transformed into an ambush. Since our ambushers had only shot up the cabs, Keith had received the opportunity to become "Vod." *I should be able to use this knowledge to our benefit.*

As my mind searched for such a tactic, the others continued to talk.

Vod said, "We're the Warehouse People."

From the way he said these words, I could tell he capitalized the first letter of "warehouse" and "people." *They don't know what they are!*

My partner seemed oblivious to this fact.

"I'm a werewolf."

The two undead looked at each other and snickered.

"Werewolves don't exist," Vod said authoritatively.

Joseph smiled at that. "Then you'll think it's hilarious that Samuel is a vampire."

Vod giggled at that comment, but his fellow zombie didn't.

Modod took a few steps toward me. "I must kill him."

Vod pulled the African American back. "No. I know he is different but we don't need to kill him."

Modod said to Vod, "He is evil. He is a vampire."

Again, Joseph was quick to get into the conversation. "Yeah, he's a vampire, but he's a good one."

Modod pulled against Vod's hand. "I must kill him. He is evil."

My partner gave me a look, then looked at the zombie. "No, he really is a good vampire."

The two zombies backed up and whispered for a few moments. I chose not to listen because regardless of what they said to each other I knew Joseph was correct. We had to convince them that we indeed were a vampire and a werewolf and we were good.

The two undead stepped closer to us. Vod said, "We know you aren't Masters."

"Yes, you are definitely not Masters," Modod agreed. "But you're not Non-Masters either."

I snorted. "Of course, we aren't. As Joe said, he's a werewolf and I'm a vampire." I examined the two of them. "And you're zombies."

This time both undead laughed loudly enough that some of the moaning of the other hundred or so zombies ceased. The huge room was very quiet.

Vod and Modod shook their heads. Vod said, "You're wrong. Werewolves don't exist. Vampires don't exist. And zombies certainly don't exist."

Modod shrugged. "I'm sorry that I said you were a vampire and I should kill you." If pale zombies could blush, I think Modod would have.

And this conversation is going in exactly the wrong direction. "Then you probably don't believe in aliens from other planets as well."

Again, both zombies laughed.

Joseph gave me a quizzical look. I think my partner didn't know what to do. He thought the zombies would just believe him.

"Okay," I said, now that I knew neither zombie was planning to kill me. "You're correct that we aren't your Masters, who, by the way, are aliens from another planet—"

The two zombies laughed again. I was finding this all rather obnoxious. *Zombies are as stupid as humans. Well, that's where they came from, so what can I expect?*

When their laughter ended, I said, "Okay, let's disregard them for a moment. Look at my chest."

The two zombies did so.

"That's a stake in my heart. See? It even bleeds a little. Your Masters put this stake in my heart—a stake that would have killed me if I were human."

The two zombies stared at each other then again at me. Vod nodded.

"Look at Joe. Silver chains are binding him. If he were human, rope would have been adequate. Ropes are tying me to this chair, but they are because I have this stake in my heart."

Modod stepped forward again. "I have to—"

Vod grabbed him again. "No. Listen to him."

Modod pointed at Joseph. "If you're a werewolf, can you transform into a wolf? Do you eat only meat?"

My partner smiled. "Yes. And yes."

Modod pointed at me. "If you're a vampire, do you drink only blood?"

"Well, I can drink other liquids," I replied, "but only blood provides enough nutrition for me to live. By the way, I can transform into a cloud of mist or a bat."

"And if you untie me and yank the stake out of his heart, we can prove it," Joseph offered.

Again, the two zombies took a few steps back and whispered to each other. They stepped forward again.

Vod said, "If Joe is a werewolf and Samuel is a vampire, and we believe that to be true, then is it true that we are zombies?" he asked for the two of them.

Now! I gazed at Vod. "Vod, I saw you die. You were a man named Keith. A crazy person shot and killed you. Your wife and two young daughters were worried about you and didn't want to leave. I told them to leave and I'd save your life. I wasn't able to because you bled out before I could get help."

Vod's mouth dropped open. "I remember that."

Modod looked at him. "He's telling the truth?"

Vod nodded. "And that means we're…"

"Zombies," Modod said.

XXXIX

Zombie Fest

Joe

If vampires with stakes in their hearts could leap up and dance and sing, Sammy would have done so right at that moment. He'd succeeded in convincing at least Vod that he was a zombie. I wasn't so sure about Modod.

The two undead stared at us sadly.

Vod said, "I remember some about Keith's life, but only as if it's happening to somebody else. My life begins only a few hours ago in a warehouse like this one."

Modod said, "And I remember about the life of somebody named Thomas. I am like Vod that it is as if that life belongs to someone else."

I glanced at Sammy. I'd swear he was smiling. He was trying to disguise it, but I could tell. *Can't hide anything from me, Sammy.*

"All right," Sammy said. "I've got to tell you some amazing stuff that your former selves of Keith and Thomas never would have believed. Will you listen?"

The two zombies exchanged glances.

Vod said, "Right now, we are hanging out in a warehouse."

"We don't have anything better to do," Modod added.

Then Sammy told them all about good and evil vampires, about aliens who disguised themselves as humans, and about his organization that did its best to save humans from both the evil vampires and aliens.

As he went on and on—he really did talk for a long time—both zombies sat down. As they listened, they also drooled. The drool made small puddles on the floor.

When he finished, he asked, "Does that all make sense?"

"I guess," Vod said. "It all sounds a bit incredible."

"If I'm not a zombie," Modod said, "I'd probably laugh. But since I'm a zombie, I guess anything is possible."

Sammy looked at me. "Okay, Joe, tell them about WOOF."

And I did. I think my explanation was much more colorful and entertaining than my partner's. My tale was about werewolves, and we're certainly more colorful and entertaining than vampires. As for what I said, I told about WOOF and fighting evil werewolves.

When I was done, Sammy asked again, "Does that make sense, too?"

Vod said, "Sure."

Modod said, "Why not?"

Both zombies stood. Vod said, "All that is very interesting, but that doesn't tell us anything about us and why we exist." He turned and looked at all the other zombies milling around restlessly not as far away from us as I would've liked. "We need something to tell the others."

"Yes," Modod agreed. "I'm not sure some will believe what you're telling us."

Sammy sighed. "Okay, I understand. But now that you understand about VATE and WOOF in general, we can tell you about how it all relates to you." My partner gave me a sharp look. "You go first. Tell them about your role in this case."

So I told them the tale that any faithful reader should understand almost completely by now. At least my part of it, which I've written well. I tried my best because it's one of my first attempts. Yeah, you know it: the werewolf/vampire group, the recruitment of other packs, the zombie delivery, the fight against the Wild Ones. I left off when Sammy and I began working together.

"I still don't get why we exist," Vod said irritably.

Modod said, "Let's just kill them and—"

"No," Vod said. "Samuel knows Keith, if only a little, and I remember Samuel as well. This must be the truth."

Sammy glanced at me. "I'll finish off the tale." And he did. You know, the vampires pursuing zombies, the vampires fighting the active shooter, the vampires getting ambushed, and on and on. He ended with us working together and being tied up here.

As my partner was finishing, he said, "So if the aliens' plan works, many zombies, vampires, and werewolves will be killed in a large battle, and the remaining ones will be revealed to humanity who will hunt us all down. Many zombies will die and not for any cause you care about. Then you won't be safe. Vampires won't be safe. Werewolves won't be safe. We can't let the aliens' plan succeed. Untie us so we can contact VATE and WOOF—"

"And if we do," said Vod. "What will happen to us?"

I glanced at Sammy. I knew the answer. I wondered if Sammy would tell the truth.

He remained silent for a moment. *You calculating, cold vampire.*

"We're going to have to kill lots and lots of you," I answered.

Sammy muttered under his breath.

The two undead stared at each other. Vod shook his head. "But you don't understand us," he said sadly.

Modod grabbed Vod's arm. "The wrong ones may die."

"Because they don't understand."

"Then explain." Sammy told them.

Modod shook his head. "No. No. We must solve this ourselves."

The two zombies walked away, and back toward the nearly two hundred who waited for them. A large group swarmed around as they approached. Most of them moaned loudly. Vod gave a sharp command. The group scattered.

Sammy told me, "You didn't need to tell them that."

I rolled my eyes. "It's the truth, isn't it? We don't have any choice. If this many zombies escape and aren't under the command of the aliens, both WOOF and VATE are going to have to round them up and kill them. You said yourself they kill humans and eat their brains."

"I saw one eat the brain of a dog, too."

I shook my head.

"Look," Sammy commanded.

"Talkers, get over here!" shouted Vod.

"The rest of you leave," ordered Modod.

Those two are definitely the leaders. There must be a way to save as many zombies as possible and still foil the aliens' plot.

But events that contradicted my hopes were unfolding.

A group of between fifteen and twenty undead gathered about ten feet away from the rest. The others bunched together even more. The moaning became louder and louder. The moans grew to almost shouts. Vod and Modod talked quietly to the others. Then Vod yelled, "Be quiet! All of you!"

The moaning ceased.

"They've got some sort of plan," Sammy said, stating the obvious.

I wanted to point that out to him but he'd be angry because he hated when he stated the obvious. *But I don't care about that. Vod and Modod are two good individuals, two individuals who took the time to listen to our long stories (and Sammy's were quite dull and arrogant).*

The group around the two undead leaders scattered into the larger mob.

"There has to be a way we can save them," I said.

My partner shrugged. "They were stupid humans when they were alive, and now they're stupid zombies."

I wanted to protest, but shouts in the zombie crowd stopped me.

"Kill the Moaners!"

"Kill the Tweeners!"

"The Moaners want to kill all the Tweeners!"

"The Tweeners want to kill all the Moaners!"

We also heard loud moaning above these words.

One zombie punched the other in the face. Two other zombies grabbed a third and yanked off its arms. Another pounced on the armless one and pulled off its head. The headless zombie dissolved into white pus, leaving only its clothes that didn't fit well. Zombies punched zombies. Undead yanked off hands, arms, legs, and heads of other zombies.

Losing heads seemed to be fatal because once an undead lost its head, its body dissolved into white pus. This fight was similar to a dance number in a musical but more destructive. The greater number of the zombies punched, kicked, ripped off limbs, and jumped on the heads of undead who had fallen to the floor. The same fifteen to twenty who'd met with Vod and Modod sprinted out of the conflict, but sometimes charged in to stomp on floundering zombies' heads. Then the stomped-on zombies dissolved to white pus as well.

"My God!" I shouted. "They're destroying each other!"

Sammy said calmly, "What do you expect from idiotic, undead humans?"

XXXX

We Are Zombies

Vod

We stand before a sea of white pus and worn clothes that only loosely fit the zombies. Modod glances at me. I survey the destruction we create. Tweeners and Moaners destroy each other—mostly by beheading each other, sometimes by yanking off all of another's limbs then jumping on its head. White pus. Floating clothes. Plaid shirts. Blue jeans. White blouses. Flowered dresses. Worn sweatshirts. Leather shoes. Bright-red stiletto pumps. Sandals with gold straps. Athletic shoes. The only remains of the Tweeners and Moaners. If the Tweeners and Moaners aren't dead, a Talker sneaks in and either yanks off the head or smashes the head in. We only lose two Talkers. But that is then, sort of, and this is now. But it's always Now.

Modod stares at me. "Are we freeing the vampire and the werewolf?"

"Yes," I say. "We can now." I look out to the white pus sea and the Talkers surrounding it. "Talkers, come with me. We aren't safe yet, but we are going to be soon."

Because we kill off the Moaners and Tweeners to save the Talkers. But we're not telling Joe and Samuel.

The Talkers gather around Modod and me. We tell them that we are leading the way, but we are possibly going to have to fight fake humans. I remember what Samuel says about the people who are guarding this warehouse. If we kill these dangerous people, Samuel and Joe trust us more. We don't have a future tense. We don't have a past tense. Because all events are now.

We walk across the warehouse floor to where Samuel and Joe are tied up. I see that Joe's face is wet. I don't understand. It doesn't rain in the warehouse. How can a face be wet without any rain? I don't ask the question because I know memories from Keith's life are providing the answer. But not right now.

"You let them all kill each other!" Joe says.

"They were going to be killed one way or another," Samuel says.

That is true. But I don't tell him.

"We think if fewer of us are here, you aren't going to harm us," Modod says.

"Yes," I agree. "Do you want us to help you?"

Both captives nod enthusiastically.

A few Talkers mutter behind us, but their muttering is quiet enough I don' t think Samuel or Joe take the time to listen. That's good. Because a few zombies say we are killing the vampire and werewolf, too. Not yet. It's not yet time. We zombies must survive.

I look at Modod. Modod looks at me. We nod.

I walk to the vampire. He says he needs the stake taken out of his chest. I grab the wooden stake and yank it hard. It pulls from his chest. Blood sprays out as the stake leaves his body. Then Samuel vanishes. Poof! He's gone. Many zombies gasp. One or two screams. I shush them. We are zombies. We are dignified. As dignified as undead can be.

Modod breaks the silver chains binding Joe's hands. After he releases both of Joe's hands, the werewolf helps him break the chains binding his legs.

Samuel reappears in his chair. His chest doesn't have a hole where the stake no longer is. His chest appears as white and spotless as if it is always this way. The ropes don't bind his hands and feet. That's quite a feat. I wonder if we zombies can do that.

"Whoa!" say many zombies.

"Neat trick!" say a few others.

I don't say anything. If we ever fight vampires, we remember this feat. Disappearing and reappearing vampires are dangerous to zombie people like us.

"Thanks," says Joe as he and Modod finish breaking the chains.

The werewolf growls at the vampire. Samuel shrugs.

"Yes, thank you," he says.

Both Samuel and Joe stand. Joe stretches because he is once bound tightly. Samuel doesn't. His trick of disappearing and reappearing makes all the pain of being tied up go away. That's what I think.

"Two humans are outside," the vampire says. "I think they probably have automatic rifles."

Modod looks at me. I look at Modod.

"We zombies are killing them," I say.

Samuel laughs. "You always talk in the present tense."

"Damn confusing to me," says Joe. "But okay."

He says that about our killing the bad people outside the warehouse.

I say to my zombies, "Moom, Kalp, open that vehicle door."

Moom, a once young female with a bobbed brown haircut and wearing a light summer dress, nods. Kalp, a once middle-aged male wearing a white shirt and blue slacks, nods as well. They walk up to the large metal door.

"Voov, Kaslik, follow. When the door opens, kill the people outside."

Voov, a once young Hispanic guy with short black hair and a mustache, strides up to a few steps behind Moom. Kaslik, a once tall, thin middle-aged female with red hair, does the same behind Kalp.

"You've got your zombies under good control," observes Samuel.

"Hey, if they're willing to fight the bad guys instead of us," Joe says, "I wouldn't complain."

"I observed. I didn't complain," corrects the vampire.

The werewolf rolls his eyes.

Moom and Kalp shove open the door. Voov and Kaslik sprint through; Voov turns to the left; Kaslik turns to the right. We hear gunshots. Moom and Kalp hurry through the open door, too, and Modod and I follow.

The man to the left backs away from Voov whose chest and back are filled with holes from which oozes white pus. The man turns to run so Voov tackles him, then grabs his head, twists, and there's one dead man.

As this happens, the man on the right keeps shooting his rifle. Kaslik strides toward him as the undead's chest and back explode in white pus. Kaslik falls to the ground, but Moom dashes toward the man, who sighs in relief. Moom pounces on the man. The man screams. But Moom grabs his head. Twist. Another dead man.

"Too bad about Kaslik," Modod says.

"No, necessary casualty," I say.

Samuel and Joe sprint out of the warehouse. They glance in both directions, then Samuel runs to the right, Joe to the left. Moom and Voov stand next to their kills. Samuel searches through the pockets of one corpse and Joe of the other. Both find cell phones. Both of them smile. I don't understand why.

The vampire dials a number on his phone as the werewolf does the same on his.

Samuel says, "Beryl, this is Samuel. We've got a situation..."

Joe says, "Hi, Grant. Yeah, Joe here. Listen to this..."

I glance at Modod. We both smile.

XXXXI

Rendezvous at the Airport

Samuel

Five black SUVs pulled up to the Des Moines International Airport terminal. They sped past the signs indicating the various airlines: Southwest, United, American, and stopped in front of the doors to Delta. Joseph and I rode in the first black SUV. We were chauffeured. Highly appropriate for the two who'd broken this case wide open. Our SUV had four FBI officers: Joseph, me, and two others not important enough to name. All the other SUVs had five. Well, some, similarly to ours, had fake FBI agents since both Joseph and I had the badges but neither of us were really FBI.

A few WOVACOM and WOOF agents were also FBI, however, and they had driven or ridden in the vehicles behind ours. Almost as one, all nineteen of us climbed from our SUVs. The drivers remained with the vehicles. Joseph and I sprinted through the revolving door closest to our lineup of SUVs. Other agents dashed down the sidewalk to the other revolving doors or the automatic doors close to the baggage claims area.

Astonished travelers arriving at or departing from the terminal stopped as these men and women in black suits barged in front of them. A few shouted and complained. All complaints died at the sight of our FBI badges.

After Joseph and I breached the building through the revolving door, we walked briskly to an area filled with couches, a food court, and a restaurant to the south. People who stood in lines for airline kiosks or were working at these kiosks or were at the counter presenting their IDs to airline personnel or giving these same personnel their bags paused in their actions to stop and stare at us. My werewolf partner glanced at me. I knew what needed to be done. *Because these humans are acting as moronically as they always do.*

"Go about your business," I said loudly enough to be heard throughout this area of the terminal. "We're FBI agents."

Joseph gave all bystanders a menacing look.

Our fellow werewolf and vampire agents hastened toward us. This time around I wasn't going to proceed without backup. Yes, Joseph had been correct that we should have had backup before our unplanned appointment with the CEO of AO Company, Inc. As readers of my previous works will understand, I didn't tell him as much.

Of course, the humans remained frozen in place—well, except for those who began filming us with their cell phones. Cell phones are wondrous devices, but sometimes I wished they had never been invented. This moment was one of them. Since we were FBI, we could have confiscated the phones from the perpetrators, but that might have taken time away from apprehending the fugitives we were pursuing.

The other seventeen agents who'd entered the building gathered around Joseph and me. Almost as one, we marched toward the escalators that led to the second story where TSA and the two concourses waited for us. And more importantly, where the fugitives we sought were still waiting to board their plane.

For those of you who wonder what we did after escaping certain doom with the zombies, I don't have much to tell. Joseph called Grant. I contacted Beryl. Both were glad to hear from us, and both had become suspicious of AO Company, Inc. when we didn't report back soon after going to their offices. Each of us briefly told his story, then arranged for someone to pick us up and to deliver the zombies to someplace less public than the front of an empty warehouse. Beryl commandeered a school bus that delivered the remaining undead to his house where he locked them in his basement.

Both Joseph and I cleaned ourselves up as other VATE and WOOF agents raided AO Company, Inc. The agents found the place filled with pseudo-people attempting to destroy all of their PCs. These actions were stopped, and enough information was obtained for VWW to track down the remaining sites where more zombies could be produced. The agents also discovered that Ms. Wakowski and her two goons had left for the airport to take a flight out of Des Moines as soon as possible.

Currently, other agents were finishing off searching the remaining warehouses where the undead could be created. Joseph and I and these seventeen others had arrived at the airport to capture the CEO and her goons before they flew off into the sunset.

All nineteen of us hurried through the terminal, flashing our badges as necessary to force the unknowing travelers out of our way. We reached the escalators. We vampires were tall, so as we climbed the escalators, we took them two steps at a time. The werewolves, including Joseph, were a bit shorter, so they trotted up each step.

Reaching the top of the escalators and not waiting for all of us to converge, Joseph and I, leading the pack so to speak, proceeded down the pre-check aisle of the TSA lines. TSA had been notified of our imminent arrival and had prepared accordingly.

Most TSA agents are humans, so I suppose they still did idiotic human stuff and probably even whispered to each other about this arrival of the FBI in as much force as we were. We'd also checked with these same agents to learn that Wakowski and her goons had gone through security nearly forty-five minutes before the time we were to arrive.

Joseph and I flashed our badges at the TSA agents as did the seventeen men and women, vampires and werewolves, who followed us. The TSA agents simply ushered us through behind the x-ray machines. One or two wished us well in our pursuit.

We didn't need luck. We had the advantage. This time around, we had the element of surprise.

Leaving the TSA area, still with our shoes on and all our equipment, that is, pistols, at hand, we reached where the hall turned into a dead-end with a restaurant. To the south was the A concourse with another restaurant to the west. To the north was the C concourse with a shop selling Iowa memorabilia, including sports products from University of Iowa and Iowa State, pigs of various materials—plastic, stuffed, metal—and not very interesting t-shirts featuring Iowa sights and sounds.

All of these shops and restaurants and those on the first floor closed at 7 p.m. every night, so if you came to pick someone up or, frightful as it may sound, were stuck in the Des Moines airport from 7 p.m. to late at night waiting for a plane, you were out of luck. Being a vampire, I never cared much because I drank blood before leaving for the airport, and my host or hostess at the other end of the flight provided me with blood soon after my arrival.

But I digress.

We turned down the C concourse. Each concourse had six gates: four on the second floor and two on the first floor. Wakowski and her goons were supposed to be at Gate C4. The nineteen of us strode as a phalanx of black suits through the concourse. Travelers ran to get out of our way. Parents scooped up their kids who were in our path and whom we might have walked over. Baby carts were rolled toward the walls. Business people chatting on cell phones as they wandered the terminal quickly walked to one side or the other.

The people at Gates C1 and C2 studied us while we passed. Rarely were this many FBI agents seen at one time in Des Moines, Iowa. (Recently, I did have a case where we had this many VATE agents, but we didn't make too much of a public show of it.)

Most of the people at Gates C3 and C4 also stared at us. With the exception of three. Three people who weren't human.

Joseph and I broke off from the rest and walked to where Ms. Wakowski, Mr. Brown, and Mr. Black sat. Standing in front of them, we gazed down upon the woman and ignored the two thugs who could practically look directly eye to eye at us, although they were sitting.

"Ms. Wakowski," I said. "Please come with us."

"You're under arrest," Joseph clarified.

The petite woman looked up at us, then stood, appearing to be taller than she was because of her black stiletto heels. Her two goons stood at the same time.

"This time we have backup," I said and motioned with my right hand at the seventeen others dressed similarly to Joseph and me.

The two goons looked from us to the other agents.

"We can take them," said Mr. Brown.

"Easily," said Mr. Black.

That means these two goons are warrior aliens. They were probably a great deal like Cecil and Theresa. Both Joseph and I had dealt with these two; however, I didn't want to fight these goons.

I smiled. "Go ahead. Already people are filming this on their cell phones."

The two goons and Wakowski scanned the gate area where almost two-thirds of the people had their cell phones out and the back of these phones pointed at us. *How will you like us pulling your planned stunt on you?*

"If you use your superhuman strength to overpower us, you'll be revealed to the world the same way you wanted us to be when we were to fight your zombie army," I said. "Joe and I don't care if we die. And neither do those other seventeen. Because we have someone already prepared to contact the local and national news stations with the story that three aliens disguised as humans overpowered nineteen FBI agents."

Joseph snickered.

"And then humans will be hunting you," I added.

Wakowski smirked. Each goon grunted.

"We surrender," she said quietly.

"Cuff 'em," ordered Joseph.

The CEO of AO Company, Inc. and her two goons held their hands behind their backs. Three other agents came and handcuffed them.

And it was as easy as that.

XXXXII

An Intriguing Interrogation

Joe

Ms. Wakowski sat in the same chair that loser Henry Borman had sat in about five hours earlier. Unlike him, she wasn't tied to the chair with silver chains. According to Sammy, aliens can be bound in a variety of means and weren't any more susceptible to silver than vampires. (I don't know how much Sammy really knew about that since VATE agents tended to kill and not capture aliens.) In any case, both her hands and feet were shackled with handcuffs. She studied us as if we were insects.

After capturing Wakowski and her subordinates at the airport, we brought them to WOOF headquarters and prison. We led Wakowski into this room, but her goons, also with hands and feet shackled, were put in the same cell as dear Henry. I thought he might learn something from these goons we could later use in interrogating their boss. Two WOOF agents, both armed with automatic rifles filled with silver bullets, stood guard in the hallway containing the cells. Grant thought these agents should be more than adequate to deal with any escapees. Not that we had any. We didn't. Prisoners in WOOF cells remained prisoners.

Yeah, I know. Sammy said we should have at least killed the thugs. Vampires in VATE (or WOVACOM or whatever other funny acronyms of organizations the "good" vampires have) lock up very few really evil vampires. Mostly they kill them. That's what they usually do with aliens as well. Berry, Sammy's boss, wanted us to question Wakowski because she was one of the highest-ranking aliens they'd ever captured in Iowa, and perhaps in this area of six states.

So here we stood. And there she sat.

"Tell us about all the operations you've run," ordered Sammy.

Wakowski laughed.

"I take it that's a 'no,'" I said.

Sammy stared angrily at me. I shrugged.

After her laughter died, she spat on the floor.

"That's rude of you," I said. "You know we could have simply killed you."

She smirked.

"We're going to find out about your operations anyway," my partner said.

"If you're going to find out about them, then there's no need for me to tell you anything," Wakowski said.

"That's true," I admitted. I thought we should lock her up and let her think about her sins for a while. That often worked with Wild Ones. Many a Wild One has seen the error in his ways and become a Friend of Humanity like me.

Sammy snorted. "You're not helping."

He's probably thinking about the stupidity of werewolves and the evil of aliens. I never asked him, so I still don't know. But if you've read Sammy's earlier works or his part of this one, you'll certainly agree with me.

"We've broken your zombie operation," I said. I thought if I laid out the facts, we might get more cooperation from her. "Right now, your last three warehouses are being destroyed." I waved my hand toward Sammy. "These vampires are even studying one of the plants used to create zombies—"

"You'll never understand it," Wakowski interrupted.

Sammy stepped toward her, hand raised. I grabbed his shoulder. *And he says we werewolves are the wild, irrational ones.* He took a step back and frowned.

I continued, "The huge zombie army went all kamikaze on itself. We've captured all your pseudo-humans who were running your company. We're checking your network and PCs. It's over. Confess."

"What's in it for me if I do?" she asked. "Will you let me live?"

I looked at Sammy. He grimaced. Vampires really hate aliens. Maybe more than they hate werewolves.

"We'll leave you to wallow in your prison cell," my partner said reluctantly.

I wished he'd checked with me first. We regularly have Wild Ones coming in and out of this prison. I wasn't sure we could spare three cells for Wakowski and her goons.

"Oh, really?" asked Wakowski sarcastically.

"Yes, really," I responded. Yeah, I know. I lied. But I wanted her to talk.

"Well, if that's the case," Wakowski said. "Then I'll tell you a little bit about what we've been doing."

If what she told us was "a little bit," I'd hate to see what "a lot" was. Wakowski told us of their plots and plans over the last ten years. Yes, ten. If I were confessing to someone to get myself out of a fix, I certainly wouldn't go back that far. A year or two, maybe. After all, I'd be confessing to the bad guys. Yeah, I know. Sammy and I were good guys. But to Wakowski, we were bad guys.

She told about planting pseudo-humans in local and state government and about the officials doing their best to ruin Iowa's waterways and soil—two of Iowa's most valuable commodities. She told about creating gargoyles that terrorized and killed people in old houses. She laughed since such incidents hadn't ever been noticed by Sammy and his vampire friends.

Wakowski told about creating flesh-eating corn. A few fields were grown; a few people died in them. The aliens had decided flesh-eating corn wasn't viable as a weapon. She told about creating a giant crocodile that inhabited the sewers of Des Moines. Unfortunately, it grew too large and got stuck in a sewer pipe and died. She told us, well, about so much more.

The alien told us about giant mutant rats, pseudo-humans who could transform into super-strong monsters, little green creatures that were like piranhas on land, black microbes that spread a potent disease, pseudo-humans who could use mind control on regular humans, and so very many other alien evils. As a matter of fact, she told us so much, I decided that none of these plots, plans, and incidents were true. I noticed my partner, too, became more skeptical the longer Wakowski chattered on and on and on and on.

"...now, if the vampires hadn't figured out about our mind-controlling humans, we would have—" Wakowski was saying.

The steel door was thrown into the room, with two large fist marks in its center, the hinges destroyed by the sheer force behind this movement. The door smashed the table between Sammy and me and Wakowski. She wiggled her chair backward as both my partner and I jumped out of the way of this large flying projectile.

Mr. Brown walked through the open doorway.

Mr. Black followed.

I detected movement behind them, but if it was caused by a smaller person, their bulk blocked him from our sight.

Mr. Brown smiled. "We're alone here."

Mr. Black rubbed one of his large fists into his other large hand. "Yeah, and we're here to kill you."

"Like those stupid werewolf guards," Mr. Brown said.

Both goons laughed.

Only to have their laughter interrupted. Their heads exploded from a barrage of bullets behind them. Blood, gore, brains, and green ooze splattered everywhere.

Both headless goons collapsed to the floor. Henry, with an automatic rifle in each hand, stood behind where they had been.

His wide, flashing eyes flared at Wakowski.

"It's your fault!" shouted Henry. "It's your fault! That's what destroyed my pack! You did!" He stepped closer to her, leveling the automatic rifles at her.

I glanced at Sammy. He nodded toward Henry. I was sure he was trying to communicate something, but a simple nod didn't tell me much.

Henry continued to rant, "Our alliance with the bloodsuckers was only a diversion. That's all it was. Your two goons told me. The whole idea of wiping out the human-loving bloodsuckers and pets was only a side operation. That wasn't even your big plan. You had us deliver zombies to bribe us to fight a battle you knew we would lose. But you wanted us to do it. That would get more human-loving bloodsuckers and pets into town for your big plot. The battle between undead, bloodsuckers, and human-loving pets. My pack died in a side operation. It wasn't even the main part of your plan..."

Tears poured down Henry's face. His eyes glistened with a wildness even Wild Ones wouldn't want to face. But he didn't simply shoot Wakowski to be done with it. As he yelled and screamed, she calmly gazed at him as if he were reciting a very dull poem at a poetry reading.

Then she yanked her hands apart and broke the chain holding her cuffs together. And yanked her feet apart and busted the chain between the cuffs around her ankles. With the fingers of the opposite hand, she twice pinched the cuffs around her wrists. The cuffs fell uselessly to the floor. She reached down, grabbed one of her stiletto pumps, and threw it toward Henry. Its heel sank deeply into his forehead. Dead Henry collapsed to the floor. White fur covered his body. The two automatic rifles dropped from his lifeless hands to the floor.

Wakowski flung herself from the chair toward the loose rifles. I leaped into the air.

And the world became black and white. Black and white. See a small woman roll on the floor, grab two rifles on the floor, and begin to stand.

Land upon her. Shove her to the floor.

She drops the rifles. Both hands shove me.

Fly through the air.

Hear gunshots fired as I hit hard against the back wall.

I transformed back into a human. Sammy held his pistol pointed at the body of Wakowski. Her head was so riddled with bullet holes she was almost as unrecognizable as the non-existent heads of her two goons.

My partner glanced back at me.

"Now that was a good time to wolf-out," he said.

"Thank you."

XXXXIII

Time to Go

We are in the basement of Beryl's house. Beryl is a large man with red hair, large ears, and green eyes. He says he's a vampire. Samuel says he's a vampire, too. I don't disagree when we are in the warehouse. But Modod and I both know vampires don't exist. Samuel disappears and reappears. So we call Samuel and Beryl the Disappearing People. But vampires? That's so funny, we laugh about it.

We do the same about Joe saying he's a werewolf. Werewolves don't exist either. Everyone knows that.

We are not zombies. We know that because the only reason we think we are is because we believe that Samuel is a vampire and Joe is a werewolf. They are lying. We know that now.

We also aren't Basement People. When we are in the warehouse, the Masters have plans for us. Maybe Samuel and Joe lie when they say that the Masters want us to fight vampires and werewolves (we all laugh about that), so they show their special powers and all of humanity are going to hunt the vampires and werewolves (and us "zombies" if we survive) until the humans kill all three groups. That's insane. But our Masters have something bad planned for us. Still, killing all the Moaners and Tweeners is good because they aren't very smart and aren't much help.

As we walk around the basement, we believe the Disappearing People (aka vampires? we laugh some more) also have plans for us. We want our own plans. We want our own lives. We don't want to live in warehouses. We don't want to live in basements. Both our Masters and the Disappearing People lock us away.

I remember the life of Keith. He has a wife and two daughters. They live in a house. He goes to work in an office. He and his friends go out to bars to drink beer. I am not Keith. Modod remembers the life of Thomas. Thomas's life is much different from ours, too. All of us zombies remember lives belonging to people other than ourselves. If what Samuel and Joe say is true, then we are undead, and we are zombies. But we know they are liars.

No, we know who we are. We are Second People. Because each of us remembers very distinct details about another person's life. We think we can see the memories as if they come from our own bodies. These other people once live in our bodies; now we live in our bodies.

None of that matters.

What matters is we want our own lives. We want our own goals. We want our own culture and society. We know we are different from the Masters, the Non-Masters, Samuel's people, and Joe's people. We are unique.

We are sad that we want to leave this place. A pool table is here. A few of us play pool well: Vaviv and Milkos. A television is hooked up to video games. We all play the different video games while others of us plan. Beryl gives us food. He gives us a big basket of apples, oranges, bananas, and grapes. He also leaves us five plates with crackers, cheese, and sausage slices. We all eat these foods but they don't satisfy us. We want to eat brains. Of the Non-Masters. The brains of other types of people don't sound as good.

Some of us will carry the food that the Disappearing People leave for us. Oh, I forget to say. Everybody has their own plans for us. But we have plans for us, too. Our plans aren't part of any of theirs. We laugh about that.

Voov breaks open the door to the basement. Moom breaks open the door to the outside.

We are leaving. I leave this recording so maybe somebody understands us. We have plans. We find homes. We find lives. We have adventures.

[The recording ends here.]

[Beryl was quite disgusted that the zombies broke out of his basement. He said he should have left some agents to guard them, but all agents were needed to bring down the alien enterprise. I told him having a few agents wouldn't have helped. The zombies would have killed them. Beryl was still sad that we won't have these undead to help us in the fight against evil. – Samuel]

[I think it's good the zombies broke out and are on the loose. They shouldn't be slaves to either aliens or vampires. Neither should be masters to the zombies. The zombies should undie freely. – Joe]

XXXXIV

A De-Briefing

Samuel

Beryl and I sat at his kitchen table, each of us with a mug of blood. After the zombies had escaped by breaking down various doors in his house, my boss had replaced the destroyed doors, but the fact the zombies had escaped had left Beryl in a very bad mood. A mood that didn't make my de-briefing very pleasant.

"Wakowski lied to you throughout that entire interrogation," my boss said bluntly.

"I'm sure a few of the plots she mentioned were true," I responded lamely. Actually, I wasn't. They'd all been ludicrous. Of course, maybe the police and the FBI had solved all these cases and killed all the creatures she'd described.

"Then you should have called her on them." Beryl stared at his mug.

Yes, I possibly could have. I told him, "Once she got talking, she blabbed on and on like an Evil One. I didn't have a chance to say anything." That was true as the observant reader well knows.

My boss chuckled. "Giant mutant rats."

I snorted. "Totally absurd."

We sat in silence for a few moments.

"The werewolves said she chattered on and on," Beryl finally said, but he didn't excuse my not calling Wakowski on her ridiculous claims.

Despite my misgivings, I thought perhaps a bit of defense about the outcome of the case was in order. "Look, we stopped the zombies from a mass attack and killed off quite a few Evil Ones. I'd say that was a successful outcome."

Beryl drank a bit of blood and made a face. His had obviously cooled to the point he didn't like the taste. "True," he acknowledged. "If we and the werewolves had gotten in a fight with that many zombies and we'd been filmed doing it, that would have been disastrous."

A point I wasn't about to argue.

"The aliens recruiting Evil Ones was new," I said, changing the subject.

"And frightening," my boss added. "Learning to pit us against each other. That's one good thing about Wakowski and her goons being killed. They can't tell other aliens how successful that part of the operation was."

I wanted to contradict him and say that Wakowski could have contacted other aliens about that part of their operation. After all, they'd known what had happened at the warehouse and acted appropriately. But Beryl was discouraged enough.

"Since the operation didn't actually succeed that might put a damper on any plans they might have to try to use Evil Ones again," I offered.

"You know that werewolf, Joseph, saved us," my boss observed. "He put together that WOOF should contact us, and WOOF warned us of the Evil Ones' attack and helped track down the aliens. We might need to develop a better partnership with that organization." I groaned. *If I never work with a werewolf again, it will be too soon.*

Beryl continued, "Using werewolves was new, too. Of course, after your time at the mall with Joseph, maybe aliens believed vampires and werewolves work together."

I withheld a second groan. *I don't like where this is going. Best to cut it off as soon as possible.*

"Even if you'd had VATE agents here guarding the zombies, the zombies would have escaped," I said. "Except they also would have left dead vampires behind."

This time my boss grunted and drank a bit more blood.

I decided to continue despite Beryl's displeasure. "These zombies were the smartest of the lot. The less communicative ones were killed when they all attacked each other."

My boss shrugged. "That's what you said. Before the mass killing, some zombies only moaned, some moaned and talked, and some only talked. Only the third category survived the self-inflicted massacre." He chuckled. "It's as if they were culling out the herd."

I snorted. "They weren't that smart. They came from stupid humans, and now they're stupid zombies." Although I wasn't sure I quite believed that. After all, vampires and werewolves hadn't killed them, they had killed themselves, and they had only done so after Joseph had revealed that, if left to us, we'd kill lots of them. *Vod and Modod decided that course of action on their own.*

"I'm still disgusted they escaped," Beryl said.

"I wouldn't worry about it," I countered. "After all, they didn't even realize they were zombies. Even after Joseph and I talked with them. You heard the recording."

"They could have helped us learn more about the aliens."

I sighed. "Again, the zombies didn't know who or what they were. And they certainly didn't know much about the aliens. They saw only the two female scientist aliens, and knew them as Masters."

Surprisingly, clones of those same two female scientists had been in three warehouses. One warehouse was filled with little green creatures that could transform into beasts to lick up goo and into beasts that could eat up rotten leaves from spent husks. I'd seen creatures similar to these on another case, but at the time, I didn't know the purpose behind their sharp teeth.

"You're right, that's probably all they saw. It just bothers me that the zombies are out there loose."

"If they appear again and are a threat," I said. "I'm sure you'll send me to take care of it."

Beryl laughed. "True. And I could partner you with Joseph."

I drank some cold blood instead of responding. *Time to change the subject again.* "We could watch the presidential debates," I suggested.

"That's a brainless idea. Human elections are only popularity contests."

And we both laughed. Regardless of the outcome of my last case, we knew human elections were idiotic, and the less we knew about them, the better.

XXXXV

The Zombie Feint

Joe

I was at Grant's place before the airing of the presidential debate that was taking place in Des Moines. We wanted to watch it because hearing the candidates' various views and seeing how they performed onstage was important. The debate could help us determine the candidate we'd support at the caucuses. Iowa was the first in the nation caucuses in the presidential campaign. For us Iowans, this is an honor and a privilege. For those unfamiliar with the system, I could explain it, but, as Sammy enjoys saying, that's beyond the scope of this narrative.

I arrived early because I wanted to talk to Grant about how my last case had ended.

We sat in his living room with a bowl of raw beef cubes before us. Each of us had a bottle of beer. A big celebration for a case well done.

"Why did you want to come over early?" Grant asked.

I smirked. "Because I have a theory you might enjoy."

"We have fun with everything."

That's the werewolf way. No cynicism for us!

"Okay," I said. "You know the alien's plan to release their close to two hundred zombies so a great number of werewolves and vampires would be forced to fight them. To defeat them, some of us werewolves would transform into wolves, and vampires would transform into clouds of mist or bats to fight them. Even if we didn't use our transforming powers, we'd still use our super-human strength or speed. The aliens planned to let the news networks know, so the fight would be filmed. Then humanity would again try to wipe out our two races."

Grant nodded and tossed a cube of beef into his mouth.

I took a gulp of beer. "The zombie attack wasn't the point. The point was getting the ensuing fight on film, then getting humanity to hunt down and kill all werewolves, vampires, and zombies. You might call it a zombie feint."

"Okay," my boss said. "Let's."

"But I think we experienced another zombie feint."

Grant gulped some beer. "Do tell."

"When Sammy and I were trapped in the warehouse with all those zombies, we told the zombies about this plan. Then Sammy told them even if they released us, we'd still kill lots of them."

My boss tossed another cube of beef in his mouth and chewed as he waited for me to continue.

Knowing that Grant had also listened to the zombie's tape, I went on, "Vod described three different types of zombies: Moaners, Tweeners, and Talkers. Vod and Modod were Talkers. Sammy had told me that he'd encountered some zombies and all they did was moan. Those had to be the Moaners. Sammy also told me about some zombies who moaned most of the time but also talked some of the time. Those had to be the Tweeners."

"All quite interesting."

"Thank you." I knew Grant would understand. Sammy might not because he was conceited. "When the zombies had their pus bath, the Moaners and Tweeners were the only ones killed. I think maybe two Talkers were." I paused. "Did you catch my use of pus instead of blood?"

"Of course," Grant replied. "And very observant of you."

I shrugged. "I try." I took a gulp of beer. "And that self-inflicted massacre was the second zombie feint. Their killing each other was a distraction to us. If we'd gone in and attacked the zombies, we would have indiscriminately killed the three different types. Maybe none of the Talkers would have survived. Since the Talkers caused the other two groups to kill each other off, we didn't have to kill any. And that meant most of the Talkers survived."

"And they would have enough sense to take off on their own."

"You heard the recording," I said.

"You disagree with Sammy's assessment of these zombies," Grant commented.

I smiled. "Right. I think those zombies who escaped are a danger. They planned so that only the smartest and the strongest survived. And they don't have any sense of good or evil. After all, they killed off most of their own kind so the Talkers could survive."

"So the self-inflicted massacre wasn't the point. The point was that most of the Talkers survived."

"To someday possibly do evil to the world," I concluded.

"That's rather grim. You know, they might just mind their own business."

I thought about Grant's comment. Vod and Modod seemed friendly enough. When they fled Beryl's house, they took the food the vampires had offered, but they hadn't ransacked the house or stolen anything. "You're probably right."

"Hey, it's time for the debate."

Grant turned on the television and flipped through to a channel where the debate was being televised.

All thoughts of vampires and zombies vanished as we sat back to watch the show.

ABOUT THE AUTHOR

James T. Carpenter is the author of four other Samuel the Vampire novels, *A Limitless Policy*, *Why I Shouldn't Work with a Werewolf*, *My Daze as a Vampire Hunter*, and *Economies of Blood* as well as the theological-fantasy *Hanged for the Few*.

He holds a BA in Russian Area Studies from Knox College and works as a senior business analyst for a regional insurance company in Iowa.

Carpenter enjoys travel. Most recently, he has made trips to Central Europe, Sicily, New Zealand, Argentina, and Chile.